Timeout 2050

ANDREW STRIBLING

For you. I hope you get the message and pass it on.

Prologue

I spent my whole life in those machines, every action measured, on time, in order and by the book. It was not supposed to be this way.

Looking out over the city I saw one, two then three dark grey plumes of smoke, rising vertically across the horizon. Their slow progress upward in stark contrast to their origin's furious descent. Bodies pulverised; their souls floating away never to be seen again.

The camera angle widened; someone hit slow motion. I could see myself frozen to the spot for a moment then falling onto my knees, head in hands until I dared look up. It was real. A tornado in my gut, water blinding my eyes; the body protecting the mind.

Now the air above me ripped apart violently, a looming shadow. I couldn't hear myself think over my thunderous heartbeat. My words flew out, incomprehensible, around my wavering arms.

'Go!' I screamed.

Franks' diary description of, "The Fall," 06/06/2030.

Part 1 Human Robots

Chapter 1
Safezone 1, 2050

Joey woke up as usual on a bright morning in the vast West City. The first thing he noticed each day was the weather for it was the only thing that changed in the Safeworld. The second, the numbers to the top left and right of his field of vision, a semi-permanent presence, one counting up; the other down.

A slow wink of his left eye changed the number on the left from the day: 6654 to the time; it was 7:31 a.m., but something wasn't right; he'd figure it out on the monorail. The blinds usually opened automatically ten minutes earlier, allowing the light to stream in and initiate the waking up process. After fumbling around for the light switch, he patted then shook them a little violently, nothing happened; they must be jammed. There was no need to panic, he'd fix it later, when he had more time.

He showered and dressed in a less than five minutes; the luke warm water stopped after three minutes and there were only two outfits available, one for home the other for work. He wiped the small steamy mirror, a bald head reflected back; the survivors, irrespective of sex, had been deprived of hair since the inception of the Freegov. It was a luxury and therefore deemed unnecessary. All resources were diverted towards the War Economy.

He popped four sustenance pills and drank a large glass of water. The pills were green, red, yellow and blue. They represented vegetables, protein and carbohydrates respectively. The blue pill, described as "mind health" vitamins, was most important for ensuring continual access to their other reality. Although there were rumours it blocked the sex hormones and contributed to the androgynous characteristics of the survivors, they didn't care. The information displayed in Joey's field of vision was controlled by his Lifechip[1]. To the right the display it showed 156 hours and 20 minutes in big bold numbering that continuously counted down. Just enough time to cover the twenty-minute journey to work, his twelve-hour shift today, then the next six days at work until he was timed-up as compensation at the end of the working turn. Indeed, that was an anomaly too for everyday was a working day in Safeworld. To the casual observer there was something robot like, almost inhuman, about the way he carried out his actions.

Joey worried about being late because there was no margin for error in West City, everything depended on time and how much you had left, there were no exceptions, no excuses; if you timed-out you were finished. Unfortunately, neither was there any thanks for being on time, no exhilaration or reward received when he earned his next turn of time for he, like every other survivor in Safeworld[2] rarely felt any real positive emotions. Thanks to the evil wizardry of the lifechip the dominant emotions that remained functional towards other survivors were of fear and suspicion. Empathy and happiness were limited to their other reality. A mixture of psychopathy and desperation remained; life had been debased to a crude survival game and Joey, like everyone else, had to be prepared to do anything it took to survive, no matter how shocking.

---

[1] Lifechip: A microchip installed in the survivors' brain in 2035. This protects from infiltration, provides entertainment and ensures compliance with the war economy; it also erases their memories on installation.

[2] Safeworld: The name given to the world under the Freegov protective administration. Broadly speaking "Safezones" replaced continents; each containing Mega Cities at the points of the compass.

The massive, dark housing blocks, towered over him as he made his way through the residential zone, there was no rush hour, for Freegov operated shift working patterns that avoided overcrowding, mixing and any sense of city life as you might know it. No car horns blared for there was no traffic, no litter blighted the pavements for there were no shops. Looking up at the impossibly small windows in the dark brick blocks Joey felt they were watching his every move with a frown.

Joey almost tripped as he scrambled to get onto the monorail before its doors swished shut, perhaps that was why he was feeling anxious that morning- any delay could be fatal; the pressure was on, nevertheless he expected an uneventful eleven stop journey to work. The monorail was a shiny grey metal and spotlessly clean; inside, the seats were numerous and of a basic construction. They were pretty uncomfortable, rather like an economy class aeroplane seat in the 2020's, the vehicle had travelled just eight stops when he heard a thud and it shuddered to a halt.

Already running late and frustrated by this unscheduled stop, Joey frantically strained his head to see what had happened, he couldn't see anything of note. The section of track was at ground level so he hit the emergency door release button and got out.

Towards the front of the vehicle, a slim figure was bent over what looked like a set of bloody legs; there had been a gruesome accident.

'What happened?' Joey asked, in a high-pitched tone that may well have given away his agitation.

As she turned her head to face him his attitude might have changed; a vision of beauty in a moment of horror, but this was the Safeworld where amorous feelings no longer existed and every Survivor was in it for themselves.

'Come over here and help,' the woman replied quickly.

As Joey approached he wondered what he was dealing with here, nobody helped others, perhaps she was scheming to get his time. But something, perhaps the angst in her eyes or more likely the need to get to work propelled him toward her.

'Remove yourselves from the monorail, you are delaying your fellow survivors from their journey,' a monotone voice said. It seemed to come from nowhere and everywhere all at once. Joey recognised the voice; it was the Freegov Helpforce[3] coming from a virtually silent drone that had appeared just above them.

'Let go, they will attack you,' he said, knowing they wouldn't ask twice.

The woman didn't move. Joey glanced up at the hovering drone and saw the countdown on its flashing red display 5,4,3,2… he grabbed her under the arms and pulled back with all his strength; as he did so it seemed she had realised the danger she was in and simultaneously loosened her grip and shifted her weight. This had the effect of making her almost weightless so they literally flew backward as the drone moved in and started removing the body parts over and above the feint groans of the still live victim.

The impact was sudden and painful. Who would have thought to put a solid titanium waste container right there behind them? It turned out it had arrived with the drone as part of the clean-up operation. The beautiful woman was raising her hand and striking Joey on the cheek over and over and with increasing vigour each time.

'Wake up, wake up!' She screamed, and even as his eyes fluttered she still slapped him. Over the pain and dizziness, he wondered if she was some kind of sadist.

'Stop now. I'm alive,' he mumbled, moving his hand up to feel the damage on his head.

'Thank God,' she replied, slowing her slap in mid-air and instead landing a soft caress on his cheek. She smiled, and Joey detected a slight accent.

---

[3] Freegov Helpforce: Military Police of the world government (Freegov) since 2035, consists wholly of robots and drones.

'I'm Cara. You saved me,' she continued.

'Joey, good to meet you.' he replied. The words he spoke shocked him and he wondered if they were strictly true, but for the first time in his restricted memory – he actually felt something.

It had been longer than he could remember what with the war and its fallout.

'Shall we link?' he asked, staring dazed, directly into her eyes. Linking was human interaction in free time. It was a thing of the past.

She looked at him with suspicion as he sat still rubbing his head gingerly.

'Err…yeah,' she spluttered.

The couple locked eyes for five seconds and the link was complete. This bizarre liaison could continue later.

While Joey had been unconscious the drone had morphed into a robot, removed the body parts and sent them on their way in the titanium waste container. It had also scrubbed and watered down the track. Freegov achieved full marks for cleanliness and the accident site looked as if nothing at all had happened.

After jogging a hundred yards or so to the next stop, Joey was slightly out of breath as he settled into an uncomfortable plastic seat for the second time that morning. He noticed a weight in the top pocket of his overalls. Closer inspection revealed a small gold coloured object with an upright post and a transverse bar. It felt heavier than it looked and there were three small, sparkling stones embedded in it. Joey held it between his thumb and forefinger for a moment before carefully returning it to his pocket and fastening the button.

Motion helped shift his thoughts back to reality; It was almost 8 a.m. and there was no chance of him getting to work on time. This meant a time penalty for violation of the Freecode, the rules governing survivors since 2035. Minor violations cost one hour and being between one second and one hour late was one of those. Being more than one hour late for work was a major violation and cost twenty-four hours; a defacto death penalty. Still it was all worth it according to the Freegov[4]; to maintain security in this ongoing emergency death meant life and life meant death.

---

[4] Freegov: The government of the (Safe)world since 2035

After the one-hour penalty had come off his time he would be in the red; unless he could make some extra-time, he would timeout before the end of his shift at the end of the turn. Joey had never been in this position before for, because as long as you followed the rules, nothing unusual ever happened in Safeworld, and until today, Joey followed the rules.

This was, so they say, unprecedented. Joey watched as the massive, dark buildings passed by his window faster and faster then slower and slower, a therapeutic hypnotising motion. Perhaps the damage to his head had done him some good, he thought.

Joey, like all survivors, couldn't remember anything about his pre Lifechip life. He could, however, still see and therefore make some assumptions. Physically he was tall and slim. He looked middle aged and walked with a slight limp, that was not immediately apparent unless you studied his gait carefully. To assist with the war economy, the survivors' Lifechips automatically expired at age sixty. They didn't know their age, nor receive any advance warning of expiry, so as not to impact on efficiency.

Joey had a deep voice with well-spoken English accent. He could be slow, shall we say 'deliberate' at times but considering the circumstances that was perhaps understandable.

He couldn't be sure if this was his natural character or the character that had been thrust upon him by circumstance. Sometimes his thoughts just didn't feel right. However, when he compared himself to other survivors, he had a presence. For some reason, perhaps his stature and voice, others seemed to pay attention when he spoke. Then and again it could have been something else altogether that had kept Joey alive fifteen years into in the daily game of survival horror.

The seconds turned to minutes as the monorail continued its passage through space and time.

Chapter 2

Joey arrived at the factory at 8:15 a.m. He glanced up at the entry camera and the display registered his details and flashed red; the minor violation equalled a one-hour immediate time deduction. There was no explaining to the boss, no exception nor excuse.

'You are late, what's the matter with you?' Tony said, as Joey slid into his workstation. Joey looked the other way, closed his eyes momentarily and held his head. He could do without his colleague Tony's bullshit today.

'Got delayed on the way in; probably an offering,' Joey replied, taking a deep breath.

'A sacrifice eh, haven't had one of those around here for a while. If it weren't for these selfless people we'd all be lab rats; something you will likely be now in…about six days.' Tony said, shaking his head as he pretended to roll up his sleeve and look at his wrist.

'Fuck off Tony,' Joey replied.

'There's no need to be rude, I could report you for that. I'll bring flowers to your grave, you might even get a street named after you, if you are a Wolf…' Tony continued regardless, 'or how about you just end it all now and you'll get your very own monument in the Cemetery!'

Joey successfully managed to block the never-ending whine of conversation coming at him for the next two hours by skillfully responding with a strategically placed "hmm," or "yeah," or "I know," whenever he detected a pause in the soliloquy. Although he was vaguely aware that Tony was making some arse licking comments concerning last weekend's Peacegames and how good it was that so many survivors had been sacrificed.

Tony was a small man with weak features and a beer belly, quite how he managed this on the sustenance pill diet remained a mystery to Joey. He was the kind of guy you would feel sorry for if you ran into him, until he opened his mouth. What he lacked in stature he attempted to make up for verbally, with disastrous consequences, indeed there were some days when Joey wished the work rotation was every day rather than every period and this was one of them.

Tony might have been a, "Civil Enforcement Officer," in the old days; a useless state apparatchik who would ask how high, to the nearest millimeter, when asked to jump by Freegov, tape measure in hand. Joey pictured Tony wearing his ironed, pressed, ill-fitting work uniform with a glowing high visibility jacket over the top holding his tablet stalking the streets; before cars became too expensive to run. In-between his deflective replies, Joey imagined a tragic accident; Tony caught between the gears of the drone part separating machine, his screams drowned out by the sound of the motor straining to crush his bones one by one. For his part Tony saw Joey as disrespectful and dangerous, he couldn't understand Joey's indifference to Freegov and the protection they gave.

'I don't get you, you're going to timeout in six days and you look like you don't care,' Tony said, as the men sat opposite one another in the upstairs break area.

'Hmm, what, did you say something?' Joey replied, realising that due to their new location he could no longer get away with ignoring the conversation.

'HELLO, Earth to Joey!' Tony shouted.

Joey was startled as if he had been rudely awoken from a daydream involving Cara. Real emotions were flooding his mind for the first time in memory. He smiled knowingly as he recalled them briefly as he re-joined the conscious world.

'What the hell is wrong with you Joey! It's that bump on your head? Have you completely lost the plot? What are you going to do?' Tony asked, struggling to keep his voice under control.

'You just realised you'll have no-one to talk to when I'm dead, so now you want to help, right?' Joey said.

'Okay, you have two choices; snitch on someone for a violation or cause an offering, which will it be?' Tony continued, obliviously.

Joey knew all those stupid enough to break the rules were sacrificed years ago. Those that remained were few and far between and exceptionally skilled at maintaining their time. Because the population decreased on a weekly basis, the more time that passed the harder it became to gain time. Eventually it would be impossible.

This unfortunate anomaly was explained away by the Freegov with various concepts of the War Economy and Peacegames. To maintain the ceasefire; weekly survivor sacrifices were carried out in the Peacegames. The number of survivor sacrifices needed to maintain the ceasefire decreased each week and would continue to do so until there were only 500 million survivors left. A permanent peace treaty would then be granted thus ending the war economy. Balanced reproduction would then be permitted to maintain the population and life could get back to, "normal." The promised permanent peace treaty was the first carrot that the survivors chased, dangling before them but never quite in reach, during these difficult times. The second; a delicious, readily available honey roasted version, was the virtual reality entertainment system they had access to via the Lifechip: Freetime V.R.

'Look Tony, we both know I'm done for, just give it a rest,' Joey replied.

'You spent your whole life following the rules, now you are going to timeout and you don't care? You may as well take control, sacrifice yourself now for the glory of Freegov,' Tony exclaimed.

Joey looked down at his scolding tea then back up at Tony's smug, bloated face. He started to move his hand towards the mug then decided against it.

'Just fuck off Tony… please,' Joey replied.

The Peacegames were advertised in such a way that the timed-out survivors from each Safezone received votes to determine whether they were to be a wolf or a sheep and thereby their role in the game. Each Safezone would hold one show each turn meaning there were shows on six days of the turn. Viewing was compulsory, a homage to your fellow survivors, the ongoing emergency and the protection from Freegov. There was, it was claimed, a way to survive the games: having killed all the sheep, the wolf would be scored under a marking scheme, out of ten, after the game. However, only full marks would achieve clemency, and nobody ever received full marks. The most recent games ended with the wolf scoring 8.9. He had timed explosives strapped to his torso, then was tied to a chair with wheels and sent down a large ramp with a hump at the end. The rest is history.

'Why were you late anyway? I bet you just slept in like a pansy.' Tony goaded, never a man to give up.

'Actually, I met a girl and we linked,' Joey replied.

'Well we all know why that is, she's after your time and you are too blind to see it- idiot,' Tony pointed to his flabby belly, 'besides women like a bit of meat to get a hold of,' he continued.

'That's fat Tony; congratulations you are an obese slob. I'll let you know how it goes.' Joey replied.

'Good luck with that, you'll be dead by the end of the turn,' Tony said.

Tony had a point there, perhaps it was the bang on the head, or the caress from Cara but Joey hadn't thought seriously about his predicament at all.

The rest of the working day passed uneventfully. The war economy saw the survivors work in one of three sectors: Armaments and defence, sustenance (food) pill production and distribution and infrastructure maintenance. They rotated job roles every three periods[5] to maintain efficiency and discourage long term friendships or subversion. Joey's current role was assembling drone parts. He oft wondered how these small drones could possibly protect them against the vast otherworldly power they faced, but that was just another one of those anomalies that didn't make sense in the Safeworld under the Freegov, and he along with the other survivors didn't have the time to question it.

---

[5] Period: equivalent of year in Safeworld, a turn broadly represented a week. Although time was only accurately measured by the day count which had increased from zero since Freegov were installed.

Chapter 3

The sun set a few minutes before Joey arrived home, he walked the journey back along one of the myriads of pathways that cris-crossed West City, surrounded by an army of imposing twenty story residential blocks. It was as if they had all been crafted from the same blueprint then mercilessly squashed together to cast their daunting shadow over the survivors. There were no trees, flowers, grass or animals. Even the cockroaches had left.

The perfectly spaced street lighting flickered on and illuminated the pathway as Joey approached his block, a slow blinking red light on the underside of the lamp reminded survivors that they were being monitored by the built-in cameras. At each intersection four drones, designed to imitate the dove on Freegovs logo, perched forebodingly on top of the streetlights in between their routine patrols.

Joey wondered what he would miss and drew a blank, then who he would miss, another blank; there wasn't anyone real anymore. Maybe this was why he wasn't too overwhelmed by the thought of death. All those years of compliance trying to avoid death and now it was upon him he didn't care. Oh, the irony. Then and again there was Freetime V.R.; a virtual reality world where every survivor could and did live out their every fantasy.

As he entered his pod, the evenings, "Respect and Remember," show interrupted his field of vision. Survivors were obliged to watch these daily briefings from the Freegov as part of their user agreement back when the lifechip was installed. The city's all-seeing C.C.T.V. cameras allowed Freegov to record and play footage of the days sacrifices along with the names of the heroes who committed them; these came under the, "Respect," part of the broadcast. They then awarded one of the sacrifices the death of the day award for achieving the best death, which meant his or her memorial would be two feet higher in the Cemetery of Heroes. Achieving hero status meant ongoing respect in the Safezone; for example, streets and monuments were constantly being renamed in their honour.

The, "Remember," part of the broadcast was an equally gory, however somehow more sinister affair. Pockets of rebels, or anti-lifers as they had become known, who had chosen to reject the lifechip and protection of Freegov, were shown living in the No-zone in the midst of the war. They would then be massacred by overwhelming firepower, played out as if it had been recorded on hidden camera. There were usually closeups of indescribable horrors to remind the survivors of what life would be like without the protection of Freegov. survivors didn't discuss or question this part of the broadcast. The horrors were enough to keep them quiet.

'Bollocks!' Joey murmured as the death of the day clip started. The scene looked strangely familiar.

This morning's calamity was playing out for the all to see on the show. "Irving" had won the award for what they were calling, "The long-jump." He chuckled to himself; I mean this guy had timed it to perfection and definitely deserved the plaudits.

The avatar hosts' analysis was making the point that a fraction of a second later and the hero would have simply long jumped into the side of the monorail, likewise any earlier and he would have missed making any contact whatsoever or the vehicle would have stopped. Irving had managed to land both legs across the track a split second before the monorail arrived, in a similar fashion to the landing of a long jumper in the sand pit when they stretch their legs out. The vehicle did not slow so sheared them clean off at the thigh before coming to a halt. As Irving recoiled from the impact he fell backward onto his back, stumps in the air spurting fountains of blood vertically upward into the air, he had a dazed but satisfied look on his face. There was no sign of the legs.

Strange, Joey thought, this was not how he remembered it this morning; he was sure the victim was stuck under the vehicle still alive without the cartoon like gore of the stumps bleeding upward. All traces of Joey and Cara had been removed. He could understand Freegov editing out his and Cara's lifesaving attempt but to somehow alter the reality of what happened made Joey uneasy. Questions flew around in his head. Was the victim in control of his actions? Did anyone really commit suicide for the cause? Were he and Cara in danger? Joey began to wonder if Freegov could be trusted; an uncomfortable feeling harboured in his gut.

Cara's face appeared in his field of vision, she looked better than Joey remembered and was a welcome distraction. Joey winked his right eye to answer her call.

'Did you see that?' She asked.

'Of course, we all have to watch it don't we,' Joey replied, immediately regretting his tone.

'Look I'm in trouble, can we meet?' Cara asked.

'Are you…'

'Yes,' Cara replied, cutting him off before he could say timing out.

'Me too, okay tomorrow at 9 p.m. at the central waterway,' Joey suggested.

Cara signed off without saying goodbye. Joey liked that, no bullshit.

They would talk tomorrow and he could check her recollection of events. Joey took his evening pills and made himself a cup of black tea. It was freetime.

Imagine all the rules and restrictions that computer games or apps or streaming sites or any type of entertainment had in the early 2020's. In particular, how your progress or enjoyment would come down to money and how much of it the developers could extract from you on a regular recurring basis. Then imagine there was no money system; it was all unlocked, ready for you to create, explore, relax, and enjoy. Then imagine the rules, laws and social constraints of society did not exist. There were no morals, no frowning, no limits. This was it, freetime "where dreams become reality."[6] The honey-soaked carrot offered by Freegov to every survivor in return for installing the Lifechip and accepting the War Economy. Considering everything they had taken away, which could best be described as everything, then the replacement had to be all encompassing. And it was.

In freetime, the user could choose from a variety of options; according to Freegov monitoring, by far the most popular was, "freetime freestyle", where your avatar joined a virtual reality copy of the old world and did as they pleased. Joey sometimes wondered what other survivors did in their freetime, for it was not a regular topic of discussion.

[6] "Where dreams become Reality:" Freegov repeated this phrase constantly, as if brainwashing the survivors, during the peace negotiations of 2035 when the war weary people were given the 'choice' to accept a lifechip.

Joey connected to his regular game and began jogging on the spot, then he reached down and touched his toes then held his arms out in front of him, then behind his back for a few seconds each. Looking from Joey's virtual reality point of view; he was inside a large stadium filled with cheering avatars, some of them waved banners with Joey's face on them. He stood on a blue concrete surface with white lines painted on it in the shape of a rectangle, which was divided in two by a taught net. Another avatar stood at the other end of the rectangle bouncing a small luminous yellow ball on the ground.

'Ready, play,' A voice said loudly, moments later the yellow ball came speeding towards him.

*

Meanwhile, in another part of the vast city, Cara was also in her Freetime virtual reality. The advanced technology contained in the Lifechip linked to the brain and allowed your body to experience the five senses in the V.R. world as if they were real.

The real world was so controlled and depressing it had become a means to an end. In 2050 survivors behaved like robots in the human world and humans in the robot world.

After a little deliberation, Cara chose time travel. She selected 2024; the old-world map appeared and she chose London.

It was the year of the General Election and Cara found herself in the midst of the chaos. The government had moved to higher ground in the north of the city, where Alexandra Palace was commandeered after the flooding of Parliament and most of central London. The devastating flood occurred after a, "Once in a lifetime," storm caused a surge in the North Sea during the summer of 2024. The deadly force made short thrift of the Thames Barrier and the dry, unforgiving ground made the flooding ten times worse according to, "The Times." A state of emergency was declared and the planned September election postponed until May the following year.

The streets were largely empty of their normal inhabitants. Modified garbage trucks, manned by faceless soldiers wearing hazmat suits and breathing apparatus, moved up and down the streets sucking up the grim contents. The putrid water harboured all sorts of bacteria; movement was restricted to allow for the clean-up operation and to protect public health. Anywhere not under water was under the watchful eye of soldiers and police in four-wheel drive patrol vehicles.

Cara wanted to explore and speak to people but this part of the system did not allow interaction; merely watching, so she turned her attention to the news. It made for uneasy viewing. The exact number of deaths were unknown but estimated to be over one million. The floods hit the whole country and these early estimates were just for the capital.

Cara sighed and shook her head; she hit the exit button and fast-forwarded time to May the following year. A televised Leaders debate between the election candidates was about to begin on the main state-run channel. Before the debate started a stern-faced commentator explained the unusual circumstances: When the flood occurred, a strange twist of fate saw the United Kingdom's 650 politicians, senior Civil Servants, the royal family, and a considerable number of overvalued, needy and vocal celebrities attending a ceremony on the River Thames. The ceremony was to mark the launch of a new part public, part private, part crowd funded and mostly hedge funded medical ship the; "H.M.S. N.H.S."

Many of the viewing V.I.P.'s were crushed between the ship and the concrete dock, the others drowned. There were no survivors. The public response was muted, indeed rumours abounded that the ships launch was timed to co-inside with the flood, and that the, brand new, thousand bed ship was really their pre-planned escape. Although this should have become a time of national mourning and tragedy, the people seemed to be of the opinion that their ruling class had long been in it for themselves, especially after the recent scandals and creeping authoritarianism, and that it may not have been such a tragedy for them to be wiped out in one fell swoop. The decimation of the established ruling class meant the evenings important democratic business would be conducted by fresh faces who had been hastily introduced to steer the course at their party's helm.

"We believe passionately in the reconstruction and rejuvenation of this great nation ...your vote will guarantee fair, just and equal distribution of ..." A politician began.

Cara listened for a moment then clenched her fist and covered her ears. No wonder they were unpopular, she thought, as she cut the speaker off and fast forwarded to the Election results programme a few days later.

The campaign had been managed in the context of the great flood and to some extent had been less adversarial and more cooperative than any election in memory. Some commentators were calling it the, "Kind," election. Others were complaining that the different parties had the same political goals.

The circumstances and clues were not enough to stem the shock on election night when a political coup was well and truly achieved. It was announced on the state broadcaster that a, "Unity Government," would be formed following an agreement between the two main parties and their smaller competitors. In an unprecedented move they had agreed to stand down M.P.'s strategically from the voting in different constituencies so that each party had the same number of M.P.'s and a hung parliament meant they set up a coalition. The election had a very high turnout supposedly due to the, hastily introduced, electronic voting system. This, according to commentators, gave added political legitimacy.

That a deal was announced on election night when it would normally take a week or so to thrash out implied a level of conspiracy had occurred behind the scenes. The fact that control of the Kingdom's nuclear red button had passed to a group of unknown, untested conspirators was beyond most analysis. The commentators sang the praises of the, "Unity government," and looked forward to it writing the world's wrongs. An onlooker might imagine all the, "United," politicians holding hands and eating marshmallows sat around a campfire singing folk songs while their citizens froze and starved and died from disease.

Cara wondered what all the fuss was about, why vote for a government who can't even protect you from the weather? She couldn't see Freegov ever getting in such a mess. I mean no wonder the world became so vulnerable while national governments full of pocket lining charlatans had been running it into the ground for so long.

Chapter 4

Daria was enjoying looking out of the oversized glass window at the beautiful view of Capital Lake until a group of paddle boarders entered her line of sight and slowly progressed toward the shore. She wished them ill and began contemplating what she would have for lunch when her virtual computer screen materialised on her desk and the inbox notification flashed. As she looked down she saw the details of two more timeouts from West city, Safezone 1.

Damn it, she thought, these two had the worst timing; until she took a closer look and realised she knew the man…before the Fall.[7] He had been one of her first targets in London, and although no further action was the outcome then, she knew there was no such thing as coincidence in her real line of work. She paused for a moment as she remembered him more clearly; even though she wasn't supposed to remember anything…a slight alteration to her Lifechip had been well within the capabilities of her long-term employer, "Mother." The group was named after its first leader who took it upon herself to nurture and push the first employees, much like a mother would. The family connotation bred a loyalty to the cause so strong that its members became fanatical in their obedience and devotion.

Joey Styles. He looked a lot older now. She'd had a thing for older guys for most of her adult life. Even when she was younger herself, she was mature enough to know what they wanted, what she had to offer and, more importantly, what she could get in return. It also helped that she was extremely intelligent, in mean physical shape and had the protection of a powerful family behind her. She had always done quite well out of her habit, she thought, however she never settled down, found true love or had a family. Being a lone wolf, along with Mother's far reaching tentacles, helped her selection by Freegov to live and work in the capital. Her career path was floorless; going from University College London to an Internship then full-time role at the United Nations. She now worked for Freegov as Coordinator of the Peacegames.[8]

---

[7] The Fall: A nickname given to the disastrous event that marked the start of the five-year war in 2030.

[8] Peacegames: Weekly event (in each Safezone) where timed out survivors competed to kill each other as a sacrifice.

Joey turning up had unsettled her. Her training kicked in and she jolted into action, down the fire escape and out the backdoor, disabling the alarm expertly with her modified smartwatch. Minutes later and she had left her mark, now she must wait. Back in the office, a vegan burger from the canteen in hand for cover, she decided to get these new timeouts uploaded on the system. She always made sure that no questions could ever be asked about her work, it was part of her training.

Once these two were uploaded the general survivor population could see their details; start voting on scenarios, weapons and who was to be the wolf. After fifteen years in the role Daria realised it was the good-looking ones that seemed to get picked more often than not. Maybe the viewers subconsciously wanted to save them in the unlikely event they scored full marks from the committee. Then again it could easily have been a baser instinct, borne out of jealousy, to want to see them suffer a final humiliation.

As she began her work uploading; which was in effect data entry from one system to another, she got to know the timeouts better. They were both from West City in the Safezone one and had timed out at the same time. This was unusual, considering there were six zones each with four megacities where an average of one hundred survivors timed out each week. This meant there were usually four hundred or so survivors in each zone's weekly game. She wondered if they knew each other and what mess they had gotten themselves into to timeout simultaneously. She also wondered if Joey had somehow managed to pull the wool over her eyes all those years ago.

A message popped up with the current population statistics; 512,366,001. There was an average of 3 million deaths a year. These consisted mostly of automatic time expiries when a survivor reached sixty years of age, then natural deaths, and finally timeouts and heroic suicides. The bulk of Earth's population had perished during the disastrous years between 2025 and 2035 when, it seemed, anything that could go wrong, did. Or so they were told.

At this rate there was still four years to go before a permanent ceasefire could be signed with the oppressive enemy force. Although Daria knew very well that would never happen. It kept the stupid survivors going.

Despite lots having changed in the world since the fall, some things remained the same; that evening the moon shone brightly into Daria's curtain-less bedroom in the Capital; bright enough for her to write three neat lines on a piece of paper then fold it in half several times and place it under her pillow. At dawn the following morning, outside and barefoot, with the destination of her wishes still visible; she scrawled up the piece of paper she had written on, set it alight and watched it burn. It burned fully without assistance, experience told her this was a good sign. Many years ago, soon after she started practising, things began to change for Daria, in good ways and bad; she became rich but was afflicted with unusual physical ailments. She achieved her goals easily but her friends and family were held back, sometimes they were hurt or even worse. But that didn't stop her.

Chapter 5

The Central Waterway was an island positioned in the centre-point of the four main canals in West City, each canal ran out from this island along the points of the compass. The monorail ran around the cities edges and stopped at the main work facilities and a tram system linked the four canals in a circular pattern within the city, like a shooting target. The canals were used to transport goods, the trams and monorail; the survivors. There were no motorized vehicles or air travel and therefore little pollution.

There was a large Freegov monument in the centre of the island, which had served as a meeting place in the early days, before the survivors had learnt to distrust each other. The monument consisted of a globe shielded underneath one wing of a dove with the word Freegov written on its other wing. What looked like a laser coming from above was deflected by the wing. Now the monument had become more of a landmark for survivors navigating their way home.

There were several cast-iron benches on artificial grass verges around the monument that faced large display screens. On them pictures of the new timeouts and voting options for the upcoming Peacegames were shown together with replays of the latest Peacegames and Respect and Remember shows. There were also adverts for new features that had become available on the Freetime V.R. system; where dreams became reality.

Joey chose a bench and sat down, he was early; sharp eyed and on the lookout for Cara. Daylight faded and turned to dusk but the air was still warm and he had no need for his overcoat. He admired the cleanliness of the pathways and the perfectly contrasting fake grass. Above him, a drone hovered while cleaning the lamp post, and its important passenger, then moved on silently to the next.

She moved quickly and he felt her before he could acknowledge her; her leg pressed against his. Other than them the bench was empty and Joey could see no reason why Cara had to sit so close to him other than to unnerve him or send some kind of energy his way.

'Hi,' she smiled, her deep brown eyes darting upward just long enough for him to detect an unsettled look, perhaps betraying what was left of the soul inside. Joey felt as if he were being controlled by an invisible force, he could not move his leg away nor reply.

'Are you okay Joey, it's me Cara…you remember?' She asked.

'Yes, hi I'm sorry I couldn't speak then,' Joey replied, eventually.

'Why were you busy or?' Cara asked, looking slightly puzzled.

'No, no I just forgot how to speak or move for a minute there,' Joey explained, again wondering what the hell he was talking about and immediately wishing he could restart this conversation.

'How is your head?' she asked, glancing up and tenderly touching the lump on Joey's head, which had reduced from golf ball to peanut size.

'Good, I mean it's good to see you,' Joey replied fumbling with the pocket of his overall, before continuing, 'what have you been up to today?'

'Working, and you?' Cara replied, eying Joey's hand movements carefully.

'Yeah, working too, in the factory.' Joey said, having successfully retrieved the item.

'We all work in factories Joey, what is that?' she asked, pointing at his now clenched fist.

'Here, it's yours,' Joey opened his hand revealing the ornament he had found after their last meeting.

'You keep it, I won't be needing it anymore.' She replied.

'What do you mean, why not?' Joey asked.

'You'll see. We should have been famous by now,' Cara replied.

'What will I see?' Joey asked.

'More than they showed on the R and R broadcast,' Cara replied. She closed his hand around the ornament and pushed it back towards him. Joey felt the strength in her will and acquiesced.

'It looked so real but we know it wasn't, maybe the Peacegames aren't either?' Joey said.

'Don't talk so loud,' she whispered looking around anxiously.

'What does it matter, we're going to timeout on Friday,' Joey replied.

'It's all my fault, I'm so sorry,' she replied and shifted away from him slightly.

'You didn't force me,'

'Well then its settled, I will sacrifice,' she said, sizing up the Freegov monument behind them.

Joey felt a lump in his throat and a lead weight in his stomach. He had, perhaps naively, not even considered this was what Cara was going to say; to offer him redemption through her own sacrifice.

'No, I won't let you do that,' he replied, holding her arm as she started to get up.

'Why, why, why? Are you crazy, I'm giving you your life back,' she exclaimed while pounding her free fist pathetically into his stomach.

Joey put his arm around her and gently exerted some pressure. Cara pressed herself against him and began to calm.

It was an odd sight in the Safezone, two survivors embracing in public, but darkness had fallen and there were few others around.

'It's okay, we will figure something out,' he said, his arm now tightly wrapped around her. There was no immediate response, just a sniffle and her head burrowed into his emaciated chest.

Joey heard a feint whining noise; he looked across to see a drone fast approaching behind Cara. Momentarily they were both shocked off the bench, which had become electrified. They left without another word. Joey enjoyed a warm feeling he didn't fully understand.

*

Cara needed an escape, she wasn't expecting to be back in her Pod that evening. If her plan had succeeded she would be at the bottom of the canal, having drowned after breaking off the Freegov Dove Monument, attaching it to her waist then jumping into the canal and sinking to the bottom. But Joey had put paid to that, *the bastard.*

Arriving in her pod, it occurred to her that there was no difference in being alive or dead in the Safeworld. She didn't need to buy milk or dinner, there was nobody depending on her; everything was the same and it would have been so if she were at the bottom of the canal. Freetime V.R. was the only activity, the Lifechip had successfully managed to replace empathy with suspicion. But, now she trusted him, the meeting with Joey had opened up feelings she had forgotten all about.

Cara sat back in a comfortable chair with a new vigour to discover more about the past. She tuned into Freetime; selected time travel and this time June 2030, London. An error message filled the screen:

"Date cannot be within the last twenty years. Please re-select."

'Zut Alors,' her native tongue returned with frustration. She vaguely remembered the instruction video had said the last twenty years were unavailable for security reasons. With a remorseful sigh she returned to the main menu and set up a night out in Vegas.

*

A few hours later, as he closed his eyes and finally drifted off to sleep, Joey wondered whose reality was more real, that of two primary sources witnessing an event, or that of millions of secondary sources witnessing an altered recording of the same event. He even questioned if his reality was the same as Cara's. Even though he knew it was wrong, Joey couldn't help but think it was the millions of people. The sheer numbers and the potential power of the discourse amongst them was far greater than the truth that he and Cara knew. 2050 where reality was no longer truth. Even if you knew it was; you thought it wasn't.

Chapter 6

Life in the Capital was unusual but acceptable; especially when it was compared to the Safezones. Interaction was common and although co-habitation was not officially banned it tended not to happen. A normal food diet was available; they lived without the perilous side effects of the sustenance pills thus sexual urges remained. The majority of the inhabitants worked for Freegov at their administrative headquarters, ensuring the various aspects of government ran smoothly. The others worked in service industries to support the capital's economy. Like the survivors; their movements, association and decision making were all recorded by the Lifechip, however, they were not time restricted.

They earned digital tokens each month that could be used for purchases. All inhabitants earned the same number of tokens. The economy was limited, for example, food was restricted to what could be grown within the city limits. Entertainment was largely via the Freetime V.R. model but unlike in the Safezone tokens were required to unlock features; this created a desire to progress and increased the time they spent in the virtual world. Sport and leisure facilities were available. One might describe this as more of a hybrid transitional economy than that of the Safezones.

The inhabitants knew what life was like in the Safezones and were thus known as collaborators. Freegov informed them of this term and that it meant they were helping the effort to survive the oppressors' threat, however another school of thought could interpret the collaborator in the World War Two sense of the word, where the citizens of an occupied country assisted in the dark purposes of the occupier.

Socially, the Lifechip controlled the collaborators with physical punishments for any violations. For example, a minor violation might lead to an electric shock, burn or disfigurement. A more serious violation meant removal of a corresponding body part, for example, if you stole then you had your finger chopped off. Persistent offending (which wasn't strictly defined) meant permanent exile to the Safezone – a fait collaborators saw as equal to if not worse than death. Much like in the Safezone, after fifteen years, the strict rules had weeded out the weaker links and people behaved.

Was this utopia? The collaborators were allowed to cultivate social links; however, reproduction was not permitted. In the rare event that a pregnancy occurred the father was immediately exiled, and the mother and child whisked away in titanium caskets directly after the birth to an unknown location. Like the survivors, all memories before 2035 were erased by accepting the Lifechip implant; families were destroyed as those under eighteen were removed by Freegov under the auspices of conscription and never heard from again. Nobody asked where they went, most likely as they couldn't remember.

Politically the Freegov was anonymous; there were no parties, leaders or politicians. They were mostly taken care of in the years of turmoil before the war broke out, and people were glad for it. Freegov was a centralised world government in a perilous time where everything was geared to survival against the all-encompassing enemy threat. Because the nature of power corrupting all previous forms of government had been exposed and admitted to; Freegov claimed a new political high ground by having no leader and a single common goal. This goal, to repel the threat to earth, meant no new direction or policy change would be required until that goal was achieved.

To ensure efficient pursuit of the single goal then everyone was equal and accepted the sacrifices necessary to achieve that goal; permanent peace. As this was a long-term effort expected to take decades the collaborators and survivors alike settled into their roles, nicely distracted by freetime, and didn't tend to ask questions. Because of this nobody really knew who or what was in charge of Freegov, if anyone at all.

Economic activity was limited; there were farmers and distributors of food, maintenance of the infrastructure and housing and administration of the Safezones. The administration of the Safezones was the largest sector; essentially a massive technological security operation. The drones and robots needed programming, maintenance and Artificial Intelligence automation software to ensure the Safezones were policed and protected. The earned tokens expired at the end of a month, everyone earned the same amount and it was not possible to save any, therefore in theory, the society was equal and would remain so.

Daria sat down and checked her inbox, expecting to see the usual timed-out survivors awaiting her directions to commence their final journey. She smiled as she thought of all the worthless survivors she had sent on their way and looked forward to her final reward. A hidden life of murder and magic tended to have a desensitizing effect on someone and she was no exception. The promised reward for a life following Mother's instruction without question was retirement in a secret location far away, a place with every luxury, without limits, where evil knew no bounds. She couldn't wait.

Amongst the ghostly candidates, she spotted a message from Freegov Command:

"Safezone 1 Peacegames requires a champion. Identify suitable candidate(s)."

Her ears pricked up and her back straightened. Could this be the moment she had been waiting for? Anything unusual they said. An old target appearing out of the blue then an unusual order from Command for the Peacegames he was in. She checked her watch, it was too early to leave the office without raising suspicions so she bit her tongue and got on with the mundane administration, besides that her response wasn't due yet.

As the clock reached midday, Daria waited patiently for the lunchtime exodus to abate; she didn't want to get caught up in any meaningless conversations and risk a companion for lunch today. *Control what you can, deceive the rest.* She remembered her training well as she walked through the now empty corridor toward the stairs. The building was low rise and constructed of wood, concrete and glass in a modern style. Money was no object and beautiful aesthetics ruled in the Capital, especially at the headquarters on the shores of the lake. The contact point was a small old-fashioned café about two blocks away, eyes up and on the lookout, she arrived at the door six minutes after leaving the office, a little faster than normal, perhaps betraying her anxiety. As usual, the door was closed and the nets drawn; the dilapidated red and white paintwork outside gave the café an unwelcoming feel.

Inside the café was furnished with six small tables, spaced evenly around its walls and glass frontage. There was a deli style counter at the back, opposite the front door, with un-appetising produce in it. She took a seat at a table in the far corner, picked up the menu and pretended to browse. Momentarily, a scruffily dressed middle-aged waiter approached with a tray and set its contents; a pot of tea, glass of water and a cheese sandwich, down on the table in front of her. She double checked the contents of the sandwich, nodded her thanks and started for the restroom.

Once inside she lifted the lid of the toilet tank and set it onto the floor. She then placed a small clear plastic zip lock bag, containing a piece of paper, inside; carefully returned the lid and left. Back in the main room, she stopped at the counter where condiments, cutlery and serviettes were available and collected a take-out box.

'Madam,' The waiter called as Daria pulled open the door to exit. She turned, without reply, to see him holding up a small paper bag.

'Your desert, courtesy of the house.' He said with no expression, having made his way toward her and given her the bag.

She was outside in less than ten minutes, anyone watching would see a collaborator, lunch in hand, diligently returning to the office not wanting to be late.

Later that afternoon Daria contemplated the situation and the evidence. Mother had responded with instructions for her to make direct contact with Joey. This in itself was unusual, normally observation orders came first, via a ham sandwich. Then there was the desert on the house, it was highly unusual and she struggled to remember the code to translate that message, she'd never encountered it before, even after all these years.

Electrical pulses shot around her head eventually finding the correct path; desert equalled the top prize- Scales. Mother had been looking for the Scientist, Scales, who created the Lifechip since 2030 when he disappeared into the fog of war. A brilliant mind, he studied at Columbia University, before a financial windfall allowed him to set up his own lab in Geneva at the turn of the century.

Mother's information indicated Scales was working on a time travelling device. This put him at the top of their wanted list; only a time traveller could threaten what they had achieved. Could Scales finally be ready to show his hand? This might be a massive coup for her, but it could also be a total disaster if she had let Joey through the net years ago and he turned out to be a player.

Then there was the bizarre email: a Peacegames champion? She read over it again; it was short and sweet. She felt as if she were being funnelled into a decision by the unfolding events and she didn't like it. She needed more information on Joey and Cara. Given an excuse to be nosey she set to work on the Freegov systems. A few moments later and access to Cara's lifechip revealed how her and Joey had met and also her physiological responses to the interactions with him.

Although it was strictly need to know, part of Mother's deal with Freegov was to share the information they had gathered over the years, especially the latter years, and this was all uploaded to the survivors Lifechips in 2035. For decades, Mother had used its tentacles to hoover up the data that humans had unwittingly revealed about themselves through years of internet and technology use. The smart grid and the cloud merely fancy terms for a virtual reproduction of their mind's deepest thoughts. There was literally a cloud hanging over everyone with their most personal and up to date information. Mother used this to gain advantages and lead humanity down the path to its sorry demise. In return they broadcast degenerative pornography and damaging media back through the airwaves to cement the destruction. Before they handed it over they had compiled a massive database which allowed them to simulate, within a seventy five percent accuracy range, the decisions people would take when faced with a certain situation. Virtual mind control. Before the Lifechip, only the few who thought differently remained out of reach.

After a short search, Daria noted an increase in heart rate and blood pressure during both Joey and Cara's meetings. After installation, the Lifechip was linked to the brain and had all sorts of neurological sensors to invoke physical sensory reality; its extra monitoring of the human bodies physiological reactions meant Freegov could simulate the survivor's likely thoughts to a higher accuracy than Mother, although their live thoughts were still just out of reach. According to the rumours, that sort of wizardry was reserved for the select few. Daria enjoyed playing these sorts of games and often wished for access to the Freegov data on Freetime usage. *That would open up a whole new paradigm of psychological study, and would allow the owner full administrator access to the human mind.*

That was that then, they met randomly and there were romantic feelings between them. That was enough to satisfy Daria's concerns that some kind of conspiracy was less likely than she feared. The decision was made, she'd nominate Joey and Cara as prospective champions; this would likely lead to a meeting thus satisfy Mother. She knew all there was to know about Joey, his love of; tennis, his daughter and excess so she stopped short of researching his past via the Freegov records. Had she done so she would have found the space where his surname should be was blank as was his picture and date of birth. Sometimes this happened when they had been a member of the intelligence or military community. Thinking herself to be ever professional she continued to research Cara a little more.

Cara Leclerc was originally from a small town in the south east of France with no children or significant other. She was born in 2010, studied History at university then had gone on to D.J. on the European dance music circuit. History rang alarm bells; there were a fair few of them in the services; as did no kids. But what a strange combination…that would be a new play book for any western agency, even the French.

Satisfied for now that she could handle these two, Daria let her thoughts run wild; a D.J. and a tennis coach; the possibilities for the first ever Peacegames champion were endless. A new musical style to help maintain survivor solidarity or the sheep buried under a sea of tennis balls. She switched to her mail programme and replied to Command with Joey and Cara's details.

A couple of hours later Daria found herself in the changing room post workout. The gym was small and exquisitely maintained. Her shower cubicle private awash with slate and marble. She turned up the heat until mint fragranced steam clouded the space. This was a standout advantage of life in the Capital, everything worked without limits, and was of the highest quality, a little like West Germany in the 1990's. It was almost as if there were no all-encompassing enemy or war economy. In the steamy cubicle, her hands drifted down below her waist, she found herself thinking of Joey, and a few minutes later, relieved, again. There was something about him that worried her. Even back then, her in all her feminine glory both physically and mentally she hadn't managed to read or seduce him. Still she got the job done, that was all that mattered and that's what she was going to do again, but this time there would be no comebacks…and the bitch would be history too.

Chapter 7

Back in his pod after an uneventful day Joey thought about the end. It was Wednesday and he would time out on Friday evening. He wondered what would happen between then and the Peacegames; where would he be taken and under what conditions? Who would take him there and how long would it take. How many other survivors would there be and would he be a wolf or a sheep. There were a lot of questions and no answers; after all nobody had ever survived in order to document this. His mind jumped back to the, "Respect and Remember," show the other day and Irvings altered death. Were the Peacegames even real? Or could they be just a show to keep up appearances and the narrative? He was clutching at straws now.

Joey sighed, then he smiled broadly, a vision of beauty. He looked up to the right of his display and winked through until Cara appeared then a blink later her face was flashing and he waited. No reply. Again…no reply. Had she timed out already? Had she offered herself to avoid the Peacegames? More likely she was in an alternative reality self-medicating. Joey decided to do likewise.

Cara had no idea Joey was trying to contact her; to activate Freetime V.R. the operator had to connect to the system. This was only possible via a device in the home that connected to the Lifechip. Once survivors were connected to the V.R. world they became disconnected from the real world and could not be contacted until they disconnected themselves. As well as a devious way to restrict socialising, this also meant the survivors were effectively dead when they were alive and alive when they were dead;

That evening Cara went history time travelling again this time as an observer to events in Europe during the mid 2020's. Paris, Amsterdam, Munich, Vienna and Rome. Cara flicked between them; compared to London things seemed less jovial, there were no celebrations or ship launches planned. In contrast there were, "European Security Force," (E.S.F.) vehicles and troops on the streets, to Cara they looked like military vehicles. Dark green and black painted S.U.V.s, perhaps Mercedes G Wagons, and armed men in boots with helmets and dark uniforms. The security forces were stationed at intersections, ring roads and large public buildings. It looked like they were enforcing a curfew of sorts; burned out cars, abandoned buildings and dark streets indicated disorder and civil unrest. The great flood of summer 2024 hit hard; particularly the lowlands of Belgium, Holland and Germany. Alpine regions suffered too with landslides destroying transport links and leaving entire regions isolated.

The Freetime V.R. history section was similar to a limited search of Primary information for the period you requested. Cara could type her search in and get several sources of information. The difference was that, for example when you looked up a news report, the V.R. mode would put you in the show, so you could experience it in V.R. The limitations were that no searches were possible from 2030 onwards; when the first Lifechips were trialled and introduced voluntarily amongst the population. This meant there was effectively a five-year gap in history from 2030 to 2035 when the Freetime Lifechip became a compulsory installation in return for the ceasefire and protection of Freegov.

History time travel was more like you being placed in the situation and being able to observe what happened without interacting with it. To find out what the E.S.F. were doing on the streets of Europe Cara's best chance was to search for news reports or articles then place herself in appropriate situations to investigate further.

A Euro News report in August 2026 announced the formation of the E.S.F. It was a merger of the European Union's military and police forces in response to continuous and serious civil unrest across the continent that decade. The report was detailed and listed long and short-term causes, followed by detailed analysis of the particular events.

Long Term Causes
- *Restrictions on freedom of movement and association following the Pandemic's led to deep divisions in society.*
- *Economic Crisis exacerbated by inflation, high debt levels and housing bubble.*
- *Political Instability after the G7 Terror Attack, 2025 and the Great Flood, 2024.*
- *Increased death rates due to pandemics and weakened immune system.*
- *Decreased birth rates due to mystery fertility crisis (miscarriages) and lack of confidence.*
- *Increase in catastrophic weather events.*

Short Term Causes
- *Police not sufficiently armed, trained or centrally commanded. Everyday consensual policing had been destroyed by years of draconian law making.*
- *Military needed more recruits.*
- *Introduction of the European digital currency (EDC); replaced the Euro and devalued assets, removed cash and increased government control in 2026.*

Cara read these bullet points and was keen to find out more, it seemed like a lot of things had happened in a short period of time and she would need to delve a little deeper to find out more. The G7 terror attack called out to her for some reason, perhaps she used to be a historian. Several pages further down she began to read:

G7 Terror Attack, Paris, France. August 28, 2025. Report from unidentified website.

The 52nd G7 Summit went off with a bang as a massive explosion disturbed the extended evening dinner with partner session on the first day of the meeting. The group of seven or "G7" consists of: Germany, Japan, Italy, France, Unites States, United Kingdom and Canada plus a European Union representative. The meeting was being held in the French capital after a late switch from the countries southwest coast that was, ironically, blamed on security fears.

The overexuberant Michelin starred menu read, "Bombe Surprise," for the desert. It certainly was a surprise for the political elite and hangers on from the most developed countries on the globe, those responsible for coining such terms as 'the international rules-based order', to be blown to smithereens as they finished stuffing their faces with the finest luxury produce known to man; whilst outside the Bercy Conference Centre, starvation, disease, misery and suffering were the status quo.

There were also mass casualties amongst the press and media who were, unfortunately, eating at the same time in an adjacent room.

The European Union has blamed the attack on homegrown terrorists who call themselves Freedom Fighters, however, no group has yet claimed responsibility.

The public reaction was perhaps a little surprising with mass celebratory rallies breaking out in Capital cities across Europe and America. Street parties were held on a more local level as an outpouring of joy, usually reserved for a declaration of peace or a World Cup victory, spread like an infectious virus. The irony was not lost on these informed members of the public that the very politicians who had increased censorship via draconian legislation to protect against terrorism had themselves become the victims of the very same all-encompassing early 21st century boogie man. The narrative that they had managed so carefully had somehow turned around and swallowed them whole.

The Speaker of the House, [9] who was not in attendance, commented:

"We condemn the terrorists and appeal for stronger security measures to protect the rule of law and maintain order."

On the public celebrations he commented that they were in fact paying their respects to the inspirational leaders who were so loved and revered for the very, very difficult and genuinely heart-breaking decisions they had made over the previous five years.

Cara thought to herself that, even from her limited learning, following years of policy failure, disease, death and disaster it was more likely the public hated their leaders than loved them.

---

[9] United States Government, Speaker of the House of Representative's. Third in line to the Presidency.

34

There was an immediate security curfew placed Europe wide, plus the G7 countries, while the terrorists were sought. Citizens were only allowed out to collect their, hastily introduced, rations once every three days.

The consequences of this attack were unprecedented. Most member states had sent their Presidents, Prime Ministers, foreign ministers plus their armies of advisors, spin doctors and civil servants. The worlds press and media institutions were also silenced, their synchronised megaphones finally quiet after years of noise. When combined with the, "Great Flood H.M.S. N.H.S." tragedy in London the year before then most of the worlds political elites had been washed away or gone up in smoke.

Cara wondered whether there some kind of takeover was going on by some behind the scenes organisation? There certainly was a power vacuum in place now; who would fill it? Would there be some sort of world government needed to maintain order?

Cara's thoughts, like Joey before her, drifted towards the nature of reality. This old report had given her an outline of what had happened but it was clearly one sided and provided nothing solid on why the events occurred. Also, she considered the author: a big press conglomerate provided with stories by one of a couple of global news agencies. Who owned or had interests in them and why were their stories cut from the same cloth? More importantly who and how big were their audiences? Like Freegovs, "Respect and Remember," many years later was it a case that the more people that saw something the more real it became? Was some kind of mass psychosis going on globally and when did it start? She had more questions than answers. Her mind switched to Joey.

Chapter 8

"Agreed. Give both same opportunities to win, ensure the deaths are simultaneous. Mandate all zones to watch. Set for Saturday night."

As soon as she sat down that sunny Thursday morning, Daria read through the email from Command and realised this was on her. She could do what she liked and wasn't in the mood to waste her time; her Spin Class with Pablo was later that evening and that meant she'd be spinning on something else for a couple of hours afterward.

There were only two hundred timeouts in total; two wolves and the remainder sheep. That made things easier. She should be able to make Joey and Cara the wolves; the votes were due in that evening but they could be fixed before being published. It was just the weapons that she needed to work out; a quick look back at their occupations gave her an idea. She would provide them with equipment that related to their skills before the fall. Despite their memories being wiped their skills might have remained intact. She drew up a list that included: tennis rackets and balls, a laptop and decks, lighting, power, explosives and a history book.

It looked like someone was setting up for some kind of sporty dance festival, maybe Joey knew Yoga and would get them all balanced on one leg before death by exploding tennis ball. She hit send and closed the screen, job done with minimal effort, just the way she liked it. Little did Freegov know their precious victors faced another threat entirely. Now for her life.

*

Cara was delaying returning Joey's call. Although she had no direct memories to recall, she thought this must be what it felt like when you liked someone romantically. She wondered what he was doing, where he was and what he was wearing. It didn't take long for her to snap out of it when she realised she knew the answers to all these lovestruck daydreams. He was assembling a drone at the factory wearing his blue work clothes. Working to maintain his subjugation. And she would be dead within the week.

A couple of blinks later Joey's face flashed in her field of vision, it was lunch time and he answered promptly. No messing around.

'Hi Cara.'

'Hi Joey.'

'How are you?'

'Great, and you?' She replied.

'I'm looking on the bright side, tomorrow is my last ever day of work,' Joey said, with a smirk.

Cara chuckled.

'Me too, anyway what did you want? I was busy time travelling yesterday,' she explained.

'Can we meet again, to……?' He started, then a loud claxon interrupted them and the call cut out abruptly.

'Take cover, incoming fire detected, take cover.' A robotic voice announced as the alarm continued, although the volume seemed to reduce slightly.

The factory lights dimmed and the survivors took cover where they could, mostly under workstations or tables but the washrooms were also safe. Joey, finally close enough to the bathroom, chose the latter hoping to get a good look out the window; he had never made it in time on other occasions this alert had gone off, usually every few months or so.

In the cramped cubicle, he manoeuvred himself onto the toilet and window ledge simultaneously, and craned his neck upwards. There was nothing; no smoke, no fire, no missile, no damage. Just nothing. Then almost as soon as it started it was over- the claxon stopped and the lights flickered on. As usual, there wasn't any damage inside the factory so the dazed survivors retraced their steps and continued their toil, no questions asked. Joey tried to call Cara but the Lifechip wouldn't let him in. He'd go to the same place at the same time later that night and hope for the best.

A few hours later Joey, Cara and 198 other survivors received an email with an attachment. Joey's read as follows:

Survivor,

You will timeout on Friday 1st June, 2050 at 7:30 p.m. when you will be collected from your place of work and transported to the Peacegames.

Thank you for your fifteen-year contribution to the war economy and the Freegov.

Your final patriotic duty will be to compete in the Safezone 1 Peacegames on Saturday 2nd June at 8:00 p.m.

You may achieve clemency by competing as a wolf and achieving a 10/10 score.

Alternately, you will be sacrificed and have played your part in maintaining the ceasefire and protection provided by Freegov. Further details to follow.

Freegov Admin

An invitation to death, no R.S.V.P. necessary. This was definitely real. Joey felt warm inside, not because he had done his bit for the Freegov, but because he had calculated the chances of him surviving. No-one had ever survived, so he had no chance.

Chapter 9

The Capital was an established international city before the fall, where the world's top scientific minds competed with suits full of bulging wallets for the finer things in life. To the north-west of the city a multi-limbed Hindu god protected the C.E.R.N.[10] research institute; whose Large Hadron Collider searched for the origins of the universe under the lake. Nobody knew whether Freegov kept it operating. With the Alps to the east and the Mediterranean coast hours to the south one might have called it the office for the elite of humanity, with the playground being just around the corner.

Daria liked it there, although life had become severely restricted, she was glad to be a collaborator and continue to live with some semblance of freedom. This came in the form of housing, friendships and liaisons, leisure activities and a normal food diet. Considering survivors and their fate was not something she, or indeed any collaborator, tended to do. In fact; their goal was to avoid thinking about them or of becoming one of them through violations.

Pablo's flat was luxury; masses of wood, granite and glass in a slightly elevated position set back from the town. The extra services he provided to the collaborators of the Capital seemed to elevate him above the station of a normal personal trainer in the eyes of Freegov. While all collaborators were equal and paid the same number of tokens, their housing allocation was unclear, however, it was clear some were more equal than others. Keeping them distracted was most important.

'Hey, whatsa the matter beautiful?' Pablo exclaimed, sweat running down his forehead and torso. 'I can't go on all night, I'm so busy, come on let go!' He continued.

---

[10] C.E.R.N: The European Centre for Nuclear Research, founded in 1954.

Daria was annoyed that she had to dismount prematurely; but she knew she was wasting her time. Concerned by the unusual events of the last couple of days, her mind was all over the place. Pablo was handsome, chiselled and well equipped for his role in the Capital but there didn't appear to be much going on up top. They had met years ago at the gym where she trained and he gave classes, following an observation order from Mother to investigate his subversive tendencies. She didn't see him as a threat then and she certainly didn't now.

'Is it your job thatsa bothering you bella?' he asked, before continuing, 'Maybe they no last forever!' Pablo said, eyes shiftily looking the room over. To discuss Freegov was subversion at the highest level; nobody even mentioned their name for fear of being exiled from their privileged life in the Capital.

'What do you mean?' she said, up and squeezing her tight jeans and top over her curvaceous figure.

'I heard of a great scientist, working on a machine that could change everything,' He replied, lowering his voice to a whisper throwing arms and flicking his long hair around the flat as he stood before a most extravagant mirror, hung over the mantle place in the centre of the bedroom. In a flash Pablo was back next to the bed hugging her and squeezing her hand tightly shut.

'Come on, get up my darling, you need to rest,' he said, prompting her towards the door.

As soon as she had left Pablo picked up the radio and hit transmit. The reply was almost immediate.

'Scales here, come in.'

'It worked, she took it,' Pablo said with not a hint of his exaggerated Italian accent.

'Good, very good. Proceed as planned.'

In the safety of her own flat later that evening, Daria retrieved the gift. She knew the all-seeing eyes of Freegov couldn't see in there thanks to Mother. As she unfolded the paper it was larger than she expected; an A5 piece of very old paper that looked as if it had been torn from a book. On it an old map of the Rijksmuseum in Amsterdam. One of the rooms on the first floor had a red pen mark in it.

A little computing time later Daria realised this was the same city where Joey and Cara would appear in the Peacegames later that week. Another coincidence, but the thought of finding Scales overwhelmed her racing mind. Pablo might be trying to expose a threat to Freegov; she figured he wasn't as slow as he seemed, in fact quite the opposite and chalked up another success to her feminine charms. Her wishes answered, the stars perfectly aligning in her favour, she wondered how much easier life could get.

*

Joey sat on the bench smiling and bobbing his head to his made-up beats. The white dove monument towering over him a reminder that he was protected; although he didn't feel it. It was like déjà-vu; Cara pressing into him all over again but this time closer, harder, more urgently. This time Joey didn't flinch. He pressed back. He liked it. He had an urge to get closer and they touched lips.

'Hi,' Cara said, between breaths. Joey moved in on her again.

'What's got into you?' she asked.

'You,' Joey replied.

Cara's eyebrows raised, her lips oversized on her face. Joey pictured how she would look with hair and clothes and a little more weight on her.

A passer-by cleared his throat loudly and the unusual couple detached; one more reluctantly than the other.

'If they faked the hero's death, maybe the Peacegames is fake too?' Joey Suggested, remembering his initial reason for contacting Cara.

'The weapons are weird but he still died, and so will we,' Cara replied; her cheeks rosy and neck blotched.

Joey went in closer again and this time received a quick slap to the cheek.

'Stop it, I'm trying to talk to you Joey,' she exclaimed. The slap did the trick; Joey jolted out of his amorous state.

'Sorry I…you know I play tennis on Freetime, I love it!' he said.

'And I love history!' She replied, touching her lip, her head tilted down but her eyes looking directly into his.

He moved his arm around her neck then pulled her toward him, their lips touched again this time more tenderly.

Chapter 10

Joey woke bleary eyed; but happy he didn't fully recall his final adventures in Freetime V.R. There were some things better forgotten. That there were no laws or limits was akin to that little devil on your shoulder being given a step ladder and megaphone to perfect his attack.

He wasn't rushing for anyone, any government or any factory robots. They could all stick it up their arse. As he showered and the hot water turned off before he was finished he cursed these bastard rules, maybe it wasn't such a bad thing to timeout. It wasn't much of a life, in fact it wasn't a life. It was slavery nothing more, nothing less.

The Freetime V.R. might distract them, but it wasn't real. He was ready to face his maker. As he dressed and glanced in the mirror, he noticed the bump on his head was pretty much gone, maybe that had jolted him out of his slumber this week. Cara jumped into his mind and he felt happy, what had happened? Did they? Yes, they had touched lips wow, he remembered her warmth, her soft skin, her aroma. Finally, alive; the day before his death.

Tony looked happy. A parasitic state apparatchik. He would sell out his own mother.

'What's the matter with you Tony?' Joey asked as he settled into his workstation at 8:15 a.m. red lights flashing and more violations, he didn't give a shit.

'I saved it since 2035, here you can wear it now!' Tony exclaimed, reaching into his pocket, he pulled out a badge and handed it to Joey. The badge was large enough to display the Freegov Logo with the words, "Heroic Sacrifice," superimposed on top of it. It was colourful and looked like it was targeted at children. There was something perverse about it. Joey undid the needle from the fastening device and stabbed it violently into Tony's hand, causing the badge to stand proudly for a moment.

'Ah, ah, ah, you bastard,' Tony screamed in shock, he pulled out the badge and rushed away in a fluster.

Joey laughed as two bots arrived, flashing and beeping. He had found a loophole in the system, once you were timed-out they had no control, after a brief pause the bots swished away toward the restroom.

He laughed again, this time uncontrollably, as he watched them leading Tony away, his face as red as the flashing violation display on the bot and the blood on his hand. Game, set and match Joey.

*

Daria's stares bounced like lasers around the walls of her flat, impatiently waiting for time to pass; all this technology available to man and she had to wait for a fucking train.

She read over the email from Freegov authorizing her to travel to the Peacegames. Maybe that's what was making her nervous; not *knowing* the full story about Freegov. She helped put them in place all those years ago but the rest was need to know. And she didn't.

After packing some clothes Daria adjusted the blinds carefully; there were two at the front of her apartment, and the signal was as simple as one being open and the other closed. In an age where everything was monitored digitally, the old methods were still the best.

With time to kill, there was only one thing for it; she headed to the gym. Squats, deadlifts and presses; heavy and hard, compound exercises to hit every muscle. Forty-five minutes later, sweat dripping from her body she spotted Pablo in the Studio. Daria looked at him but he seemed to look directly through her. The music was off and clients around him were picking up bags and waving at each other so she headed over. As she reached the door, her lace was loose so she stooped to tie it. Moments later in the studio and Pablo was gone, his bag abandoned on the floor and the fire exit door slightly ajar. Instinctively Daria followed, stairs up to ground level then an open, grassy space where cars used to park before the fall. No sign of Pablo and her wet skin getting cold, she retreated back to the warm studio, neatly picking up his discarded bag on her way out.

It all added up perfectly, Pablo was spooked after giving her a tip he shouldn't have; and preferred to run rather than face his fears. What a pussy.

With time to kill she grabbed an energy bar in the gyms café and looked over the travel instructions.

- *5 p.m. Board monorail and take to last stop; "Esportif," on Northern artery.*
- *5:15 p.m. Walk north for approximately thirty minutes. This will take you past the city limits. If you are approached by any Helpforce bots produce your travel permit.*
- *5:45 p.m. Enter, "Gare Invisibles," station and proceed to platform. There will be a train waiting; board rear carriage.*
- *6 p.m. Train will depart.*

'Fuck,' she sighed and a shook her head; a walking expedition after training, what a ball ache. As she was readying to leave she almost tripped on Pablo's bag that she had strewn under the table; it had a handy carry strap feature so what the hell, she popped his map into a side pocket and left.

Things were going to plan as the monorail hummed into, "Esportif; stop 15," on the Northern Artery. This was the location of several sporting retail outlets and Daria remembered being here before, she rotated until her Lifechip display confirmed she was pointing North then started to walk. She passed a parade of sport shops, tennis, golf and football then saw a park with a pond and some food outlets beyond her. This was all very nice, she thought, perhaps beginning to appreciate the life she had more; now that she was headed into the unknown abyss that was the Safezone. She had noted the time when she started walking and kept up a decent pace. As she was leaving the built-up area she could see a large fence in the distance and it dawned upon her that she was about to violate the code for the first time. Do not draw attention to yourself they said, still she *was* on mission.

The punishment for leaving the Capital would count as a major violation; meaning exile to the Safezone and a life of slavery. Even her protected status could not stop her heart thumping, she proceeded until something willed her to turn around. There was a man in the distance behind her blowing a kiss and tapping his shoulder in the same place she held Pablo's bag. She reached for her glasses, blinked to focus and he was gone.

Daria threw down the bags and sprinted to where she had seen the man. When she arrived, there was nothing but a Freegov waste bin on the side of the road. She kicked it hard in frustration and winced at the pain in her foot.

'Minor violation- damage to property. One-month recreation ban applied,' said a metallic voice from the drone as it appeared above her with a flashing amber light.

'Approaching city limits, state your intensions,' the drone continued.

The latest turn of events was not helping Daria's mood, but at least she could find out now whether the travel permit worked before going past the city limits. She removed the printed version, with its QR code, and held it up to the drones display scanner. After what seemed like an age the drones light flashed green.

'Proceed,' it said, then flew away.

Daria double checked and frowned. They had more power than she expected; she'd heard rumours the light-poles, bins and even some wild life had cameras in them, recruited by the Freegov to enable their dastardly social engineering experiment. However, drones were rare in the capital and their powerful, grounded cousins the bots were non-existent. That most authoritarian method of policing was reserved for the survivors in the Safezone. Maybe they just increased patrols at the city limits. She sped her pace toward the station- completely forgetting about the waving man.

As much as passing through the city limits would have been a monumental moment for a collaborator, it turned out to be as simple as opening a gate that had been built into a twelve-foot-high fence and walking through it. The pathway she had been following continued on the outer side, it was made of the same material and in the same state of repair. She couldn't help wondering if she hadn't attacked the bin would going through the gate have set of any alarm or had any consequence? In fact, she wondered why there was a gate in the fence at all considering anywhere outside the Safezone or Capital was apparently unsafe. Perhaps it was all part of the illusion to keep them in check. A little like airport security.

As she walked a large brick building seemed to appear from nowhere next to her. There was an archway in the centre behind which stood a pair of barriers, one for entry the other to exit. A digitised drinks machine on the wall and a cleaning bot mopping the floor betrayed the secrets of the Invisible Station. She scanned her travel permit and the barrier opened then proceeded to the platform. Everything like clockwork; maybe travel wasn't a thing of the past after all, depending who you were of course.

Moving forward onto the single platform, she stopped in her tracks. In front of her stood a silver, shiny train engine with what she assumed was a driver's cabin at the front. It seemed to be suspended slightly above the track. The Freegov Logo was emblazoned across the side. Linked to the engine were three dark, decrepit carriages with dents, cracked windows and no doors. Then another modern carriage at the rear; it was a silver metallic colour with mirrored windows. It was bullet shaped and could almost have passed for a horizontal space-rocket. The back doors slid open as she approached. She entered, deposited her luggage and sat, as she did the seat reclined and a menu appeared in the table top display.

The seats carried the Freegov Dove stitched neatly into their headrests. She felt motion, the windows transformed into vast inward displays of the Peacegames, Respect and Remember shows and adverts for new additions to Freetime V.R. Classical music played in the background.

Chapter 11

Daria's words composed then launched, flying through the ether with a swish, then landed for decoding. Joey and Cara's chances of survival had both increased and remained the same. They were still 100% likely to die, but they had 100% more chance of survival than the sheep.

After reading the message Joey fell backwards from his workstation stool, unbelievably hitting his head in the same cursed spot as before, although this time the impact was less severe.

Joey soon got fed up with blinking or winking or whatever it was and grumpily went back to his workstation. What could possibly be more important than answering his call? Even putting their blossoming love to one side, which clearly hurt the most, he had a lifeline, the cards drawn heavily in his favour and she couldn't answer the call. Time was nearly up and still nothing from Cara. Joey began to get worried, it was 5 p.m. His remaining time read 02:30 hours. His hands sweaty and unsteady; he threw down an awkward drone part in frustration. What was she doing? Was she okay?

*

Daria couldn't remember much when she woke up, a glance at her Lifechip showed the time was 6 p.m. Forty winks. On the empty seat to her right were two old looking metal and rubber devices. She couldn't be sure if they were there when she got on. On closer inspection the device was sturdy and about the size of a small bottle of water. It almost fit into her hand. There was a knob, a slim protruding part at the top and two buttons while the material on one side had holes in it. She was just about to pick one up when it started crackling, and a small red light flashed on the top.

'Daria, come in…come in,' a voice said. It was an unknown male who spoke slowly in good English but with an accent she hadn't heard before.

'Who is this?' Daria asked. She picked up the device hit the button and spoke back.

'Ah good, you worked out how to use it,' he replied.

The man had manners, it couldn't be Freegov, Daria thought and wondered if this was her time.

'This is Daria, who are you?' She asked.

'You can call me Scales, these devices are Radios, I've modified them to extend their range. Keep one for yourself and the other for the wolves,' Scales explained. His voice was calm and measured, his speech methodical.

'Okay. Do they need a battery?' She asked, keeping up the pretence she didn't know what a radio was.

'They should last a good while, you don't need to think about that now. I need to warn you not use them near the bots, they can detect the interference, only if it's an emergency then make it quick,' he continued.

'Okay,' Daria replied. As she well knew; Freegov had everything covered with technology, so regression a chance to defeat them.

'I need you to listen very carefully to me, then you can ask questions when I finish. I have sent you to begin a very important task. You will investigate time and space with the help of the victorious wolf. The purpose of your investigation is to discover how humanity was defeated between 2030 and 2035. We may never meet, as we exist in different versions of the programme, but you can reach me with these Radios. Your work is very important. You have been chosen for this task because of your background and skills. Me and my team have infiltrated the Freegov systems, and now we need someone in the Capital and the Safezone. Freegov is not all it seems. We need your help, a physical presence; a time traveller,' Scales explained.

Jackpot repeater. This idiot didn't even realise she was part of the plot in 2030, some scientific mastermind he was. Daria took a deep breath and exhaled for longer than she inhaled, a crooked smile on her face. She felt excited; a weight lifted from her shoulders, no more waiting- and it had all come to her on a plate thanks to her role in Freegov.

'Thank you for choosing me, I will gladly help you Scales,' she said, sincerity personified.

'That's good,' Scales replied, 'you have made the right decision, I'm sure we will make a good team. Please maintain discretion and be careful who you trust.'

The radio crackled again and the light went out. Daria took her leave to the restroom, splashed water on her face and allowed it to drip down without drying. She admired herself in the mirror without registering the significance of Scales' last words. She was too busy thinking of the glory that awaited her upon bringing in Mothers most wanted or better still killing him. But first she'd have to find him and there were no operatives outside of the Capital, this was all on her.

Chapter 12

As the years passed by and the disobedient were filtered out, so the lonely procession became less frequent. It had become tradition for the remaining survivors to stand and applaud their departing colleagues with nods of respect and appreciation.

The clock approached 7:30 p.m. Right on time two bots approached their lights atop their heads flashing red. The Freegov anthem, a military style tune, played from their built-in speakers.

'Timeout activated, you are no longer a protected member of the Safezone,' one said.

Joey looked around hoping they had the wrong guy but was resigned to his fate as the bots enclosed him and cuffed his hands then started to move away.

Joey struggled to walk properly with his hands cuffed to the bot behind him, the bot was only three feet tall and it made Joey look as if he were squatting to relieve himself when finally, he saw a sign on a door near the entrance that read, "Holding room." *So that's what it meant*. The bots deposited him and swished off, Joey winced and rubbed the red mark on his wrists gingerly, then almost immediately a door at the rear of the room slid open allowing a loud claxon sound inside.

A new bot swished in and locked him to its arm, then moved of outside, faster than Joey cared to travel. It wasn't long before he was unceremoniously deposited into a large cage with other survivors sat on benches along it's wall. It was unlit, but Joey estimated there were at least ten soulless timeouts in there. They were all linked to cables behind the bench and Joey realised they were self-medicating with Freetime, their final dreams becoming reality. He tried to walk further inside but the bot had attached him to the seat. Still no sign of Cara. *Where was she?*

The cage moved off quickly, it was crudely attached to some kind of motorized vehicle and caused an uncomfortable, fast and bumpy ride. Not long later they stopped. This repeated itself several times. Joey realised they must be collecting all the timeouts from their respective work locations. Sweat dripped from his torso, he thought of cold water. Every-time they stopped he strained for a view outside, but it was no use, the sides of the cage were covered by a dirty old tarpaulin. Finally, they travelled for a longer period then came to a halt.

'Prepare to transfer, prepare to transfer,' a tinny voice repeated over a loudspeaker.

Light flooded in as the tarpaulin was lifted, the timeouts shielded their eyes and were led one by one out of the cages then ten meters walk to a dark train, with three old carriages attached to a modern engine. There was still no sign of Cara.

Inside it was smelly and damp; had they removed the toilets? Joey felt like an animal as he sat on the floor in a corner and watched as his fellow timeouts walked in zombie like, then sat and connected themselves again, surely those dreams were now a nightmare.

As his eyes became accustomed to the dark carriage, he noticed a faded logo adorned the walls, with pictures of men in uniform below them. There was a faded flag too, he thought it had been red and black in its day, but couldn't be sure. He considered the broken souls that had been on the train before him. Still no sign of Cara, tired and thirsty, Joey closed his eyes. A constant barrage of aces thundering past him; surely, they couldn't maintain this level.

Chapter 13

The Central City Arena had been built in the late 1990's and was located to the south east of the City. It was constructed in concrete with a grey and sand coloured cladding. It was more oval shaped than the previous era of rectangular sports stadia and had a former capacity of 55,500 spectators.

By 2050 the Arena had been modified for its gruesome purpose; the grass replaced by a mass of concrete with small channels cut into it that sloped away from the centre into larger troughs that ran around the sides of the playing area. Many of the seats had been removed in favour of mirrored glass executive style boxes. There were large accessible storage containers pitch-side. From afar the stadium and the station looked as if they had been placed in their positions from outer space; for everything else in this city had been long since abandoned. Two light sources in an overgrown forest of dark shadows. The eerie silence gave no indication of the former glories of this old cultural city.

There was little walking necessary, the on-screen maps indicated that the train had arrived at Arena Station which was located directly opposite the stadium. Daria began to gather her bags and straighten her clothes, then moved towards the door expecting it to open.

A few moments later and no change in status, the doors were shut and still displayed the glorious achievements of Freegov on their built-in video screens.

A few meters away, the emaciated timeouts were being led in a chain gang off the train. An army of bots co-ordinated the transfer, lights flashing yellow, while moving C.C.T.V. cameras on the station and stadium opposite followed their every move.

Darkness had fallen, the powerful floodlights that woke Joey moments earlier the only light for miles around them. They gave the scene a most disconcerting energy, as if something altogether untoward were about to happen.

Each timeout was linked right arm in-front and left behind to complete the chain. Joey, eyes down, did as he was told. Maybe it had all been a dream, or another one of Freegovs created realities. The gang walked awkwardly down a slight ramp and into the underbelly of the Arena. The floodlights snapped off as the last timeout got inside; Freegov- always efficient.

Moments later they entered into a vast space where dim strip lighting ran in columns as far as Joey could see illuminating the dreary grey concrete floors, walls and ceilings. There were hundreds of titanium caskets, their lids ajar, positioned spaced out a few meters apart on the floor as cars in a car park would be. Underneath them a rubberized conveyor belt system that was currently static. There were cables running to the caskets.

Ahead, just as he feared, the bots directed timeouts into the caskets, overseeing the destruction of the chain. As he trudged closer to his resting place, Joey's eyes opened a little wider as he noticed some breathing holes in the top of the caskets, how generous, the Freegov would keep them alive until the games. Then it was his turn, quick thinking wasn't his speciality, but he knew he had to do something, anything to give himself a chance.

Just after the timeout in front unlocked from his right hand, Joey seized his moment, pulling the ornament out of his pocket and concealing it in his palm, the bot was behind him now unlocking his hand from the next. Joey got in slowly and placed the ornament skillfully in the clasp just as the bot closed the caskets lid.

*

After a while Daria became impatient and approached the train door for a closer look, she had no idea about the grim procession she had missed outside the carriage, nor that the train was about to leave. After some fumbling around the doors, she found an emergency door release switch concealed at the top.

About to step off, noise and movement outside alerted her and she moved back into cover, then looked to the left twenty metres ahead where a second chain gang of timed-out survivors could be seen being led by bots into the stadium. A few moments passed and they had disappeared inside what looked like a service entry point. Suddenly the area was dark again and she seized her moment, darting across the road and into a doorway opposite the train which looked like the main entrance.

She used her travel papers on the door entry system. Nothing happened. *Fuck this.*

She kicked the door in frustration. There was slight lateral movement. Looking closer she noticed there weren't any lights on the entry system and she pried the sliding doors open, they gave way easily and the she moved inside before closing the doors manually. What a shit show. Still it was to her advantage if Scales were incompetent, but these bots might be another matter.

Inside it was cold and dilapidated. The reception area looked like it had not been touched for years, decades even. Before she had time to settle a crackle and a flash, Daria pulled out the radio.

'Come in Daria, Scales here,' he said.

'Receiving,' She replied curtly.

'Is everything okay, you sound a little distressed?' Scales asked.

'No…I mean yes it's fine, I'm here and everything is fine.' Daria replied, having fought her attitude into check.

'I'm glad to hear that Daria. Now, I've disabled the bots and the security systems, you have free reign of the stadium and the games tomorrow. Make sure you turn the cameras on to broadcast the games at 7:30 p.m. otherwise Freegov will get suspicious. They are in the control room. The timeouts are in the holding area; the weapons are in the pitch side lockers. Your goal is to escape with the victor after the games to a safe place in the old city, you have the location.' Scales explained in his methodical, calm voice.

'Okay,' Daria replied, wondering how much easier this could get.

'If you don't know what to do follow your instinct, call me when you are ready to turn the cameras on. Over and out.'

Daria settled herself in the first room she came to after her mini strop, who the hell did this scientist think he was bossing her around? She gathered her thoughts.

Dust plumes enveloped her midriff as she sat down in the abandoned, cold waiting area in what she assumed was the stadiums reception. She coughed. On the table in front of her a pass marked "Guest" with the Freegov Logo sat, covered in several years' worth of dust. There was a self-service drinks machine to her left, it's digital display dark. Beyond the webs and dirt, posters on the walls showed previous glories of the resident football club in happier times. To the right a door marked, "Restrooms." The only sign of modernity a static, lightless yellow cleaning bot at the far end of the corridor, behind it a large door with a sign marked "Members and Guests Only." Perhaps the bot was headed this way, she thought, as there was precious little sign of any cleaning there, but at least it showed Scales had actually managed to do something.

Daria sat and laughed out loud. Then she started giggling uncontrollably, her face slightly crooked; she looked possessed. After a few minutes she slowed to a throaty cackle and lit a cigarette. She should be making a 'plan A' and a 'plan B'; checking exits, entrances, lights, power that sort of thing but she really didn't feel the need. This buffoon, top of Mother's wanted list for years was leading her straight to him so she could help stop the very thing she had masterminded all those years ago. She couldn't have made this shit up in her wildest dreams. Cigarette done and her thoughts shifted to Joey; she liked to be dominated and wondered if he had it in him. Unlikely, her answer, but she needed to find him and build up some kind of rapport, tell him the story he wanted to hear, all that bullshit she'd done a thousand times before. Still, she was closer than ever to her reward after all these years of devotion to the cause. Mother would be pleased.

'Waahhh, waahhh, waahhh.' A bot approached fast from her right red-light flashing.

'You are in violation, no humans permitted outside the Safezone.' The bot said in tinny tones.

Daria startled and began to rise but before she could the bot shocked her, clasped its robotic hand around her belt and swished off dragging her unceremoniously behind it.

*

56

At this moment, it became an advantage to be slim, the casket was the usual size but Joey barely filled half of it width wise. Length wise was more of a challenge, however he was able to shift onto his side easily and get a view through the gap provided by his improvised door stop. A little adjustment and he had the side raised an inch giving him a view up the row of caskets toward the lift.

He heard a siren noise, then the lights flickered from emergency mode to full brightness, heart thumping he resisted the urge to close the lid and hide. He had to take risks now.

Up ahead he saw the flashing red light moving steadily toward him, it's progress along the floor wasn't as smooth as normal, maybe it was malfunctioning. No, it was dragging something behind it. As the bot came closer Joey lowered the lid slightly, but enough to see, it was a woman, but not a survivor. For a moment he worried, it could have been Cara; but as she passed he soon realised it wasn't her; the woman had hair and had been roughed up. There were scratches, cuts and a small trail of blood marked her path. He heard a casket slam shut somewhere behind him then watched the bot retrace its route and remove the evidence.

Joey waited for the lift door to close then exited quickly, the lights were still on fully so he ran to the lift before they went into emergency mode again. He figured there was a sensor somewhere. He hadn't accounted for the fact he'd have to call it, sighing he moved into a shadow until it arrived. The woman could wait, whether she had the time or not, she wasn't Cara. Inside there were three options, Car park, Holding Area and Surface, and no visible cameras. He hit surface and waited.

The corridor was empty of immediate threats but he saw something on the floor at the end, he passed pictures of men in a red sports kit with a small ball and shiny trophies. What a life.

Getting closer to the object he realised there were two bags and a shiny wrapper. As he opened the zipper of the large bag a buzzing noise caused him to drop it in shock. His instinct was to run, but where, back to the casket? No, after a deep breath he opened the bag for a second time to see a small flashing red light, maybe the bot had given birth.

'Joey, take the bags and go through the doors behind you and into the restroom, quickly.' A calm voice said with urgency. Joey did, passing a yellow cleaning bot on his way.

'Now, barricade the door with the wastebin, tell me when you're done.'

'Done.' Joey replied, small beads of sweat running down his face, he sank down on his haunches next to a wash hand basin and wiped his brow.

'Well done. Now tell me what you saw in the basement,' the voice said.

'Wait a minute, who are you and how do you know I was in the basement?' Joey asked a slight wobble in his voice.

'Just tell me what you saw and I'll explain everything.'

'Where's Cara?' Joey asked.

'Did you see a woman dressed casually, a Collab?' The man persisted, his voice no longer calm.

'A what? Is this some kind of joke?' Joey raised his voice, he gulped, then continued, 'yes, I saw a woman down there and she was out cold.'

'And where is she now?' the man asked, still tense.

'Locked in a casket, she had some injuries.' Joey continued.

'We need her alive for this to work, do you understand?' The man said passionately.

'No, I don't fucking understand. Who are you and where is Cara?' Joey shouted.

'Keep your voice down, remain calm Joey, the bots are dangerous.' he replied.

'You think I don't know that? I've lived with them for fifteen years, I know they are fucking dangerous. Why do think I'm sweating like this?' Joey replied.

'I'm sorry. Let me explain, so long as she is contained, we will be okay. My name is Scales, I was the leading scientist who invented the Lifechip, I wanted it to be used to help people; cure disease or overcome mental illness, for example, but my invention was discovered and its use was changed by dark forces whose goal was to destroy humankind. The woman in the casket is Daria, and she played a crucial part in the event that left people begging for the lifechip.' Scales paused.

'Yeah sure, and my names Bob.' Joey remarked under his breath.

'I heard that. Open the sports bag and find the file. There's a page on Daria. Read it.' Scales said sharply.

Joey pulled out the file and began to read. A single page in a plastic folder. There was a picture of a young woman in military uniform in the top right. Then details below under several headings; Name, Alias', D.O.B., Height, Weight, Locations, Education, Work, Strengths, Weaknesses, Opportunities, Threats.

'You'll notice she was based in London for a couple of years. She lived at your mother's house while doing studies. She spied on you for her organisation.' Scales interrupted Joey before he had a chance to fully read the information.

'Me, why?' Joey gasped.

'The same reason I chose you, you have a powerful gift and it brought you to their attention.'

'What gift?' Joey scoffed.

'To unite people, to see through the fog and break down barriers.' Scales replied.

'Chose me for what?'

'To escort Daria back in time and change the path of history for the better.' Scales explained.

'Bollocks, I just want to find Cara.' Joey replied.

'And do what, die in the Peacegames? Live happily ever after in the no-zone, with Freegov hunting you down for eternity.' Scales replied. Joey remained quiet.

'I'm offering you a new life, in the past, you can take Cara too. I just need you to get Daria there, the rest is up to you.' He continued.

'I need to find Cara first.' Joey replied.

'Find Cara and get out of there. Take Daria and you'll both have a new life, with the chance for so much more.' Scales said.

'Okay, I'll do it.' Joey replied after a pause.

'There's a map in the other bag, the Rijksmuseum is ten miles north, that's where you need to get to. Once you are there I'll do the rest. There are hundreds of bikes in the car park, it's not far. I can open the gates down there but I can't disable the bots, you'll have to avoid them.' Scales explained, an excited vigour in his voice.

'What about Daria, she will come willingly?' Joey asked.

'She thinks she can reach me through you, so yes, but Joey be careful; the devil is in the air. Over and out,' Scales replied. The radio crackled and the light turned off.

Joey exhaled deeply and stood up, stashing the file in Daria's rucksack, then putting it on over his shoulders, an action he'd later relive over and over. He already had a plan; find Daria and blackmail her into finding Cara. If she was even here that was.

Chapter 14

As usual, there was no time to waste, Joey wondered if he'd ever get to rest. Still, this new development renewed his focus with the chance to escape for good with Cara. But the bots were a problem. If he got caught, he was toast, or would be in a couple of days. It was the middle of the night now, not that they needed sleep, but they would likely be running to a program and not expect any problems from the timeouts until morning. It was now or never.

Joey retraced his steps, passing the disabled yellow bot, through the door and beyond it to the lift. Something didn't feel right; like he was being watched. He was, in fact, being watched. Somewhere, far away, eyes were watching him through the limited vision of the arenas cleaning bots.

As he moved hastily beyond the doors the décor took a turn for the worse and the corridor was even colder. This place hadn't seen any maintenance for years, there was accumulated dust on the ceilings and mould around the corners of the carpet. He kept moving and came to a small screen on the wall which flicked between different camera views. Holding Area, Pitch, Entrance, and Basement. He was concerned to see the Arena had a power supply and cameras; Freegov were all seeing.

Joey entered the lift first and hit the button; back down to the Holding Area. As the lift jarred into action he saw someone on the screen moving in the shadows. The lift slid open and for the first time he realised there were doors on the far side of the massive room, as he got closer he noticed androgynous figures on the doors and a sign in the middle reading unisex-restrooms. The pervasive social engineering had reached the continent too and although they may not eat, they still drank, and sure enough relieved themselves regularly, together.

Joey stood for a moment looking back at the rows of caskets, and wondering how the timeouts got out to visit the restroom, if they were locked in. Then it dawned on him, they weren't. His heroic, lock jam device was totally unnecessary, he just needed to push the lid. The timed-out survivors were so taken up in Freetime and obeying the instructions of Freegov, they didn't even need to be locked in when they were about to die.

As Joey looked out over the caskets, and pondered this development, he heard a noise from behind then found himself being forcefully dragged backwards through into the restroom. Upon turning, he feared the worst; a blow to the face or an electric shock, but the reality was far better; a smiling Cara. She looked at him with her big eyes, and for a moment they locked eyes.

'I missed you, where have you been?' Joey asked.

'In my casket watching some Freetime V.R.' Cara replied. Just then the door swung open and another Surv came into the restroom and entered a cubicle. To avoid any suspicion Cara stripped down to the waste and began washing herself in a sink while Joey turned toward the dryer and turned it on. This sort of behaviour was completely normal in the desexualized world they lived in. Thanks to a couple of mirrors Joey was at just the right angle thanks to see that Cara's torso had an unusual feature; a large birthmark above her naval. His eyes were drawn to her curves but before he got a chance for a closer look the sound of the cubicle door opening broke Joey's gaze and he knelt down to tie his boots until the imposter left.

'I think I have a way out of this mess but I need your help to get a Collab out of here, follow me.' Joey said quickly, his tone betraying enough raw urgency for Cara, who had dressed, to move immediately.

In the main hall, Joey shivered as if he were being watched. On the wall to his right there were two buttons; one green the other red marked start and stop. In front of him, on the floor, there was a lever that could be swapped between pitch and exit. His mind raced.

A noise distracted him as he was about to operate the controls, then a slight movement in the corner of his eye. Trying to locate his empty casket he moved past the comatose army. Hundreds of defeated souls silently awaiting their destiny. Leading Cara by the hand he darted toward his casket, he easily identified as it was still slightly ajar. He grabbed his trusty ornament and moved past trying to remember how long the bot dragged Daria for after they past him earlier. It didn't take long before he saw one with its clasps down and a small blood stain on it.

Joey lifted the lid; both Joey and Cara stepped back. Cara gasped. Daria's eyes were open, staring coldly upward. She seemed to look right through them as she got up of her own accord.

They stood a metre apart and observed in silence, survivors and a collaborator together, but were they on the same side? One of them should speak; the one in charge, but no. Stasis; looking, assessing, thinking, but still silence. It was as if their hidden energy forces were entangling; communicating around them in an unseen space in time.

Tossing the coin, who would serve first? Then a force moved them closer; Joey reached out and touched Daria's side. They moved apart, had a hidden power betrayed the past?

'Come with me if you want to find Scales,' Joey said.

He meant to start fast and not let her get her bearings. He knew he had to maintain his position of power; she had no idea, none whatsoever, that he knew all about her and was leading her back to the past to face her karma.

'You're not in charge here slave boy, now give me my bag.' Daria said reaching towards her rucksack.

Cara delivered a swift jab to Daria's side, where a bloody stain had seeped through her clothing. She doubled over in pain, holding her side and wincing uncomfortably.

'Shut up bitch,' Cara hissed.

'Move,' Joey raised his voice and pushed Daria forwards.

As they moved Cara noticed scratches and dirt marks on the caskets; they definitely were not new. They looked as if they had been used and re-used again and again. The dirt was a grey, black colour that had been part washed off, it was present on all the caskets. She was beginning to think this whole Peacegames operation didn't seem real.

There was nobody from Freegov here to oversee it and she wondered about spectators due to the condition of the Arena. If the titanium caskets were reused then it meant they didn't go to the oppressive force as an offering. This brought up two problems; where did the bodies go and was there an overlord at all? Was Freegov real or had the survivors and Collabs just succumbed to a cleaver narrative and elaborate technology-based scam to control them forever more?

Reaching the centre of the massive room, they came across a table with bottles of water and a large sustenance pill dispenser. Joey stopped to grab some supplies, and nodded to Cara to carry on, pointing toward the conveyor belt system which looked like an airport baggage handling machine, to see where it went. After a few twists and turns they came to the edge of the space and could see a tunnel leading upward towards the pitch outside. Parallel to it was another conveyor leading back inside which they followed; past a sign marked exit that pointed to the other, as yet unexplored, half of the large underground space.

They continued to follow the conveyor belt along the outside edge of the space until it stopped towards the corner of the room, where a steel framed machine that looked like it fitted around the caskets stood. Immediately adjacent to the machine there was an empty pit. Cara wondered if it were a swimming pool or something until she noticed a retractable steel lid and air ducts halfway up. There was other smaller metal piping at the bottom of the pit. Water wouldn't stay in there because of the vents and she noticed black charring around the sides of what she now realised was a massive steel container with a lid, vents and pipe input. She did not notice the plastic water pipe system and eight spaced out industrial sized shower heads above the container. It certainly didn't take a genius to work out what wet on here.

Joey stopped and directed Cara past the container. Survivors die here, that was the story they, and everyone else had been told. What difference did it make how they died? Was it as it as simple as being told a story to achieve these horrors, was that all it took? What was it all for?

Daria, who had been walking awkwardly between Joey and Cara, slowed her pace until her legs buckled and almost gave way. Cara supported her from behind while Joey descended a small ladder on the container then reached up for Daria, unsteady, eyes half closed. They manoeuvred their cargo carefully then settled in the near corner, suitably hidden from view.

'She's bleeding from the head and side, see if there's anything in her bag we can use to patch her up; we need her alive to escape!' Joey said, handing the rucksack to Cara.

Daria's injuries didn't look bad enough to warrant her condition. He tilted her head back and gave her water and a sustenance pill. Her dark eyes fluttered. Then he fed her part of an energy bar, with more water.

'Get off me,' Daria pushed Joey away forcefully, then winced in pain again. Cara shook her head while tying a sock around Daria's head, successfully stemming the red flow, then used a similar method with a t-shirt around her midriff.

'You had a daughter, did Scales tell you that? I know where she lived.' Daria continued, glaring directly at Joey.

'A daughter? What's that?' Joey asked. Daria was blissfully unaware that the survivors had had parts of their vocabulary and reproductive urges removed by the Lifechip.

'Check the bag, Freegov papers. It's all there.'

There was silence while Joey opened Daria's bag and found two pieces of loose paper with the Freegov logo on the top. The information was sparse but he saw a picture of a young girl in his file and slowly began to join the dots.

'And me?' Cara asked.

'No family, they died when you were young. You were a keen Historian then a D.J., you lived in near Toulouse in France,' he answered softly. The couple stood, enlightened and educated, pasts becoming present.

'Bastards,' Joey exclaimed, discarding the papers angrily. Cara moved closer to Joey and held him.

Despite the circumstances and the Lifechip, Joey knew himself well enough to stay silent when he was this close to the edge. His mind raced. Questions. So many questions.

Amid the revelations; neither Joey nor Cara noticed Daria reaching into a small zipped compartment of her rucksack and pressing a small button twice. Daria leant her head back on the container, looked upward and smiled crookedly.

*

Far away, in an underground bunker on a historically disputed island, a tech nerd sat in front of a bank of screens where dots blinked and flashed continually. His attention was slow to turn, most of these were false alerts and they disappeared after another sweep of the radar screen. But this one had now stayed on now for a good two minutes, a distress signal from the no-zone; he got up and went to check the mission log; he actually had some work to do for the first time in years.

Chapter 15

All things considered, it was probably a good thing when the noise from a bot's alarm broke the silence. Joey climbed a rung on the ladder and raised his head cautiously to peek over the containers edge. He saw the machine stationary and flashing amber next to Daria's casket, its door still open. They had to move fast.

'Get up now,' he shouted. The two women followed Joey up the ladder, Daria first then the trio moved past the pit away from the bot. Joey spotted another elevator on the far wall and made directly for it. Daria moved slowly now as Joey and Cara sped ahead. He still hadn't decided what to do with her. Inside, he pressed B2; lower into the arena's underbelly. The doors slid shut without any indication that the bots had discovered them. *Yet*. Moments later as the lift bumped to a halt and the doors slid open revealing a massive, empty car park behind a room to the right marked, "Staff area."

Joey led the way and waited not so patiently for Daria to arrive then closed the door. He resisted tripping her as she passed him. There were lockers, some open some shut. The open ones were empty save the odd clothes hanger. Several washing machines lined the far wall. Layers of dust carpeted every surface; Cara coughed as she swung a locker door closed and wondered when the last time it was actually used could have been. She guessed before 2035, when Freegov took over, but probably longer.

'Okay there's nothing useful here, are you ready to move?' Joey said. Cara nodded her agreement while Daria smirked at them both.

Joey opened the door cautiously, seeing the coast was clear he moved out slowly walking through the deserted carpark towards an upward sloping ramp with a massive steel gate. That must be the exit. Joey's heart rate reduced slightly as he realised Scales was telling the truth. Then, just as promised, to the left they approached a large area marked, "Cycle Storage." The gate was open and there were hundreds of bikes in there. He wondered what happened to their owners.

They each entered and chose a bicycle. Their only consideration whether the tyres had air in them, it wasn't long before they exited the room successfully.

Joey and Cara began up the ramp, slightly ahead of Daria who, still weak, had stopped to adjust her bandage and catch her breath. As she was distracted, a loud claxon style alarm sounded causing Joey and Cara to turn and look back. They saw two bots approaching fast, not far behind Daria, red lights flashing.

They watched on as Daria, alerted to the danger, realised her predicament. Neither stopped to help. She lifted the bike and used her remaining strength to launch it at the bots, turned and ran. The impact took out one of the bots and slowed the other. Joey sighed, then signalled to Daria to hitch a lift with him and the two cycles made their exit. As they exited the basement area Cara turned back to see the second bot stop dead at the threshold and continue to flash red. How these bots controlled the known world was indeed a puzzle.

Joey peddled hard, physically struggling to balance with his passenger against the strengthening wind, mentally struggling to understand his role. An unusual energy came at him from his passenger, the opposite of Cara, something dark and lifeless. His visibility was restricted by the driving rain and the darkness surrounding them, the only light source now the distant waning moon.

After ten minutes or so, and fearing exhaustion, he saw a shelter and headed for it; perhaps it was an old tram stop. Plants and shrubs had long ago overwhelmed the city; it had become an unusually shaped homage to the insignificance of humans and the strength of nature. There was something raw and powerful about the scene as the three insurgents sheltered from the storm.

Daria was worst affected by the conditions, handicapped by her injuries and light clothing she had become a sticky mess; shivering uncontrollably. Joey and Cara fared better, their overalls offering more protection and no hair to become soaked. The three huddled under the shelter; the two better equipped making a sandwich of Daria who didn't have the energy to resist. Cara pulled and scratched away at the medium density shrubbery and vines that had grown across the shelter, revealing the Tram stops name and a map.

'Fredericksplein!' She exclaimed while Joey studied the map tilting his head awkwardly to see in the darkness.

'We are about a kilometre away from the Rijksmuseum, it's to the south-west, there should be a canal over there we can follow. Come on.' Joey shouted, beckoning them back to the bicycles.

After a few minutes cycling they saw a massive building that looked like a cross between an old Palace and a Gothic church with a large water feature front of it. There were two towers divided by a great archway, with two smaller archways either side of it. The moonlight lit up a portion of the building and showed its former splendour and current dilapidation all at once.

Some of the windows were smashed and the intricate brickwork on the façade was partly overgrown by shrubs and ivy. The wind seemed to intensify as they moved closer causing Joey to lose his balance and deposit Daria roughly off the makeshift tandem.

With the destination now in sight the trio continued on foot with Daria propped between Joey and Cara in a line of three. Joey and Cara dragged Daria as best they could directly into the harsh wind. Soon they reached an archway leading to a covered area, drenched and finally able to take shelter from the storm. Daria collapsed in a heap on the floor, Cara sat next to her while Joey struggled out of the rucksack, threw it down next to Daria and headed back to retrieve the bikes.

Moments earlier, the driving rain and dark sky provided the perfect cover for the small chopper to land undetected in the garden behind the museum. Four armed men, dressed all in black moved silently toward a rear door, and not long after were inside. One of them looked down at a flashing red dot on a mobile device, it was less then fifty metres away now to their north-west. Next to the dot was a mugshot of Daria in her military uniform. He waved his arm, and the group followed in silence, two each side of the great hall, toward their target.

Far away, in the command centre, and away from the jurisdiction of Freegov, an old looking group of men in military uniforms watched the action unfolding from a camera on one of the armed men's helmets. One of them wore a two-way headset.

'Target identified, threat detected; permission to engage.'

'Permission granted.'

Two silenced shots zipped into their target. The men approached, picked her up and left. They were back on the chopper banking away toward the airstrip within minutes.

'Mission accomplished.'

'Copied. Return to base.'

Chapter 16

The bikes crashed to the ground the instant he rounded the corner, he put out his hand and steadied himself on the brick wall. He knew instantly- mouth open wide but no sound emitted, Joey rushed to her and knelt. Her head snapped back awkwardly against the wall, eyes open looking wildly upward, he shook her. Closer now he saw a small hole in her forehead and a bloodstain on her chest. At least she didn't suffer. Not like that bitch would.

He closed her eyes then looked away, then back, then away again. He began to sob. Tears mixed with rain now as he struggled with his beloved passenger. He tripped then stumbled but somehow managed to regain his balance. He struggled for grip as he navigated down some stairs and the surface below foot became loose. Looking down around her limp limbs he almost lost his balance again.

Heavily panting, he scoured for a suitable spot amongst the stone statues now hidden by the hedges that were once so neatly coiffured below them. His back creaked and shoulder throbbed; this would be her resting place; under the painted murals still visible on the outstanding stone and brick walls at the rear of the museum.

Joey thought he could make out a soldier with a sword and a flag with three X's on it. They would protect her better than he had. A final kiss, then he held the ornament Cara had given him, looked up to the battle hardy warriors and willed their strength into him.

Soaked through to the skin now suddenly the rain eased, the fast-moving clouds dancing past the moon bringing the shadows around him to life. Scales said she was dangerous, but she wasn't armed. Where was she? Didn't she need to find Scales? Joey's eyes were drawn up to the mural that guarded Cara. They likely wouldn't have conquered the world sitting around asking themselves questions.

'Scales, come in,' Joey spoke calmly, a cold separation in his eyes.

He was inside now, away from the bloody scene, with the bitches bag by his side. The radio crackled with interference. There was no answer. He emptied the bag out on the floor, stripped using some of her clothes to dry himself, then put some joggers and a t-shirt on. He noticed a tiny electrical device and crushed it angrily with his boot. *Why had he brought her rucksack?*

After some water and two energy bars, Joey began to study the A5 piece of paper. It was a plan of the museum, with a red cross mark in the second-floor library. The hard floor echoed as he moved through the shadows, past the cloakroom and information desk. Massive skylights in the ceiling aided his progress; the main hall preserved as if time had stood still.

Up a small flight of stairs and into the first gallery, he struggled to see, after a moment the shadows began to reveal themselves, broken glass and large picture frames littered the floor, betraying the lawless years. Perhaps these great works now adorned another reality. Through this room then out towards glass windows; at last some light. He strained his eyes to check the map and confirmed he was in the corridor and on the right track. He followed it around the windows looking out to a courtyard then through a door towards the steep stone staircase, he figured he must be in the tower. He climbed up two floors then moved through an open doorway onto the gallery, which had also been looted.

Around the corner to his left, there was a closed door; excited now he pushed hard and it hit the inside wall with a bang then slowly shut behind him. A musty smell of old paper and dust brought on a cough and splutter. He had reached the Library. Joey looked up and thanked the architect for the three huge ornate windows opposite him and the skylight above. The room must have been the size of a double decker bus, spread over three floors with three levels of shelving around the outside. The original contents in all their glory appeared to still be in place. The plunderers didn't value education or history. Immediately in front of him stood a smashed glass display case, two or three meters wide, there remained a few small coins scattered on the floor. This was definitely it.

*

By the time Daria came around she was aboard a jet flying south-west high above the Ocean. Her eyes remained closed as she tuned into the sounds; a little distant and muffled by the whirr of the two small jet engines that powered the plane, but she was sure she recognised the tongue. Her mother tongue and the tongue of Mother all in one.

She opened her eyes and approached the men at the back of the plane, commandos; she didn't know any of them.

'Where are they?' She asked expectantly.

'Who?' one of the men replied, cigarette still in mouth. Daria snatched it from him and pulled hard.

'The two people I was with when you extracted me; Joey and Cara.' She said through gritted teeth.

'There was only one…and she's dead.' The first commando said, lighting another cigarette.

'Argggggghh.' Daria bit her tongue.

'We were ordered to extract you, that's it, now sit down and stop bothering me.' The man said sharply.

'To where?' she asked, puzzled. The commando had returned to his game of cards and ignored her. She made eye contact with another and raised her brow.

'America South,' he answered without changing his expression.

This was the first time she had ever heard those words spoken, the place of rumour and legend that all Mother's children aimed to reach. A place where they could live in peace, luxury and excess. Where a lifetime's duty and dedication were recognised and all their wishes come true; it was rumoured they could even stop the sands of time from flowing.

'Deal me in, brother.' She said with a crooked smile.

*

'Come in Joey, Scales here.' Static and interference crackled from the rucksack, struggling to break through into the world of nod. Every route was blocked. Mind Avenue closed for urgent repairs. Body Road off the power grid. Soul Street no answer, try again later.

'Daria, Cara, come in,' he repeated.

Scales frowned and looked down at the floor. In his hideaway on the outskirts of the capital, he had no idea of the latest events, but thanks to his hack on the cleaning bots was aware that the trio had managed to escape the Arena.

He was old, maybe eighty years or so with a slim build and healthy complexion. His short trimmed afro hair was still black and he wore a long white gown.

73

'Joey are you there?' Scales raised his voice for the first time in centuries. Circuits linked and Joey pressed the button on his radio and mumbled.

'Cara; she's gone, you bastard,' Joey slurred.

'No, you will meet again. Is Daria with you?' Scales replied.

'What, how?' Joey stirred and opened his eyes.

'Is Daria with you?' Scales repeated.

'No, I don't know, she's gone too,' Joey replied, eyes wide now, 'we arrived at the museum and I left them alone for a moment; Daria was injured. When I got back Cara was dead, shot twice in her head and heart, and Daria was gone,' he explained.

There was a medium length pause. In his retreat outside the capital Scales closed his eyes tight, clenched his fists and let out a long, controlled deep breath.

'There is still a way Joey...' Scales started.

'You are a liar, Cara's dead, I had a daughter, Freegov isn't real, why should I listen to you?' Joey screamed, standing up and smashing his hand into the broken display cabinet in front of him.

'Oh, Freegov is very real, believe me. The Peacegames are an illusion sure, but the survivors still die. Daria works for Mother, a secret organisation who paved the way for Freegov. Help me and you can stop it all.' Scales explained, having just worked out a plan B. His radio went quiet.

In the museum Joey's radio landed in a puddle, damaged beyond repair after flying through the large stained-glass window that allowed just enough moonlight into the Museum's Library. Joey paced around, kicked the cabinet, then began to fling books down from his third-floor perch to the ground floor, where study desks sat empty. He laughed as he imagined students sat there being hit by his projectiles before they bounced upward and came apart at the seams. He reached back into Daria's bag and pulled out her lighter.

*

Somewhere over the Atlantic Sea, whether that was its name or not, Daria drifted in and out of consciousness. The small plane was being buffeted around by the jet stream, not that she noticed after several whiskey tonics with a dash of lime.

'Good-morning, your breakfast service will be available in ten minutes, I have dressed your wounds and administered painkillers,' said a tinny female voice. Daria opened one eye to see a five-foot-tall robot, dressed as a female airhostess. It looked almost human in that she had skin and hair. Daria perked up.

'I'll take black coffee' She replied, thinking that would be the end of the conversation.

'Do you require any other services? I am equipped with all relief programmes, male and female,' the bot asked, leaning forward toward Daria, touching her arm.

Daria immediately figured out what was on offer, she'd heard rumours about this sort of thing and how good it was, being able to specify exact parameters and the rest. She reached forward and touched the bots' leg, noting its skin felt human.

'Yes, full service,' she said, smiling her crooked smile. The bot produced a pen and a form with various sexual acts and tick boxes next to them. Daria ticked a few hastily and handed the paper back, the bot scanned the paper and smiled.

'Very well, your wish is my command' the bot said, smiling as she knelt down and began to remove Daria's clothing. Through a mirror on the seat in front Daria looked on at the bot's impressive curves for a moment until she was overcome with pleasure.

After the event, Daria sat still and wondered if she was dreaming, she rubbed her head; there was a smooth, well fitted bandage in place now. She checked herself downstairs; it was real. Feeling elated she couldn't stop herself from squealing in delight. What other pleasures could she look forward to in America South?

The stewardess bot came out again with coffee and pastries and placed them on the table in front of Daria's large luxurious leather chair.

'Breakfast is served. Madam, please let me know if you require any further services, I am equipped with both male and female relief programmes' the bot said, reaching over toward Daria's hand.

'That won't be necessary, you are dismissed,' Daria said, brushing the bot away and picking up her drink.

No memories, no commitment, no boundaries, no comebacks. Do what thou wilt; she lit a cigarette, smirking. She was going to enjoy this. I'm in charge now, to be obeyed, the opposite of that shitty place.

'Hey, Mother wants your report now,' A Commando at the other end of the jet shouted, just at the wrong time causing Daria to choke on her hot coffee and spill it over the side of her chair.

'Yeah, give me a minute.' She said. It was only then she noticed the men were large and well built; almost super human looking.

Daria winced in pain as she got up. There was a bag on the floor with her coffee dripping down it. She opened it and began to examine its contents.

There was a purse, a scarf and a hairbrush alongside some peculiar looking clothing. Daria opened the purse and was disappointed to find only a credit card. The words, "America South Lifecard," were printed across the top. There was a shiny eagle crest and a small microchip visible toward the bottom of the card which was transparent. The stewardess bot appeared.

'What is this?' Daria asked.

'A Lifecard, it entitles the holder access to America South. Everything is included for the lifetime of holder; accommodation, food and expenses.' The bot explained in monotone.

'Dismissed,' Daria replied, a smile breaking on her face.

A lifetime holiday camp, just as the rumours said, picking up the pass to take a closer look.

'Prepare for landing in fifteen minutes,' a monotone voice said over the tannoy.

*

As Joey thrust his arm forward again something stopped him releasing his grip on the soon to be projectile. He let out a deep breath and brought the book closer to his face. He had no idea what the title said for it was written in an unknown language, but he stopped and gently placed it back where he had found it on the shelves. He pulled out the ornament Cara had given him, it was the same shape as on the front of the book. The radio began to blink and crackle.

'Scales here, come in.' Joey looked with disbelief toward the bag, then fished around for the large device and pulled it out. He had completely forgotten there were two of them.

'Spit it out old man, I don't have time for your crap,' he said.

'Help me and you'll be free from the Lifechip. I need you.' Scales said.

'I've already timed out, what difference does it make?' Joey asked.

'You should get your memory back for starters, besides what other options do you have now Joey?' Scales replied.

'I need to find Daria,' Joey said.

'That will be your first task, find her and stop her, however you want.' Scales said.

'I'll make her pay,' Joey replied, through gritted teeth.

'Get to the library up the spiral staircase and near the cabinet with the coins, there's a large chair, sit in it.' Scales said.

'I'm here already and there's no chair.'

'Okay just stand by the cabinet, yes, I see you now, hold on…remember Daria's file.'

Part 2 Robot Humans

"All that is necessary for the triumph of evil is that good men do nothing."

Edmund Burke

Chapter 17
2030, London

Joey figured Scales had a pretty good sense of humour when he realised where he had landed: London Heathrow Airport, Terminal 5, Arrivals. Luckily, not airside, for he had no documents or whatever was required in those days in order to fly through the air. The man from the future had landed somewhat ungracefully in a disabled toilet near a large coffee shop in the terminal building.

Joey landed with a bump and was drinking water from the basin and dousing himself in an attempt to cool down; travelling faster than the speed of light sure was hot work, he thought to himself, as he looked in the mirror he saw her face again and braced himself for some turbulence.

'What the hell Joey! My lifechip display has gone, where are we?' She exclaimed, her face flushed and eyes darting around the small room.

'I'm not too sure, have some water,' he replied, moving away from the sink and beginning to dry himself. He looked up expecting a reply, but it never came. *What the fuck?* As he did so he saw the apparition was right; the numbers that had permanently adorned his waking field of vision had disappeared! Finally, he was free. He stumbled over a black backpack that was on the ground next to the toilet. Opening it up he found two small rectangular devices made from metal with a glass screens, they were slightly different on the back. There was also a large bottle of water, two small cardboard boxes with something enclosed in them and a brown silky item. Finally, a hand-written note:

"You are in London, England at Heathrow Airport, the busiest airport in Europe. Your arrival here will have caused the deaths of your old selves, as the same person cannot exist in the same reality. These are mobile phones. They can be used for identification, purchasing goods and ruining your life amongst other things. Do not lose them. You are no longer sustained by the Lifechip. You will need to eat food three times per day and your hormones and growth will return. Start with these sandwiches. The map on the phone has been programmed with your home address. Get there without delay. Do not draw attention to yourselves."

'Airport!' he exclaimed, looking both impressed and confused. He saw her in the mirror; she picked up the wig and adjusted it over her head, she must have paid a lot of attention to Daria's hair as she seemed to know what to do; she looked beautiful. Then she was gone. Joey ripped up a hand rail and smashed it into the mirror with all his might letting out an anguished scream at the same time.

'Is everything okay?' A knock at the door, he had pulled the red alarm cord while destroying the toilet. Joey flung open the door almost knocking himself out and glared at the man in the cleaner's uniform.

'No, it fucking is not, this place is a shit-hole. Clean it up now.' Joey said, several years too late.

The terminal building heaved, it being the height of summer and the airport now being one of only two left functioning in England. Fucking people; everywhere, like mice, rushing around in their own little worlds in pursuit of their food. Joey headed for the sign that said, "All trains," as per the directions. Despite being in the arrivals section they still rushed as if their plane was on the tarmac ready to depart, not undergoing an environmental clean to remove the virus.

Most of the other people were well dressed, wearing hats and pressed clothing, and looked down on Joey's scruffy attire. The carbon exchange economy championed inequality, with valuable travel credits the first to be sold by the poor; airports had generally become a place for the rich.

'Fuck you,' Joey said, as a man with a smart suit on bumped his shoulder. His vocabulary had certainly become a lot more colourful after the removal of the Lifechip, he noted.

Joey noticed several men in dark blue uniforms walking around the terminal in pairs. He went down a moving staircase, there was another couple of them stood at the bottom, looking sternly at the new arrivals.

Joey strained his eyes and made out a label saying U.K.S.F. on their arms and chests along with a shiny circular device. He made a mental note to find out what that stood for later. There seemed to be a choke point up ahead as ques formed. Joey noted people stopping and touching their phones onto a scanner near the barrier then looking up at a screen which mirrored their face and gave a temperature reading before the barrier opened.

'Copy me,' he said, nodding to the line ahead.

Joey got through the barrier without fuss and turned to wait for Cara, then realised she wasn't there.

'Fuck!' He screamed. A man in uniform was now approaching.

'Come with me Sir,' said the uniform.

'Can I see your I.D. please?' The uniform asked. Joey handed over the phone.

'Okay, do you have a problem Mr Styles, your behaviour is aggressive and upsetting, I have therefore applied a social penalty to your profile,' he continued.

'Good for you Officer, are we done?' Joey asked, smiling broadly.

'Yes, do remember the cameras will recognise you by your facial structure. I'd suggest you consider your behaviour more carefully in future,' he said.

Joey moved off in silence toward the platforms where a sign read Elizabeth Line. A few minutes later a train arrived, Joey stepped into the carriage and took a seat. A voice coming from above said repeatedly, "Please find a seat, anyone not seated must disembark," the people seemed to listen to the announcement well as there were no spare seats, nobody standing and an orderly que on the platform. It was as if the rabble from the airport had suddenly been through prep school on the stairway down.

Then again, half of them had died since 2020, so the transport network actually worked. As the train started its motion Joey observed as silence descended upon the carriage and everyone bowed their heads.

Perhaps they are mourning a lost friend, he wondered. Nope, it soon became apparent they are staring at these mobile phones. A bizarre solemn ritual.

He shifted himself a little in his seat to look at the screen the person next to him was so engrossed in. This was harder than he imagined as the young lady seemed to be changing the content so rapidly that all Joey could take in was pictures of other young people with a few words and numbers next to them. Her finger was moving in a repetitive motion across the screen to enable this constant flow of happy, beautiful people. It seemed to Joey like she must be looking for a certain photo or be in some kind of a rush as the photo barely had time to settle on the screen before she moved onto the next.

'Staring is an offence.' The young lady said, glaring sideways at him.

'You'd better stop it then lady.' Joey replied.

After a few minutes, an enthusiastic sounding voice spoke over the loudspeaker as the train slowed.

'This is Hayes and Harlington, please take all your belongings with you. If you see any unaccompanied baggage press the alarm button to alert the driver, please do not travel if you feel unwell, emergency medical equipment is available in the central carriage. Stay alert.'

'What the hell was all that about?' Joey said aloud, before he remembered that life in the 2030's was hell. Either you were a robot, attached at the hip to your screen; letting it dictate your life, or some other form of robot was constantly telling you what to do, how to think and who to report at all times of the day. You weren't safe from the Commy bastards anywhere. Do this, do that, don't do this, feel sorry for them, they are right, he is the big bad wolf... it was a never-ending attack on the human mind. Maybe that's why most people stayed at home. Or just died. It was easier.

All the heads in the immediate vicinity stopped their scrolling and looked up directly at him. Joey slowly moved his finger to his lips to mock these robots.

'Three more stops and I'll be out of your hair,' he said to nobody and everybody all at once.

Joey stood as the train pulled into West Ealing station. A myriad of barriers and screens confronted him; a phone and a beep later and he was on the street wondering where to go next. A voice from Joey's phone instructed he turn left. On the display, he could see a blue line which lead west then south and under that a display that read twelve minutes' walk.

At first, in the area around the station, there were rows of much smaller buildings than in the Safezone. They were separated by large tarmacked areas with different heights that initially confused Joey. The buildings were dilapidated and probably unoccupied, although Joey thought he saw movement in one of the windows as he passed. He walked back parallel with the train tracks before turning left towards a modern looking bridge.

A sign above the bridge said, "Welcome to West Ealing Residential zone." There was a scanner below it and barriers restricting entry. This was becoming a bit of a habit Joey thought to himself as he reached for the phone again. A beep and a scan later the way became clear and he continued across the bridge. He hadn't come across any people since leaving the station.

As he exited the bridge and continued straight ahead there was a loud noise, followed by the screech of rubber on tarmac. To his left he realised a small vehicle had almost ran into him.

'Watch it, tosser,' Joey said angrily. The vehicle had one person in the back and nobody in the front, it made no sound as it approached until its emergency stop. A robotic voice emitted from the front of the taxi:

'Incident number 211, no damage detected, recorded as near miss, fault of human,' the passenger in the back shook his head and the car moved on. Joey raised a finger then remembered; cars- they have fucking cars here. It would be useful if his memory was either there or not there. This was going to confuse the fuck out of him. Still, it was better than being toasted by Freegov or fucking a robot.

Not more than a second later his phone chimed happily. Pressing the screen a message appeared from UKGOV:

"Social contract violation, 2nd Strike: 24-hour movement restriction enabled, 1-mile radius of home."

Joey looked again, there was one above it from the airport; Social contract violation 1st Strike warning for threatening or harmful conduct. They may as well have said he was unkind. Phew. What were people made of these days…glass? More likely multicoloured glass with a tint to ensure maximum obfuscation.

'Get me the fuck outta here fast. Less than a mile from home, this isn't a problem,' Joey said to himself.

The man from the future walked onward following the blue line on the phone's display for another couple of minutes until he arrived at a large yellow brick building. It reminded him of the apartment blocks in the Safezone. Soul-less and blueprinted. A small sign adjacent to an entry door read, "Kindness House," and an entry system scanner blinked red.

Joey laughed out loud and started pressing his phone onto the door. Nothing. Again. Nothing. 'What the fu..'

'Can I help you?' a tall, middle-aged man in non-descript clothing was standing just behind him with something in his hand.

'I can't get in,' Joey replied.

'Do you have a key?' The man asked, waving a small set of keys in his hand.

'Yes' Joey replied feeling a little stupid after fishing around in the bag. There was a note saying the address. Flat 911. That number had a nice ring to it, he thought.

'Okay, after you, I'm Franks. Nice to meet you,' the man said.

'Joey, likewise.' Stretching out his hand. Franks looked surprised but shook it firmly. A real man.

'I'm in flat 909 if you need anything,' Franks said, as he walked away towards a wall of small metal containers.

Joey managed to navigate from the lobby to the flat without further ado. It was on the ninth floor and he had travelled up in one of two elevators. As he exited lights turned on illuminating a grey carpeted corridor, he turned right and walked to the south eventually reaching flat 911.

He sighed with relief as he closed the door behind him. What a journey. He entered into a hallway with some hooks to put your coat, then two doors off to the right and two to the left. These turned out to be two bedrooms, a bathroom and a utility room. There was furniture in them and they looked like good solid pieces, but it was sparse and definitely lacked that homely feel. As they moved into the last room at the end of the hall Cara gasped in awe.

'Wow, I've never seen such a view, it's amazing,' she exclaimed. They had walked into a large kitchen diner that contained massive floor to ceiling windows giving 180-degree views from central through south then to west London.

Joey resisted the temptation to smash the window where he saw the latest apparition of Cara. He was losing it here. Fuck. The cupboards…yes. Bottles. Not many but it would do. He sat down at a small table and drank. The liquid tasted horrible but he continued drinking it anyway. Maybe his old life was coming back to him faster than expected.

'Hey, cool- they fly!' Joey remarked, pointing directly out the window to a que of planes on final approach over west London toward Heathrow Airport. Looking out over the panorama, he could see four planes lining up with the runway at various altitudes.

'Yes, they used to be the main form of travel in the old world. This place is nice; Its certainly an upgrade on the Safezone,' she added smiling, before pulling Joey back towards the larger bedroom.

Chapter 18
2050, America South

Daria entered the dark room at the rear of the jet, limping slightly, she made her way over to a chair in front of a desk and sat down. Her face contorted unhappily as she approached her judgement. There was a phone with loudspeaker on the desk with a flashing red light. She tried to recall her training.

'Interim Report; Target Joey Styles, Unusual Behaviour. Made contact, May 31. Threat Assessment Medium. Target associated with Scales. Recommend further surveillance. Injured in pursuit of target who escaped.' Daria said.

There was a pause on the line.

'Detail all information on Scales.' The voice said.

'He made contact via modified radio with no encryption and wanted me to travel back in time.'

Another pause.

'This is not your best moment, Daria. You will recuperate in America South. Go to the Palm Tree Complex. Stand by for further orders.'

Daria sighed and lit up, she went back into the main cabin, opened the coffee stained suitcase and pulled out all the clothing.

There wasn't much to choose from; Mother had packed light, the commando's looked on intently as Daria stripped down to her purple silk underwear. One of them approached and offered to help as she struggled into a velvet textured green gown. She couldn't help notice his massive muscles and the glow to his skin and hair. Still feeling weak she allowed him to help her into the undersized garment.

They were interrupted by the pilot bot asking them to be seated for landing, which they did. Daria looked eagerly out the window; small angled white ripples on the vast blue carpet below them; up ahead to the right a thin strip of grey amongst the lush greens.

Minutes later they were stationary; the stewardess bot opened the door and a blast of hot, humid air rushed into the cabin. Moving forwards into the open air, Daria took a deep breath, lifted her head and pushed her shoulders back, she felt an energy within growing, flowing like a current around her body.

As they stepped down onto terra-firma Daria pushed away the puppy-dog Commando who was still fussing around her like a bad smell, wrestled her bag from his clasp and walked forward confidently. Something in the air agreed with her here.

There was no airport, no passport control, no hustle and no bustle. Just perfection everywhere. Plants, flowers, trees all lined the runway. They were perfect shapes, as if cut out by the original creator, perfectly proportioned, vivid colours. Daria picked at a leaf to check they were real. Tropical birdsong and the hum of cicadas followed her as she walked toward a line of cars with, "AmSouth" written on the side of them.

A bot wearing a chauffeur style uniform opened the rear door and ushered her in. She was pleasantly surprised to be asked her destination then told the journey time, no apps or Satnav here. Just good old-fashioned road signs.

After a twenty-minute drive, the car stopped inside a complex with several two and three-story high villas linked by a central glass domed area. The building was a shiny silver colour likely designed to reflect the sun although she could not tell what it was made from. A concierge bot opened the door to a reception area that was floor to ceiling marble, with huge mirrors and more perfect looking plants; these ones looked double the size of normal plants.

'Welcome, Lifecard please,' the bot said.
Daria handed it over and waited. The bot looked at it and gave it back.

'Thank you. Condo 3, porter, expect a medic shortly Daria,' the bot said. She handed the card back. The porter bot arrived wearing a stupid uniform and an even more stupid grin. He certainly wasn't getting hired for any extras. Daria slid into the golf buggy and they drove off.

'Amal, Amal is that you?' A voice said.

'AMAL, wait that IS you!' The voice shouted. The penetrating and harsh female voice was clearly shouting at her. They sped further down a stone pathway in between lush velvety green grass.

'Keep driving,' Daria said, 'I don't know this madwoman.' But it was too late, Daria felt a hand on her shoulder and turned around.

'Oh, my goodness, Amal, wow. You had another treatment. It worked this time and oh, wow you've had your breasts done and oh my, oh my, you've got a man. Oh, you look so wonderful darling so young, so fresh, so new you must tell me the formula!' The lady said loudly, not pausing for breath. She prodded Daria's body and looked the porter up and down.

'I'm not Amal you are mistaken,' Daria said.

'Nonsense you are just having one of those hazy days, you remember me; Cruella?' The lady replied, grabbing both her hands.

Daria got a good look at the woman while she removed himself from her clutches with disgust. She looked about seventy with white hair and a gravity defying curved figure squeezed into tight colourful clothing. She had outrageous fluorescent coloured makeup on her lips and eyes and wore a large pink top hat with glowing gold pendants hanging from it. Her skin glowed just like the Commando's and her hair glistened in the light.

'I need to rest,' Daria said.

'Oh, your voice changed too, my goodness so young, you can tell me all about it at the entertainment later, good day,' Cruella screeched. She was gone in a flash faster than she had arrived.

The crazy old bat had really cold hands. Daria shook her head slightly and they resumed their journey down the scenic pathway. The porter bot stopped and left her bag by the front door of condo number three then left. The door opened automatically as she got within a couple of feet of it.

'Welcome, room temperature twenty-one degrees, pool temperature twenty-six degrees, air quality high, you have mail,' a computerised voice said as they entered.

Daria took a look around the home, it was constructed from a silver coloured metal, concrete and glass. It felt fresh and clean, but somehow soulless inside. She gave the ground floor a quick once over then decided to explore from the top down.

Up on the third floor, two glass doors slid open leading to a roof garden. There were four loungers, numerous potted plants and a medium sized rectangular pool all located in the atrium. Everything was enclosed by a glass roof; a kind of solarium, leisure area. She allowed herself a smile and wondered whether the roof was keeping good air in or bad air out. It was hot so she stripped off and lay down, closing her eyes and enjoying the peace for a moment before was interrupted by a bot.

88

'Welcome, what service do you require?' The bot asked. Daria looked up to see a bot of similar construction to the ones on the plane, this one was human looking too and dressed in a maid's uniform.

'I am equipped with all relief programmes, male and female,' the bot said, moving close enough for Daria to see some detail on her natural looking flesh.

'Not now. I need some clothes,' she replied. The bot made its way downstairs to a bedroom while Daria lay prone. There was a small sheet of paper on the bed placed deliberately so as not to be missed. The bot picked it up along with a dressing gown and returned to the roof depositing the gown on a small table made out of a natural boulder next to Daria's lounger.

'Weekly entertainment rescheduled for tomorrow. As always; dress to impress. Collection time 7p.m. lobby. Palm Tree Condos, administration.' The bot read out then swished off, leaving sleeping dogs to lie.

Her head throbbed and she felt her heart thudding against her ribs, through blurry eyes Daria identified something in white moving around her, then felt a sharp pain in her neck. She also noticed she was inside now on a bed.

'I have removed your Lifechip, you will feel pain there for a while as it heals. The air here is pure so you will recover faster than normal. You will receive monthly injections that work with the pills, do not miss them. The live pills will help to dull the pain amongst other things, you need to take a pill at least once per day. You should start to feel better immediately.' The medic bot said, then placed several boxes onto the bedside table.

The box was constructed from paper-thin white cardboard with, "LIVE" printed in black lettering on the front. Daria tore open the flimsy container and popped some pills, leaving the box in tatters at an angle. From her position, prone on the bed, head spinning she read the letters, backward, through the box.

"E V I L"

Chapter 19
2030, London

Joey stood in front of the mirror, happily it was only him this time. He turned on the cold faucet and let it run, and run then splashed his face over and over, while looking into his eyes and trying to reconcile these last days. There was a dim throbbing in his head and he thought of then regretted the drinks. Looking more closely he noticed black hairs on his chin and neck and even on his bald head. Then came a rumbling growl from his stomach immediately followed by an alarm; 'beep, beep, beep…' from somewhere. He followed it to the utility cupboard, where a meter flashed, he hit a button and it stopped. Overuse warning, Green Global Water. *Fuck off.*

As he took in the other sights of the utility room he was rudely interrupted by a rustling noise that sounded like it came from the front door so he followed to sound and turned the corner to see a folded piece of paper had been slipped under the door. Quickly, he pulled open the front door and looked into the corridor, the motion sensor-controlled lights were on but there was nobody to be seen. Back inside, he unfolded the paper to find a handwritten note in black ink, which he read to himself:

"Welcome to London, we have had to change plans a little, due to the circumstances. It is now imperative that you find and stop the 2030 version of Daria urgently. She orchestrates the Fall in a few days. Pablo's file details her regular haunts and cover stories. Hurry, time is running out.

Most things here revolve around your mobile phone so get to know it, you will need your eyes open to see what's really going on, nothing is what it seems. Your phone has details of your bank account and the currency in it. You receive the Universal Basic Income from the government on a monthly basis, this is approximately to 1,500 Ukc[11] dependent on other factors which you will discover. All currency is digital although there are black markets which you might discover. You'll probably need some food today from a supermarket. Your cover is that are looking for work as an electrician on construction sites after being in the north of the country looking after your sick aunt who died leaving you some currency.

Note that public opinion is influenced here by a combination of information given in various formats. Most of it can be seen on your phone and is called the internet but you also have television and printed media. There are a few printed newspapers left which you can buy in shops. They all say the same things. There is a television in your living room that people here use to watch for entertainment, but it is also used to disseminate different types of information via 24-hour news channels and state sponsored channels. Get to know these mediums and how they work, look for and identify patterns in communication and analyse them. Also get to know the laws of the land. I see you have fallen foul of a couple already. The penalties for breaking these laws restrict your freedom, integrity and self-respect. Be aware.

Finally, here you have writing devices; pens and pencils. I know they were not available in the Safeworld. This is an old-fashioned way of communication that you can use to ensure privacy for your work and thoughts. Anything you send through the internet or phones will be watched. Make use of them to log events and discoveries. I'm working on it but for now I cannot communicate with you directly but I can hack into C.C.T.V. cameras and watch.

Good Luck.

Scales"

'Secret agents,' Cara said, nodding her approval.

'Secret lovers,' Joey replied, picking up a pen he had found in the bedside table drawer and starting to imitate the letters on the pages, then looked up and noticed he was talking to himself. Again. Stomach churning, grumbling, he grabbed his keys and phone.

He missed the digital banner advert as he walked into the supermarket, it would soon become apparent. "Food rations back to protect your environment."

---

[11] Ukc: United Kingdom Coins, digital currency introduced in 2025 after the financial crash.

There was a scanner between the double sliding doors. Joey walked through the first set aggressively; there was a large display screen above head height. It contained a grid with several lines of writing on it: Physical and Mental Health status, Environmental (Carbon) Impact status, Financial status, Criminal Justice status and finally Social Justice status. There were ten small boxes to the right of each category which began to fill up like a petrol gauge after Joey tapped the scanner. Once they had reached over five the gauge turned from red to yellow, then again over seven from yellow to green. There was a logo and a badge saying Lifepass[12] on the scanner. The logo was a picture of a phone and a smiling human with green colours; it was a very basic almost childlike design. Joey noticed his Social Justice status only reached five therefore was coloured yellow, however, the door opened anyway and he entered the shop; making a note to check the rules later. He turned expecting to see Cara but she was nowhere, he was blocking the way and people behind were staring and becoming agitated. A large sign above the door read, "No Exit."

'This is a one-way system, collect your trolley and carry out your shopping sir,' a voice said. It came from a mean looking security guard who approached and directed Joey towards some baskets with wheels.

Again, the other people were scanning their phones in order to unlock the trolley from its docking station. This time though some people were putting on gloves and covering their face. Joey copied these lemmings and the trolley released. There were shiny back scanners on all four sides of the vehicle and a small display on the handle that read 29:56. It was counting down. *Not a-fucking-gain*, was he going to timeout eh? Part of him wanted to just wait for it to expire to see what would happen, his stomach growled louder; that's a negative. He took a deep breath and started down the first aisle; copy the others, a robot human.

"Face, Space, Pace remember the safe shopping protocol," rang out from the store loudspeaker system. They had made it into a jingle. *Tossers.* Joey half expected the national anthem to play next. Or a colourful flag to descend into his face and smother him for his unkind thoughts.

---

[12] Lifepass: A mobile phone application that enabled access, payments and services in UK in 2030.

He wasn't in the mood; he picked items, and threw them into the trolley. 'Error, place items slowly, one-by-one.' The display flashed. Red. Joey the bull. Why couldn't it be blue or grey or…Joey removed the items and inserted them one by one, he noticed three numbers on the display; health 88/100, Carbon 68/100, price 4.39Ukc and heard a beep as the item received approval to land. The time display flashed the cumulative price and displayed; "Broccoli." Joey soon worked out this was some kind of underhand way to alter behaviour and made his way to the meat isle. He was pleasantly surprised to find a steak and placed it into his trolley. No worries but the price was 35Ukc. He went for another but instead of the beep there was a two-tone noise and the display flashed red.

"Carbon limit reached. Return item," scrolled across the display.

'Wow,' he mumbled, under his breath as he returned the item to the shelf and chose another. The same alert sounded. He wheeled the trolley off and only stopped when he reached an isle with no shoppers, where there were lots of smaller items in shiny wrappers on the shelves and it was warm again. He remembered the energy bars Daria had and started shopping again. The General Secretary of the shopping trolley kept quiet while he added items.

Then just as it seemed he was on a roll the trolley calmly informed him via the two-tone alarm, red flash and display that he had now reached the Health limit and needed to put the latest addition, a chocolate bar, back. That was it; his eyes grew large, he grabbed the chocolate bar aggressively and bent his arm back over his shoulder, about to thrust forward and obliterate the item and the shelf when he felt someone grab his wrist.

'You do not want to do that,' a voice with a slight accent that he recognised said slowly.
It was Franks who lived at the apartment block. He was smiling; despite his anger levels Joey was disarmed and accepted the advice; putting the chocolate bar down slowly.

'This bastard machine, it won't let me buy things,' Joey said, steam still figuratively coming from his ears as he gestured to the trolley.

'Just rest assured every decision they push you into is for your own good, so they say,' Franks explained, eyebrows raised, possibly a hint of sarcasm. He pressed a couple of buttons on Joey's Red Army issue shopping trolley.

'Right, you have ten minutes left and several empty slots before your quota is full. Follow me,' Franks explained.

'Okay,' Joey replied. No-nonsense. He liked this guy.

Franks directed him around and picked up staples. As they walked, Franks explained that as well as the health, environmental and time limits on shopping there was also rationing going on due to shortages and the current emergency. This meant you were only allowed to shop for yourself and your financial dependents and only for three days at a time. These parameters were all recorded on your phone.

'Is there a war on or something.' Joey asked.

'Yes, a war on the mind,' Franks replied, with a slight shake of the head.

'What do we do here?' He asked approaching the exit seeing no tills.

'Nothing, the shop will take the payment automatically when we leave the store. Just pick up the bags and return the trolley there.' Franks replied, picking up his own bag and depositing his trolley.

Joey hadn't noticed that the bottom of the trolley was pre-lined with two large reinforced paper bags with the colours from the supermarket on them. He breathed a sigh of relief as they exited into the fresh air and sunlight.

Before he could even catch his breath, a scruffy looking slim woman with a pitted face approached him, phone in hand.

'Carbon credits for sale, 50Ukc per gram.'

'Fuck off,' Joey barged the woman aside and the men continued.

'Listen, they can be useful when you need stuff, especially when you hit your limits,' Franks added, nodding toward a group the woman had returned to.

It turned out Franks' flat was directly opposite Joey's, so Joey invited him in. As they entered the living area Franks let out a slow whistle.

'Perfect view, right,' Franks said, as he followed Joey onto the balcony.

'They are amazing,' Joey exclaimed, not taking his eye of a small jet disappearing toward the runway just before the control tower.

'Tell me about it, I used to fly the big foot[13] in and out of there once a week.' Franks replied, in a regretful tone.

'Really? You sound like you miss it?' Joey asked.

'Nothing comes close to that feeling of opening up the thrust on those engines; I'll always miss it, but things got crazy there for a while so I'm happy to have moved on. Hey, I've got some binoculars; I'll go grab them. You sure do have an ace view from here,' Franks said.

Joey filled the fridge, gorged an energy bar and cracked open two beers. Franks walked back in as Joey finished chewing.

'Come on I've got the binoculars,' Franks reported, before continuing, 'That's the regular westerly approach into runway 27 at Heathrow. Look you can see them lining up over London, keeping 3 nautical miles apart on their final approach, there's about four separate jets in sight now.'

Franks pointed to out to the east then back across the south and finally to the west where a tall slim building with an inverted pyramid shape on the top could be seen in the distance.

'That's the control tower, where they guide the planes in and out. Those guys in there are very professional, even the Scottish one who I could never understand. Here, you have a look,' he explained. Joey took the binoculars and was disappointed to see less clearly than with his eyes.

'Adjust the range finder on the top,' Franks said, reading his mind. After a while Joey got the hang of it and focussed in on a plane to the east over the city.

'That's looks like a Guppy; a Boeing 737. They fly short distances regularly. You might hear when the pilots reduce throttle and extend the flaps. There look it has dropped the landing gear!' Franks continued. Joey watched in awe as three sets of wheels dropped out of the planes' undercarriage. He was enjoying Franks commentary.

'Now it's on short final, the weather is fine, no wind the pilot flying will be in full control, the co-pilot on instruments will be watching the runway counting down the altitude,' he continued. They watched on as the plane disappeared to the west just before the control tower.

---

[13] "Big Foot": A nickname used by pilots for the Boeing 777 in reference to its massive landing gear.

'And she's down, full reverse thrust and hold the nose straight, job done,' Franks observed.

'Awesome power, ever had a smash?' Joey asked. Franks looked away.

'No... but, err how about we eat?' Franks replied, shifting uncomfortably.

With a little help, and some more beer, Joey managed to order Chinese food for the two of them, laughing out loud as he chose the carbon neutral seaweed and the green drone delivery option.

'If you got money, I mean Ukc's, then you can just about do what you want. It's the poor bastards who have to sell their credits just to eat those nasty Crickets and Ants I feel sorry for. Ugh.' Franks continued.

'I thought everyone got the same income?' Joey asked.

'They do, but it's not enough and some started with more and earn much more. The poor sell to live a restricted life and the rich buy to live their regular life without feeling guilty about climate change.' Franks explained,

'Fucking Commy bastards!' Joey exclaimed.

Franks spluttered then choked on a chicken wing.

'Just where have you been Joey? You seem fairly intelligent to me. Surely you know what's going on here, it's just nobody talks about it, you know...'

'Know what?' Joey interrupted.

'The Report and Reward scheme.' Franks whispered, eyes shifty.

'Oh, yeah of course,' Joey somehow cottoned on and nodded, getting up from the small dining table. He returned momentarily with a piece of paper he had scrawled a few words on and placed it on the table.

"Is someone listening?" Franks took it and wrote back.

"They could be, or watching. It's a smart home. Everything is connected."

'Nice to meet you I'm going to get some rest, it was a long journey for me.' Joey said deliberately.

'Yes, I owe you dinner, let me know...' Franks replied handing the paper to Joey.

"My flat is clean come over anytime."

Chapter 20
2030, London

Franks stayed up most evening's researching, his flying career with the U.S. Navy involved him with several conflicts and he had developed a strong interest in history. That was before his commercial flying career came to a premature end just after the turn of the century. His best friend, who flew for the same carrier, was tragically killed on duty during a terrorist attack.

Franks investigations into the event rubbed his employers and the establishment up the wrong way forcing him to leave the United States. One of the contacts that hadn't deserted him was his brother who'd spent his career as a military aerospace engineer at the top-secret facilities in the Nevada desert, who had a few interesting theories himself. Since leaving the states, he'd felt more able to pursue his interests freely as he wasn't breaking any contract he'd signed or a threat to National Security, not theirs anyway.

Tonight, he'd decided to do some research on the G7 Terror Attack to compare it to other similar events. The search screen pulled up several different options to choose; after spending an age scrolling through them he settled on an article titled, "Uncomfortable Coincidences; Terror and the Security Services 2001-2026." Pleasantly surprised the article loaded correctly and was not censored, Franks began to read.

The article was a few pages long and used three terrorist attacks as case studies, briefly describing the events as they happened, then the results of the investigations and enquiries afterward. The third case study was the G7 attack in Paris which he read through to compare with what he remembered from the news reports, after all it wasn't that long ago.

He was interested to read that the investigation had identified and found suspects very quickly after the attack happened. They were members of the European Liberation Army (E.L.A.) a group that formed after the pandemics, energy and food crises in the early part of the decade, to protest against the removal of fundamental human rights. It appeared three members of the group had infiltrated the events kitchen by securing jobs as kitchen support staff. The French security service, the D.G.S.U., found the conspirators identity cards, an E.L.A. branded bomber jacket and a small piece of the same explosive that made the bomb in a car parked near to the arena that very evening. The report also revealed that the suspected ringleader had been a D.G.S.U. informant up until 2025. Finally, that all the suspects had died in the explosion.

Franks thought that the security services must have been working to a very high standard to have found out the identities of the suspects on the very same evening of the attack; and wondered why they hadn't done so a little earlier.

Then he read the conclusion of the report and it became clear that there was a pattern; in all three attacks identity documents, plans and parts were found the very same day as the attack; in one case a terrorist's passport survived a plane crash then explosion followed by a building collapse and fire. Franks wondered if his homeland had been testing a new fire retardant, indestructible passport.

Likewise, the terrorists had links to the security services; either as targets or informers. In two of the three attacks, there were drills carried out at the same time as the attack that mirrored almost exactly the events as they unfolded. What were the odds of that!

Finally, all the terrorists were killed during the attacks, meaning there was no trial, testimony or evidence to be gleaned directly from them.

Franks closed his computer, went over to the open window and took a deep breath- his head ached.

*

Next-door Joey was getting to grips with the television having thrown his phone down in disgust after a zombie like scroll session on the couch. It was all coming back to him pretty quickly now. He didn't need to boost his ego or bank balance by becoming a director and star of an advert for himself on social media, nor was he interested in throwing his Ukc's away to online companies for some "fun" while he watched virtual sports. And, what really got his goat that evening- he most certainly didn't need to watch videos on the small screen to satisfy his human urges. Maybe that's what Franks meant earlier when he said a war on the mind.

He needed to find Daria but he had the 24-hour movement restriction to contend with. He'd already searched for her online which, unsurprisingly, came up blank. Even her job title at the University came up blank, perhaps her cover story had been erased, it now being so close to the attack.

Loud noises from the television interrupted his train of thought. It sounded as if a military parade were beginning. Behind the sounds an authoritative female voice could be heard.

'Welcome to the U.K. news. Our main headline tonight; The United Kingdom State of Emergency has been extended for a further three months,' the presenter said. Joey glanced over at the screen noting the presenters' photogenic features.

'The government has today announced that the state of emergency, first introduced in 2025, has been renewed under the Emergency Planning Act; which allows for the threat level of all known threats to be assessed on a quarterly basis. Government experts then produce a score out of five for each threat. When the separate threats average over sixty percent a state of emergency is declared with various contingency measures put in place to mitigate the threats and protect the population. Parliament was not required to vote on the renewal due to the measures in place requiring Politicians to stay at home for their own safety following the pandemic, recent floods, terror attack and energy crisis. Food rations, timed daily electricity breaks and 10 p.m. curfews will remain in place. Any other restrictions will be determined personally via your Lifepass,' she continued.

Then a graphic titled, "U.K. Threats," was shown on the screen. It detailed the threat levels for several categories including Environment, Health, Terror, Cyber (Including Misinformation) and finally War. The total combined threat level was three out of five or sixty percent.

'We cross now to our Emergency Correspondent, for further analysis,' said the presenter.

'Well, if we take a closer look at today's events we can see that nothing has changed in terms of the actual numbers reported by the governments' Threat Advisory Panel.

However, inside sources tell me that there was a heated virtual debate over a reduction to the terror threat, as it has been over four years since the last major attack, which occurred abroad in Paris. However, I understand, a classified threat has been decoded via international listening stations, as a result they decided to err on the side of caution,' he explained.

'Thankyou. A poll conducted by U.K. News has revealed overwhelming support for the measures. 92.3% of people surveyed gave positive answers regarding the continued state of emergency. In other news a group of Anti-deniers[14] have been arrested today for threats to national security. Now we cross to our Home Affairs Correspondent, for more details,' she continued. The screen cut to a middle-aged lady, who looked like a librarian, wearing expensive clothes. Joey turned it off.

Emergencies eh, the gift that kept on giving regardless; past, present and future. Joey wondered what would happen if there was a real emergency. Chaos. Then again, he knew the answer to that; 2050 Timeout-that was the plan.

The self-loathing part of Joey urged him to continue watching the news despite the damage he knew it was doing. The next link reported record economic growth across the country but that it was not expected to reflect in wages for twelve to twenty-four months.

---

[14] Anti-denier: A derogatory term coined by the government and media in the mid 2020's to describe those who questioned the official narrative.

The same report went on to explain how wholesale prices of gas and oil had reduced but the reductions would not reach the consumer for at least six years. People in expensive suits talking bollocks to scared, scarred, distracted, broke people who believed them because of their job title, then did as they said 'cos their on-demand series had run out. Morons. Joey hit the off button fast before the social interest story to get everyone upset came on. He knew the programme…programming.

Chapter 21
2030, London

The next morning Joey opened his eyes and looked around; disoriented and slightly startled, it took a while for his brain to catch up. When it did he checked the time; his movement restriction ended in less than an hour so he could get on with finding young Daria instead of bumming around doing nothing. He was going to make her pay, and enjoy it.

As he thought about breakfast there was a knock on the door.

'I made coffee, you want some?' Franks beckoned him over.

The flat was a similar layout but had that "lived in" feel that estate agents go on about while peddling their charms to their unfortunate victims. They settled in the front room and Joey smiled at the two defrosted croissants Frank's placed onto the cluttered table. A copy of "Professional Pilots Network" lay on its front half open over a pile of unopened letters.

'Cheers,' Joey nodded, mouth full, then noticed the egg boxes on the walls. 'You play loud music in here or something?'

'We can talk in here, no one can hear, so long as you leave your phone in another room.' Franks said, a twinkle in his eye.

'I'm getting the feeling you aren't so on board with these idiots in charge?' Joey asked. Franks offered him a knowing glance and for the first time in a long time, he smiled.

Connecting with someone who was actually human and not brainwashed was like your team winning the Super Bowl in 2030.

Joey got up and returned with Daria's information sheet. He placed it down on the table, downed his coffee and lit a smoke; the last one from that bitches' bag. Franks signalled him outside and whistled.

'That's quite a piece you got there, what'd she do to you?' he asked. Taking a closer look at the full body shots; particularly the partially clothed side view.

'I've got two days to find her before she blows up London. She's a state sponsor... no... I mean intelligence agent.' Joey said between puffs. 'Oh, and she killed my girlfriend.'

Franks glanced up to the shelf, eyeing the half empty bottle of Jack. No, it was too early. 'She looks mean, what have we got to go on?'

'You tell me, I've only just got here.' Joey said.

'It says her hobby is physical training and that she worked part time at a large gym chain. There's one in our local shopping centre. How about we check it out?' Franks suggested.

Joey glanced up at the old analogue wall clock, then nodded.

'Get your phone, it is illegal to leave the house without a form of Identification which the U.K.S.F.[15] can request at any time. There was a physical Identity card available but this was phased out last year so, unless you have one, it is de-facto illegal to go out without your phone.' Franks explained.

Joey retrieved his phone and noticed a text message.

"UKGOV Info: 24-hour movement penalty expired."

Then a gradual low rumble grew from outside. They moved quickly to the balcony and looked up to see the undercarriage of a plane directly above them, the balcony shook as the plane screamed past them.

'Whooooooaaaa!' Joey screamed, at the sheer power almost within reach.

It was a couple of hundred feet above the flats and flying normally, however, the wind had changed direction so the runway operations had changed their orientation to easterly.

'Come on, the car is here,' Franks said, looking up to the sky as if remembering a long-lost friend.

The duo sat in the back of a silent, white coloured taxi.

'You go shopping?' The driver asked, looking in his review mirror.

'No were going to the gym,' Joey replied.

'I'm going to the bar.' Franks added, meaningfully.

'It's expensive to visit in person, most people go virtually online to get the old prices and Lifepass credits. Maybe you are rich sir?' The driver asked.

'What do you mean online, fuck that buddy,' Joey replied.

'Ah, okay mate, no trouble please.' The driver replied.

'He wears woman's clothes,' Franks interjected, helping to shift the conversation.

'Okay good then you can shop at home its cheaper and better for the environment.

---

[15] U.K.S.F.: United Kingdom Security Force. A merger of Police and Army following civil unrest in 2024.

You know so many troubles these days. Government pay me more currency to stay off road and not work. Most taxis drive themselves. Nobody go out. They scared,' the driver explained. He was getting into it now; a self-therapy session.

'You mean the state of Emergency. What exactly are they scared of?' Joey asked.

'They are scared of everything and nothing. I see no change except the behaviour. After the flood and the bomb five years ago, everything changed. But since then nothing happens; only people are scared and restricted,' the driver replied.

Suddenly car horns blared, interrupting the driver, and their car came to a halt as two large vans came within inches of a crash ahead of them.

'Bloody smart vans, oh my, I die in this car one day, help me,' The driver exclaimed.

He drove on past the large navy blue and brown vans with some lighter coloured writing on them.

'What's your name? I'm Joey and this is Franks. What's your phone number?' Joey asked, seeing an opportunity. The man gave Joey a small card with writing on, which he gave to Franks.

'Thanks Abdul,' he said. Joey jabbed Franks in the arm. 'Nice one, thanks.'

'Don't worry there's a shop in here.' Franks said, chuckling.

They got out and faced a large complex of buildings ahead of them as the road turned into a pedestrianised area. Up ahead Joey noticed what looked like scanners and security staff.

'Here we go again,' he said, shaking his head ruefully. The duo arrived at some barriers that looked similar to those at the train station. There was a small hut on each side with security staff in them, plus a few more standing around busily engrossed in small screens. Clearly security was tight. They wore dark blue uniforms that looked very similar to the U.K.S.F. at the airport. There were no other customers at the entrance but there were some up ahead beyond the barrier.

'Welcome to Westgrass Shopping Centre, do you have a slot booked?' A female guard said to them, with a forced smile, as they stopped.

'Yes, but I had some trouble confirming the booking.' Franks replied.

'Due to the state of emergency you must book a slot in advance before you can shop here,' the guard replied, in a disinterested tone.

'Okay, how do we do that Brenda?' Joey asked, taking out his phone.

The security lady's nametag betrayed her and Joey took up the gauntlet of getting them past the shopping centre boss. She looked at him and thought for a moment, then took his phone and pressed some buttons.

'Okay, it's not exactly busy. You are booked in to the next slot, tap your passes and go through, enjoy,' Brenda said, almost managing to smile.

The visitors tapped through and some blurb appeared on the screen about time limits, air quality and routes to follow.

'Fucking joke, do they want my money or what?' Joey said, spotting a shop on the corner that looked like it might stock cigarettes.

They walked past several dark, empty units to their left, some had menus outside with bird crap all over them, tasty. Then Joey noticed some neon lights and a sign, "The 19th Hole," it said, as they passed he noticed there were mostly men inside and several large television screens.

'Come on, there's plenty of time for that later.' Franks admonished.

They veered off to the right and entered the large grey building with glass frontage. As they went up an escalator the place came to life, there was some pleasant music playing over the tannoy system and more people milling around with the buzz of conversation in the air.

Franks walked at a decent pace, and had to stop and turn when he noticed Joey no longer at his side. He sat on an empty bench, slightly annoyed with himself, under the watchful eyes of a security guard.

It wasn't long before Joey emerged from the store bag in hand. His proud smile disarmed Franks and they continued.

The men arrived at the large glass windowed, 'Sustainable Fitness 4 All,' Gym. Franks tapped his phone and chose day pass, Joey reciprocated. Inside the stale smell made Joey heave and Franks nose turn up, it was virtually empty with nothing resembling the young Daria in sight.

There was a tattooed meat head, dressed like a weight lifter on a bench in the corner; he was too busy grunting and looking in the mirror to notice them. Then a group of teenagers with unusual angular hair styles were busy focussed on their screens while occupying a rack in the other corner.

'You guys need something?' a guy in jeans and a cap with the gym logo pulled down low said, seeming to come out of nowhere.

Joey glanced behind the man to see a door swinging shut then pulled out Daria's picture, which he had torn off Pablo's file.

'Never met her.' The guy replied quickly, looking away.

'Me either,' Joey answered with a shake of his head, putting the picture in his bag and pulling out a t-shirt, 'I meant to ask if this is suitable clothing for this establishment?'

'Sure, you can change in there.' The guy nodded his head toward the swinging door.

'He knows her alright,' Joey concluded in the changing room, 'it's just a question of how.'

'There's only one way out of this place,' Franks replied.

'It's settled then, come on let's get this shit out the way old man,' Joey said, a rueful look on his face as he tightened his laces and pulled up his socks.

Forty minutes later, after some running, cycling and weight lifting, the two men sat sweating in the locker room. Their phones chimed in unison as they scanned out at the front door, Joey was first to react. A notification read: "Heath bonus awarded," and a green bar filled in on his heath screen, he clicked detail to see how many calories he had burnt along with other data from the exercise session.

'How does it know all this?' He asked.

'Sensors in the machines communicate with your phone, the rest is history,' Franks replied carefully looking around them as they walked, 'come on, she could slip by while we're in here we need to get to the entrance.'

They walked in and took a look around the aforementioned drinking establishment; there was a guy sat at the bar and group in the corner. A plump, middle aged lady stood, arms folded, behind the bar with an array of glass bottles behind her. While Joey ordered two lagers, Franks took a seat in a booth by the window.

'What now?' Joey asked as he sat down.

'We wait. Tell me more about Daria.' Franks replied after a large sip of the cold golden liquid.

'She works for a shadowy organisation called Mother, whose goal is to enslave humanity by turning humans into robots. They are working on a major event that will happen in two days.' Joey explained.

'Robots eh!' Franks exclaimed, looking down at his phone, 'they are doing a good job.'

'Yes, but this is the final piece in the Jigsaw, an event that makes humans so scared they beg for the ultimate draconian solution, giving up their minds.' Joey replied.

'Sounds like an old government ploy. Stage an event, control the reaction with well-placed media sources then let the people ask for the solution. They will think the government is acting in their best interests and not mind giving up their fundamental rights.' Franks explained.

'What would make you accept a chip?' Joey asked.

The question hung in the air as Franks walked to the bar. Joey's attention fell on the escalator opposite where an athletic looking woman bounded up it; her long dark hair flowing behind her. Joey's chair crashed to the floor as he rose and flew out the doors toward his prey. She was only yards ahead, but safely out of sight now inside the building.

Joey's feet skidded on the hard floor as he turned the corner, then without looking up he ran straight into a security guard. He heard sounds but did not translate them and ran on, desperately looking for the hair, the leggings the bright trainers, but nothing. He arrived at the gym and scanned his phone. Nothing happened. Again. The screen bleeped and a message appeared on the screen "Daily entry limit exceeded."

About to kick the door in frustration it opened, revealing the same woman, now carrying a bag and wearing a cap. Alarm over.

'Where the hell did you go?' Franks asked, as Joey sat back down.

He shook his head and took a drink.

'It wasn't her, this could be a long night.' Joey gasped.

'No, it won't, we're are reaching our alcohol limit and outside entertainment venue time limit.' Franks said, shaking his head, 'these fucking communists are already in charge here.'

As the men contemplated their predicament; a commotion erupted from the other side of the bar, where some guys sat near one of the large television screens started shouting and the volume coming from the screen seemed to increase as virtual horses with virtual jockeys riding them raced around a track.

'Go on the Loser!' One shouted.

'On the inside!' Another exclaimed.

'No!' The first shouted again.

Moments later, all except one in the group sat down deflated and quiet

'Result confirmed from Windsor. First place; Blinkered Loser, second place; I've Never Won and third place; Deluded Nag,' a voice said from the screen.

They watched intently as one of the loud men from the television area approached the bar. It was the employee from the gym.

'Four pints and four surf and turfs love,' he said, smiling and holding his phone up as if it were a trophy.

'Coming right up, what's the matter you look happy?' The barmaid replied, in a deadpan tone.

'I won in the last race,' he replied, taking a large sip of his fresh drink.

'First time for everything, eh,' the woman said, while pressing some buttons on a screen and placing three other drinks on a tray. The man still wore his cap and as he turned to walk away he caught his ankle under the foot Joey had just stuck out.

'You'd better start talking, Pal. I know she works with you,' Joey said.

The man looked shocked as the drinks crashed to the floor, he turned and ran to the bathroom. Joey followed with Franks not far behind.

'Taking photos of women changing, eh, that's a sackable offence,' Joey said, pulling out the photo of Daria, wearing only her underwear.

'That, hey, no' the man started as Franks came in and grabbed him around the neck.

'Okay, okay, I know her, she works twice a week' he squealed like a baby.

'When? Where does she live?' Joey slapped him around the head as he fired.

'Wednesdays and weekends. I can't access the records, that's all I know, I swear please leave me alone.' He said.

'Who can access the records?' Joey asked, pushing the man towards the stinking urinal.

'There's a guy called Larry, he owns the gym and couple of pubs in Ealing. Try him, but please don't tell him- he'll kill me.' The man continued, as he did so the door swung open and the guys friends entered, younger and fitter; not a fair fight.

'There you go, everything is fine, don't drink so much in future,' Franks said, as he straightened the guys shirt collar and turned away. Joey followed moving past the puzzled looking younger guys quickly.

Chapter 22
2050, America South

Daria reached the reception area alone a little after 7p.m. She handed over her Lifecard and a taxi driver bot appeared beyond the glass front door and beckoned her toward its car outside.

The reason for her tardiness, she had walked extremely slowly down the winding path from her condo, in order to avoid Cruella whom, she had spotted just ahead of her. The last thing she wanted was that oversized overexuberant lunatics company.

'Great Tropical Hall; ten-minute journey time.' The driver bot said as she got in.

'Shut up and drive.' She replied, opening her purse and checking her face in the mirror.

As she exited the vehicle Daria drew in a breath, smiled and feasted her eyes on a building the size of a large banquet hall; constructed out of a material she hadn't come across before. It seemed to change colour and consistency before her eyes; the majority of the time it was a see through, glass like material, but it flickered from that to a jet-black colour then more metallic. Positioned equally around the building, although they blended in, Daria could just about make out monitor screens that cycled through portraits of the mother's greatest heroes, in full military uniform, medals shining upon their sleeves. There were several steps leading up to the entrance, giving it a grandiose national monument impression.

As she approached she was glad for her bold decision to allow her maid bot to dress her for the occasion. Clearly the more outrageously you dressed, the more you fitted in in this new world. Her long flowing yellow gown and shaped stuck up hair, which looked like it had been electrocuted, kept all eyes off her. She stumbled on a step in the black high heels she had squeezed into and cursed, before a man helped her up and smiled.

He was short and round and dressed in an oversized black suit with a large top hat on his head. His face was contorted and ugly and his eyes hidden behind a pair of sunglasses.

'Come on, live a little,' he said, winking as he helped her up and put some pills into her hand.

'Thanks,' she replied.

She put the pills in her bag then tried to keep on walking but the man blocked her path. He had his hand down the front of his trousers and was moving it around and smiling at her. She gave him a slap and continued. Reaching the front door, she stopped and looked back; the man was busy continuing his task unperturbed.

A security bot sat at the door with a Hawaiian shirt on.

'Hoola, hoola, the fun starts here,' he said.

His eyes swivelled around in his head like a crazed clown then he dropped his shorts to flash Daria his strange looking robot penis, feeling well now she decided to get involved, downing a couple of the pills the hatter gave her and copping a feel of the bot's schlong.

As she walked into the lobby; to her left she saw a waitress bot on all fours with a bathing suit around her ankles. Daria laughed loudly, picked up a cocktail then accelerated forward into the hall. There were large, ornate dining tables and chairs laid out like a royal banquet.

Four massive screens positioned high up on the wall in each corner of the room looked down at her, on each a clock counted down from forty-five minutes. She was right on time and looked around appreciatively until she heard a familiar voice screech at her.

'Amal, over here darling, here I've saved you a seat!' Cruella said.
Daria looked toward the voice and saw Cruella, who looked even worse dressed up, sitting at a large rectangular table to her left. Without any other option, she made her way over and sat down. A smorgasbord of Caviar, oysters and roasted meats adorned the table. She had made it.

'Who the fuck is Amal? Stop calling me that.' Daria said, pulling up a chair.

'Don't you remember darling? We worked together getting those idiots to transfer the last detail of their lives into the cloud. Then poisoned their minds in return. It certainly had a silver lining for us!' Cruella replied.

'Yeah,' Daria answered hesitantly, wondering if she might be being mistaken for her mother who had worked in the U.N. department for future technology many years ago.

'Oh dear, you really are gone, there's plenty more here for you anyway darling. Here have some pills,' Cruella continued, as she scrambled around in her bag then handed Daria a few pills that looked the same as the perverted hatter had given her.

'Thanks. I err,' Daria started.

'Well go on then!' Cruella said. She picked up a couple of pills and put one in her mouth and another in Daria's mouth then raised a glass of red liquid and toasted; almost smashing the delicate glasses in the process.

Now three "live" pills down; time seemed to stand still and accelerate all at once. Daria's point of reference was the countdown clock but somehow, she forgot about it. She remembered eating and drinking then an incredible noise as a ringleader bot stood on a raised platform at the front of the room.

'Let the games begin!' It announced.

Her memory became hazy after that but she could remember thinking the show seemed familiar.

Then she felt contact around her face and looked to see Cruella jumping up and down and cheering wildly looking up at the screen.

'Kill them, kill the cattle, yes, yes, yes!' She shouted uncontrollably.

'Don't you mean sheep?' Another voice asked. It came from a masked female. Daria made eye contact with the woman who raised her mask and smiled provocatively.

'You are very beautiful, where did you get your treatment? I love your breasts,' she said to Daria, as if talking about the weather.

'The usual, do you want to go outside?' Daria asked, feeling the need to escape.

'No, but I know a place we can go,' she replied smiling, then led Daria away toward a staircase. They went down, then through a door and into a large, cool underground area.

As soon as they were alone the woman started to remove her clothes. Daria touched her smooth skin, it reminded her of silk, then allowed the woman to remove her dress, and start caressing her breasts.

'That feels so good, don't stop,' she said.

'Here have another pill,' the woman replied, forcing a pill down Daria's throat.

Daria lay back and closed her eyes while the woman went to work on her.

'Mm, yeah,' Daria exclaimed between heavy breaths, writhing around until she was about to reach a climax when the woman bit her hard in the crotch.

'What is the matter with you? You fucking psycho!' Daria screamed.

The woman looked up and smiled a full blood-stained grin. Daria, still wearing her heels, kicked sharply into the woman's face. The toe landing squarely in one eye and the heel her mouth. The vampire lady doubled back; a bloody mess now.

Daria inspected herself, realised the damage was only superficial then quickly regained her composure. She retraced her steps back toward the main room, passing a waitress bot on the stairs whom she told to go and clear up the mess.

As she entered the main hall, the ringleader bot was announcing tonight's competition winner who had correctly predicted how long it would take, to the nearest minute, for all the sheep to be killed. A man in a dark suit, which changed colour a little like the building itself, went up onto the stage to collect a trophy. On the big screen a close up of the trophy revealed it had a miniature human head fixed to a gold challis. The head wobbled unnervingly and looked real, although it looked too small to be real, Daria thought.

'Congratulations, your prize will be delivered to your home after next week's shipment,' the bot announced, geeing up the crowd who cheered wildly.

The man in the dark suit made some celebratory movements but said nothing before leaving the platform.

Daria smiled to herself and looked forward to winning her own little plaything. Do what thou wilt, they had said. And they did. She staggered outside and got in a waiting taxi, not paying much attention, she sat down, slumped her head back on the seat and closed her eyes.

She felt the motion of the taxi stopping but something told Daria not to open her eyes. They opened themselves regardless and she instinctively tried to move away, but she was momentarily paralysed. Recovering, she tried the door nearest her but it was locked, then the other door; it too was locked. She looked down at the floor, trying desperately to control her breathing.

113

A message appeared in her mind that told her; "You are nothing until you defeat Scales, not even Grandfather can protect you." She actually felt it arrive and nodded her comprehension, the power was like nothing she had ever felt before, an irresistible force moved her eyes up to look. She thought to shield them with her hand but it wouldn't move. Cracked skin, pointed, enlarged features. Heat, she felt so hot.

A clunk in the doors around her and she was free; running away now at top speed. Too fast and still under the influence she tripped and fell. She felt pain; looking down she saw a sharp twig protruding from her hand. Then home at last she slammed the door and collapsed against the wall; panting, shaking; trying to reconcile. Could it have been the one whose magic she had summoned so often over the years? It can't have been. Maybe there is more than one…it was.

Chapter 23
2030, London

Franks and Joey sat in his living room frustrated they couldn't take their search further that evening. The Lifepass controlled access to all venues, and outside entertainment was time limited, so they simply could not go anywhere else to pursue their lead. Franks reached up for his bottle of Jack, retrieved two glasses from the freezer, and poured them a drink.

'Listen, thanks for your help today, I couldn't have done it alone.' Joey said.

'Don't mention it, I haven't had this much fun in years!' Franks replied, 'did you ever hear about the War of the Worlds incident?' he continued, a sigh of pleasure as he took as sip of the ice-cold liquor.

'No.'

'On Halloween eve, in 1938, New Jersey, America. The local radio station, C.B.S., broadcast an adaptation of a science fiction novel called the War of the Worlds.[16] The broadcast began by describing a meteorite crash in the nearby vicinity then cut to a reporter on the scene who described the craft as extra-terrestrial. He then went onto describe E. T.'s coming out of the craft, the woods on fire and vehicles exploding before screaming and going off air. The broadcast switched to the Ministry of the Interior who declared an emergency situation, with scores dead, the Army mobilized and placed New York under evacuation orders.' Franks explained, before continuing 'there was pandemonium as other radio stations tuned in and broadcast the C.B.S. wire; police switchboards were jammed, people fled the city and hospitals began admitting people for hysteria and shock.'

'But it wasn't real, right?' Joey asked.

'Exactly, it wasn't real at all but it showed how easy it was to evoke mass panic and control via the use of technology, in this case radio.' Franks said, taking another sip of his drink, 'I was thinking about what would make people accept a microchip; they'd need to be petrified and an alien invasion sure was petrifying then, without 24/7 news channels and social media, can you imagine it now?'

---

[16] The War of the Worlds, H.G. Wells, Heinemann, London 1898.

'I sure can, I mean they've done everything else; world war, terrorism, economic crashes, viruses, energy crises, cyber-wars, food shortages, mass dis-order. There's only one thing left to try.' Joey said.

'*La piece de la resistance*!' Franks exclaimed.

'Yes, but how?' Joey asked, as Franks flicked on the television.

'Welcome to the U.K. News at six, tonight with a special report on population changes and the future of humanity by our virtual technology correspondent,' said the immaculately presented, girl next door type newscaster in commanding private school English.

'The population of the world has decreased by 500 million since 2020, compared to an increase of 1 billion in the previous ten years from 2010. Tonight, we investigate the causes of this decline and ask whether this is good or bad news for humanity as a whole.

Population change is determined by two factors, fertility and mortality, put simply birth rates and death rates. From here more factors come into play such as the reasons for changes in births and deaths; they can be economic, social and health related.

Broadly speaking death rates are more likely to be related to health-related factors and birth rates to economic and social factors. Firstly, death rates have increased due to antimicrobial resistance and immuno-suppression. Over the past ten years we have seen an increase in so called Superbugs that were able to resist antibiotics due largely to their overuse and maladministration over the years.

The, "Aquavirus," caused 300 million deaths in 2026 after frequent floods in Europe and heatwaves worldwide left humanity overwhelmed by disease and starvation. The increase in superbugs has been worsened by immunosuppression amongst the general populations of the world since the turn of the decade.

Various reasons have been given for this including the long-term effects of both the Coronavirus and of the resultant vaccines amongst the general population. There has also been an increase in deaths due to heart related conditions which remain largely unexplained by scientists. These, so called, "Sudden Deaths," have plateaued and decreased off in recent years, therefore, many consider them to have been a result of the psychological stresses caused by the long pandemics.

Secondly, birth rates have declined sharply in what has become known as the, "Emergency Decade." This gives us a clue why; people do not choose to have children while they cannot be sure of their social and economic security. The years of heath crisis, followed by environmental, economic and social upheaval have directly affected birth rates. The number of births in the U.K. has more than halved since 2020 when there were 700,000 births compared to last year's figure of 300,000. This trend has been reflected around the developed world. However, it has become more difficult to compare statistics since the decentralization of the N.H.S. in the middle of the century, when most antenatal responsibilities were subcontracted out to private providers. There has been some suggestion that more pregnancies have failed to reach their full term as a result of miscarriage but unfortunately the statistics are no longer available for analysis.

Finally, it has been argued that people are scared of intimacy due to the perceived risk to their own health following the years of infectious virus's and diseases during the decade. Scientists find this the most plausible cause of the decline; however, their modelling predicts that there will be a turnaround in line with the expected forthcoming improvement in the public health and therefore confidence.' The virtual reporter said.

'Other news now and the terror threat has been increased following a credible threat to aircraft…'

Franks turned off the television before the presenter could finish and sighed. People were dying more and being born less but there was nothing to worry about; an immortal man with a sleepy voice will be on in a minute explaining the wonders of the natural world. Just keep doing as your told and everything will be okay.

'Why do you watch that shit?' Joey asked.

'So, I know what not to think,' Franks replied, with a wink, 'how about we split up tomorrow, so we can get in both this guy's pubs before our limits kick in.' Franks suggested.

'Sure, where are they?' Joey asked.

'I'm just about to find out.' Franks replied, flipping open his laptop, 'there aren't too many pubs left in Ealing.'

'Won't that leave a trace, everything is monitored right?' Joey asked.

'Well yes; but they are mainly looking for Anti-deniers these days.' Franks explained.

'Anti-what?' Joey said, lighting up on the balcony with a fresh Whiskey.

'People who ask questions, who don't believe the narrative-they are like modern day conspiracy theorists. A guaranteed way to shut down debate before it begins.' Franks continued.

'Shit that sounds like us,' Joey chuckled to himself while admiring the view over London.

'We don't really have a choice.' Franks replied.

Chapter 24
2050, America South

Daria lay motionless staring up at the modified fresco on the ceiling; demons, downward spirals and faceless figures looking down upon her. She wondered if Mother was having a fucking joke with her and resolved to sleep in another room from now on. Still it was better than the other option, for every-time she closed her eyes she saw it, each time a different expression and outcome; but each of them bad, very bad.

She always knew this moment could come, not that she really ever thought it would. Nobody she knew had seen what she saw yesterday, nobody living anyway. Although they all used the power for their own gain, when things went wrong it normally manifested in physical pain or loss to the self or those closest to them. She had fucked up and there was nothing she could do about it but wait.

It came back faster than she expected; being moved unintentionally around the bed by an invisible force, trying to stop it but being too weak, then a vision resembled a dark moving cloud in human like form but faceless and continually moving so it could not be identified. She heard a scream and opened her eyes again, this time not making the mistake of staying put she went out to the upstairs solarium area and fiddled with the control unit until the two panes of roof glass started moving. Relieved by a little fresh air, Daria dived into the pool and got straight out the other end. Donning a dressing gown, she went down into the living room. A few commands later; the waitress bot duly obliged, bringing out coffee and toast.

Sitting around really wasn't her style, especially when the Damocles sword was hanging over her own head for once. Feeling better but annoyed at her situation she searched the house, it was very tidy, and she was about to give up when she had a brainwave.

'Waitress get me contracts,' she said.
The bot appeared seconds later with a see-through plastic folder. On it a label read:

"America South Contract."

It looked like a legal document, but it was only a few pages long. Then there was a glossy brochure with bright pictures and finally a two-sided leaflet. Daria perused the document and noted the following down on paper:

- Contract Start date 06/06/2033 – no end date; ends upon death.
- All services included; food and accommodation, transport, entertainment and maintenance in a choice of locations around continent.
- No laws, no government, no institutions, no police.
- Exclusive invitation only club.
- All needs serviced by lifelike A.I. robots.
- Blood renewal treatments. *Subject to availability.
- Pure air guarantee.
- Motto: "Where reality is a dream."

She moved onto the brochure, it was like the type you would expect to have seen in a travel agency before they were replaced by the internet, with glossy full colour pictures of enticing scenes. The gluey smell of the pages made Daria want to taste them.

The brochure was divided into four sections: Tropical, Temperate, Polar and Desert. Each section was then subdivided into different settlements that were available to live in depending on your preferences. There were only twenty settlements at the time of publishing but the promise of more under construction. Daria realised the awesome scale of the operation; construction must have started straight after the Fall to achieve so much in just a few years. *Oh, the wonders of slave labour.*

Finally, she perused the leaflet. It was called. "Live; your everyday life companion with happiness guaranteed," then there was a picture of a beaming woman holding a handful of small white pills in her hand. She turned it over and read the back.
- The only pill you need; feel good all the time.
- Promotes accelerated growth.
- Take daily to guarantee a good night's sleep.
- Natural opiate / herb mixture.
- Increased libido.
- Decreased inhibitions.
- No comedown.
- No overdose.

Daria put the leaflet from Mother down and sighed. She should be enjoying all this with not a care, this private utopia; a lifetime holiday camp. There was no mention of Freegov. This the escape route for Mother employees only once they had finished using humans for their evil ends. And good for them, fuck the herd.

She liked that there were no government or police to watch and control people. They'd have to police and settle disputes themselves- she'd have no problems doing that in fact it should be easy. In theory with everything provided there would be no inequality therefore no need for theft or violence. Hah, she chuckled, tell that to the bitch last night. She'd only been there a day and already murdered someone.

It was a good theory, one that had never been tested in practise before, perhaps the, "live," pills had something to do with the maintenance of America South; she wondered as she popped another one and looked in the mirror, she felt strong again.

Chapter 25
2030, London

Joey woke early with a dry mouth and sore throat. He panicked for a moment until he checked the date, tomorrow, it was tomorrow- he still had time.

He poured some cereal out, made a coffee then sat down and flicked on the television. His attention was taken by an advert for, "Brand New Air Crash Investigation Series 22," available on demand now.

'Verify email; click here, take live photo, what the fu..' Joey mumbled, as he attempted to link his Lifepass to the television and set up his on-demand account. He heard feint laughter from the kitchen and looked over to see Cara chucking to herself as she prepared her breakfast.

It was like a role reversal; Cara calm, Joey about to light up the place.

'Yes!' Joey exclaimed, as a list of all Air Crash Investigation Series appeared on a blue index screen in front of him.

'Well done,' Cara said, smiling, as she brought her plate over and settled down to eat. Joey reached out to hold her hand but it wasn't there. A tear dropped from his eye onto the glass coffee table, then another. He gulped trying to hold it back but it was futile, then he let go.

He wasn't sure how long he'd been sat there for but he found himself holding her cross; he knew what he had to do. He rifled through his sparse belongings until he found it, Daria's printed email on Cara. He carefully cut out the picture of Cara and pinned it to the wall by his bed. He looked at her and smiled.

Joey ate while watching the story of an aircraft that lost its windscreen during flight, causing the pilot to be sucked out. Miraculously the plane, passengers and crew all survived after the co-pilot landed the plane while holding on to the pilot simultaneously. The pilot suffered severe frostbite but lived to tell the shivery tale. The accident was blamed on a faulty repair job when the suspect windshield had been recently changed using an incorrect fitting.

It was still early so Joey selected another episode, which focussed on a fairly modern airliner, a Boeing 777, which had disappeared of radar after transmitting the emergency code for hijack, 7500, in June 2028.

The plane landed at a nearby airport half an hour later and all the passengers were evacuated safely. However, both pilot and co-pilot were deceased when the cockpit door was forced open. In this incident, investigators were able to reveal the existence and activation of a hijacking safety system called; "Boeing Uninterruptable Autopilot," which was patented by the Boeing Company in 2006.[17] This system allowed for the plane to be remote controlled from the ground in the event that the pilots lost control of the cockpit, therefore land the plane safety. In this case no terrorist group claimed responsibility. The events in the cockpit proved difficult to explain; there was no communication with air traffic control and the cockpit voice recorder was silent. The plane did record the emergency transmission for a hijack but either pilot could have actioned this. Autopsies failed to determine their causes of death. Although many questions remained unanswered, the overall conclusion of the show was positive; despite two disabled pilots, the plane landed safely with no injuries to the passengers thanks to the uninterruptable autopilot system.

A vibration and a beep on the glass coffee table jolted Joey from the world of avionics; checking the device he saw a message from Franks to meet him outside in ten.

'One of the pubs he owns is right outside here, apparently he's American. How about you go in and I'll wait outside for you?' Franks said as they entered the elevator, 'you have the pictures?'

'Okay.' Joey replied, tucking his new polo shirt into his jeans, a mirror of Franks attire.

Joey scanned his phone and entered the large public house. It was a brick building with dark grey painted frontage, there was an outside area at the front but nobody was sat in it as Joey walked through. Inside there was a yellow hue from the lighting that gave a warm feeling.

---

[17] https://patents.google.com/patent/US7142971B2/en

There were a few men spaced sporadically around the room where cosy tables lined the walls. The bar was circular and crossed two rooms, both of which had large television screens in them. Joey went to the bar and ordered a lemonade, then over to a table at the far end of the room with a good view of one of the large screens. As he surveyed his surroundings he noted most of the other guys in there were looking at their hand-held screens, giving away their minds, and the televisions were not on.

'Yo, What's up?' A man said, he was a medium build, medium height dark skinned man with a friendly face. He approached Joey and sat down opposite him. The man wore light coloured baggy jeans and a sports jacket and his hair and facial hair were all the same, very short, length. He had an accent similar to Franks that Joey understood easily.

'Ain't seen you around here before, where you from?' The man asked.

Joey resisted the temptation to inform the slightly overbearing man that he was in fact a man from the future and shifted on his seat before replying.

'Joey, pleased to meet you, Larry,' Joey said, whilst extending his hand with a knowing smile.

'What the hell kind of wizard shit is this man, we've met before right, how'd you know my name, shit,' Larry replied, in an animated tone as he shook Joey's hand and jumped back, feigning surprise, simultaneously.

'You own this place right, I need your help,' Joey replied, placing the photo of Daria in military uniform on the table.

'Shit, Daria, in the army!' Larry exclaimed, picking up the photo and examining it closely.

'It's worse than that, look I need to find her now, I'll pay you.' Joey explained.

There was a silence, while the men contemplated their positions.

'Smoke?' Larry asked, as he got up and nodded towards a door at the rear.

Joey followed without reply. He handed Joey a cigarette and took a deep breath in.

'So, what you doing here?' Larry said.

'Don't worry about me, this place could do with a lick of paint, some new tables, ten thousand Ukc's if you lead me to her.' Joey replied.

'I own this mother fucking place man. Don't come in here and tell me what I need. You her boyfriend or something? She's a bit young for you.' Larry said.

'Look at the photo, here there's more. She's very dangerous I need to find her today for all our sakes.' Joey replied.

'Highly trained, judo expert, intelligence, suspected murders…' Larry mumbled as he perused the file; eyebrows raised.

'She's is a terrorist, planning an attack, here…tomorrow!' Joey continued. Larry flicked his cigarette into the ashtray, tossed the file on the table and walked away.

'He's at the bar now, short guy and he's American, show him the other photo and we might be in.' Joey whispered to Franks over the phone.

Joey watched Larry sat at the bar sipping a small glass of golden coloured liquid through the glass window set in the top of the back door, as Franks walked in from the front. He was a big man, and towered over Larry's hunched figure.

'I'm here with the C.I.A. We need to find this woman and I believe you can help us. It's a matter of National Security.' Franks said, holding up the photo of Daria. Larry looked across at Joey through the window, blood draining from his face.

'Look, she works for me at my gym, but she hasn't turned up for the last two weeks, and she's not returning my calls.' He replied.

'Okay, you have her address?' Franks asked. Larry pulled out his phone and scribbled something down on a beer matt. The door swung open, Joey walked over and patted Larry on the shoulder.

'That wasn't so hard now was it, call me if you hear anything.' He said nodding towards the exit. Game, set and match.

'What about my Ukc's?' Larry shouted.

'We haven't found her yet, buddy.' Joey replied.

As Joey and Franks walked away, Larry unlocked his phone, selected Lifepass, and navigated to the, "Report and Reward," section.

Chapter 26
2050, America South

Far, far away; awaiting her personal judgement Daria mulled her situation. She thought back to how it all began, the day her conscription ended. The ceremony confirmed adulthood and allegiance to the small, isolated country. The conscripts handed back their weapons and were given certificates. Proud parents flashed large old-fashioned cameras to mark the occasion forever. They were allowed to keep their uniforms in case of a short notice call up. She never saw active service but excelled in her training, particularly close combat and shooting accuracy, but it was another skill altogether that got her selected for further employ.

In a makeshift office behind the barracks, a short masculine woman she had never met before sat sternly and offered her a scholarship to study in London, at a well-known University, all expenses paid. She wasn't short for money, her mother being a highly paid diplomat, but the offer of independence attracted her. They would even set her up with a part-time job and pay a retainer. All she had to do in return was report back monthly and attend occasional training from people she'd meet there. It seemed a small price to pay and she readily accepted.

It wasn't until a few months in, after several training sessions, that she realised what she was really being paid to do, but the rewards were so great, both financially and in terms of the knowledge she gained; that she continued. Morality wasn't ever a problem for her, she enjoyed power and control regardless.

It was the early 2020's when things really started to kick off; as the western democracies became more and more authoritarian; cancelling anyone who spoke out against their controlled narrative. She knew that everything governments said was inverted. For your health meant to kill you and bombing another country was certainly not to achieve peace.

She knew that political power naturally corrupted, and that power in the hands of compromised psychopaths was genocidal. And that's where she came in. She'd lost count of the number of operations she'd set up to record a politician or business leader doing something unspeakable. It was usually sex, but sometimes other vices came in handy. Everyone has a desire; therefore, a weakness. And she would identify and then exploit it, ruthlessly, to progress Mothers plan.

That's how she got the gig in 2030, it would be hard, air traffic was one of the most secure roles, heavily protected by its home intelligence community, but that didn't bother her, nor Mother, they would just target them too.

She smiled and lit a cigarette as she remembered the pathetic look on the guys face when he realised she'd used him, and then his eyes large as she aimed her silenced weapon at his head. Ahh, it was all coming back to her now. What a day, weeks of planning and then poetry in motion as they dropped, one by one. The final nails in the coffin of humanity. And now that idiot Joey was going to experience it all for himself.

Daria's trip down memory lane was interrupted as the phone rang. It was reception saying her taxi had arrived. Mother. She knew their style, keep you guessing, but she was ready. She collected her pre-packed case and made her way down the perfectly set pathways, through the freshly cut grass, beautiful flowers and huge palms. This reality was a dream.

Daria arrived at the airport slightly agitated not knowing her destination. Success in these missions was about preparation and this time she had little. Happily, this was no normal airport and there were no draconian procedures in place to ensure she wasn't going to blow herself up or spread an extremely scary virus.

Daria showed her, "Lifecard," to the security bot and walked out onto the tarmac toward a small plane. A stewardess bot stood at the door and invited her aboard.

'Where are we going?' Daria asked, looking around the deserted airfield.

'Patagonia. People do not fly unless they are moving areas, most people don't move areas.' The bot replied in tinny monotone.

'Please make yourself comfortable, I am equipped with both male and female relief programmes,' the bot continued.

Daria got on and made herself comfortable. There were holiday style brochures on a table, she opened one and began to read. Patagonia was to the south west of the continent, a mountainous area with a harsh climate. She had heard about it before and was a little annoyed she hadn't packed warmer clothes and more solid footwear. Perhaps she could get some when they landed.

The plane was fitted out luxuriously in a very similar fashion to the last jet; carpet, leather, mirrors and display screens adorned the cabin. The pilot- bot emerged from the cockpit, closed the entry door and waved at her with a happy robot expression.

After an uneventful, but bumpy, flight it was immediately apparent from the rocky terrain and much colder temperatures that she was in the right place. She picked up a heavy coat and some boots in the deserted airport store then got in the waiting taxi. The taxi had larger tyres with extra tread, but Daria was more concerned with the driver who seemed far more human than any of the other bots they had come across. He was tall, muscular and his skin had blotches and freckles on it.

'Welcome to Patagonia, the most sparsely populated area in America South. I am your driver for today. I will …' The bot said, sounding suspiciously like a tour guide.

'Just drive, I assume you know where I'm going. Dismissed,' Daria interrupted.

Something about this bot had set off her internal radar in alarm. She estimated he was over six foot and 95 kilos, she couldn't see any weapons. The rear doors locked as she shuffled over out of his view, then the taxi moved off.

'Are you fitted with both male and female relief programmes?' She asked.
There was no reply.

'I said are you fitted with both male and female relief programmes?' She repeated.

'I do not have these programmes fitted,' the bot replied, after another pause.

'That is inconvenient, I was hoping you would be able to assist me,' She continued.

'No, the journey will be another hour,' the bot replied, seemingly having forgotten his manners and the dynamics of the robot-human relationship in America South.

Daria moved fast, grabbing the key from the tray behind the gear stick and shoving into his neck before he reacted, then holding him from behind in one armed strangle hold, while the other stabbed again and again. Judging by the mess, he certainly wasn't a bot. It was over in seconds but the car continued, she pressed the handbreak and held the wheel steady. Then, after some minor contortions, she knocked his foot away from the pedal and the car decelerated eventually coming to a halt.

She released her grip and collapsed backward into the seat, panting. What had she done? They trained her; they should expect this, it wasn't her fault, they should have sent a robot, then she would have gone along with it. Her fears were confirmed as she checked his shoe to find a concealed 50-gram gold bar; standard issue. She had killed one of her own- what now? Stick or twist?

Outside, snow was beginning to fall, the soft patter calmed her thoughts and she began to drive. Not long after the emergency stop, the dual carriageway changed to a single lane road and the terrain became more mountainous, she past a sign saying, "Patagonia Settlement," with a large blue arrow which pointed up a steep looking road to the right. She turned up the heat and started the ascent. There was snow on the ground now, getting deeper by the minute; clouds began to enclose the vehicle as if they were trying to suffocate it. Daria smiled, feeling herself again and enjoying the challenge in the freezing conditions.

The road surface was white ahead of her and she was glad for the four-wheel drive system; there were no tracks to follow so she had to make her own path, judging her location on the snowy road by the orange and black marker poles to each side. She turned on the headlights and wipers and slowed the vehicle down; keeping the engine revs steady.

Snow was falling harder now and visibility was down to only a few meters but the tyres were gripping the dry powdery snow well so Daria continued, bit by bit making progress up the massive mountain. Finally, as dusk fell, she saw her chance; a sharp bend at the top of the peak, she pulled her coat on and dived out at the last second, sacrificing shelter for her chance to live. Then she began walking.

After what seemed like an age, as her hands and feet began to lose feeling, Daria spotted yellow flashing lights up ahead. The road levelled out and the lights were now to her right side. As she approached she heard the ticking of a diesel motor then recognised a huge snow plough, getting ready to go down the pass. There was a sign, but it was caked in snow. A little further on she made out the silhouette of a large building with lights on in the windows. It looked warm.

She was so cold now the only thing she saw was the light as her boots crushed then compressed the fresh snow with a crunch and a squeak. The large snowflakes fell silently, an ode to nature's power, until she entered the large double wooden doors, stained into a dark brown colour by the aging process.

'Welcome to Patagonia, Lifecard please. What is the duration of your stay? Leisure or new resident?' A bot asked, it was stationed behind the counter and dressed in winter clothing and a red woolly hat. Daria might have laughed at the absurdity were she not covered in the cliff diving agents' blood. She handed over her pass.

'Daria, we have been expecting you. Are you alone? The bot asked.

'Yes, there was an accident on the mountain pass. I am alone.' She replied.

'You have a suite. Follow the porter,' the bot said.
Daria, reached out as he handed over a key and touched his hand.

'Not human,' she murmured. She left the room towards a dark corridor that the porter bot had scooted down.

The porter stopped in front of a large door and held it open. Directly opposite the door in the hallway there was a large window, whose curtains remained open. Darkened by snow and the fading light, it gave no clue as to what lay beyond its temporary veil.

Inside, Daria immediately collapsed onto a large, copper coloured sofa, that matched the earthy décor well. She reached for some pills and gulped down some water. As her body temperature slowly increased she took the chance to undress and shift into the bed. She adjusted the thick, feather duvet until it was tightly wrapped around her, cocoon like, allowing her breathing to finally slow to a light snore.

Chapter 27
2030, London

In a dark, dusty office in Whitehall, an older aged gentleman sat at his desk, from where he had a good view of the clock in the background. It read 5:39p.m. His turn-based strategy game had not gone at all well that day, and he was looking forward to getting home to a nice hearty dinner, made by his wife of 30 years, and then walking his two trusty Labradors in the fields.

A knock on the door; and a young, over-exuberant man dressed in a cheap department store suit with an ill-fitting shirt barged in before being invited. Lucky it was the strategy game on Tuesdays. He'd already been demoted once after an embarrassing discovery on his hard drive; now he spent his days waiting for these damned sheep to tell on each other.

'Sir, emergency sir. Station Chief authorised this for immediate escalation sir.' The man shouted, in between breaths, as if he had climbed ten flights of stairs.

'Yes okay, okay, put it down there.' The older gentleman said.

'Sir, this is urgent.' The younger man said.

'Give it here then, any other copies?'

'No, sir, just this one.'

'That will be all.'

After a rapid read, pleased his memory still worked, the man fed the paper carefully into the machine until it gripped, seconds later the noise quietened down and he turned it off. He then took a small old looking mobile phone from his bag and placed a call.

'I need to get a message to Mother, it's urgent.'

*

Joey passed the coaster to Franks as they emerged from the pub.

'I know that place its right by the southern perimeter at Heathrow, she can probably see the control tower from there,' Franks said, while Joey called Abdul.

'Are you thinking what I'm thinking?' Joey asked, looking up suspiciously at a passing plane.

'It's been done before…and it worked.' Franks replied.

'And it would be fucking scary, especially if there's a little green man in the cockpit!' Joey said, getting in the silent, small taxi.

'What's the plan?' Franks asked.

'We find her and I kill her.' Joey replied, matter of factly.

As the taxi turned left onto the A30, it was overwhelmed on both sides by flashing blue lights. Four U.K.S.F. vehicles; two estates and two S.U.V.'s, overtook and sped off into the distance. Neither man said anything. As they approached the address their fears were confirmed.

The road was blocked at the top end by one of the S.U.V.'s and its four occupants. They bore arms, sub machine guns, and looked like they were not to be messed with.

'Go around,' Franks said to Abdul, who was beginning to mumble and getting himself in a panic. They continued fifty meters until a roundabout. It was blocked by the other S.U.V. and its occupants.

'Let us out over there,' Joey said pointing a little further down.

'Looks like they beat us to it.' Franks said, in the fresh air looking at the roadblock.

'C'mon, we have to check, just front it.' Joey said.

'What are you doing?' The U.K.S.F. troop asked, as Joey and Franks attempted to walk directly past their barricade, 'can't you see the road is closed?'

'My friend lives there,' Joey replied, pointing past the barricade.

'It's okay, we'll come back later.' Franks said, leading Joey away.

'Are you crazy, they'll arrest you.' Franks said as they got out of earshot.

'But we don't even know if all this is for her.' Joey argued.

'Okay let's get closer. We might be able to see the house.' Franks replied.

After some scrambling, dodging and following their noses, the two men crouched between a bush and a tree just in front of a small river.

There was no hiding from the smart cameras though; a little like the post-boxes of old they were placed strategically at the start and end of each street, with no attempt to disguise their purpose in fact quite the opposite; a pair of eyes stood proudly above the slogan, "keeping you safe." They monitored movements and data of the citizens via their mobile phone transmitters and facial recognition technology.

The hideaways would just have to hope they weren't being monitored live. At the top of the road, one of the estate vehicles blocked the junction by an old public house. A little closer to them the fourth U.K.S.F. estate car was parked directly outside Daria's address.

Two troops stood guard; one at the drive the other the front door, which was slightly ajar. The house was part of a run-down estate that looked like it was built in the post war period. It was small, one up one down, of brick construction with recently upgraded windows. Daria would have had a good view towards the control tower from the first floor.

'That's her place alright,' Franks said.

'No sign of her.' Joey replied.

'We aren't getting in there now.'

'I don't like it. Coincidences make me nervous.' Joey continued.

*

Earlier that morning, the young, attractive (and bubbly) for this case anyway, Daria indeed did have a good view of the control tower from the first floor. Through her military issue binoculars, she was able to have eyes on her target, one of the thirteen Air Traffic Controllers, as well as ears through the wires she had taped to him in the bedroom that morning.

His job was simple, to place a device in the tower that would allow her team to take control of operations and the safety net; the Uninterruptable Autopilot. Daria watched as the weak, excuse of a man carried out her instructions word for word. Her crooked smile adorned her face as the man trembled whilst placing the device under a desk, that was it. She did a quick sweep of the house and cleared out, stepping on a picture of a plane on the front page of that morning's newspaper as she slammed the door. The headline read: "Air Terror Threat." Feint sirens blared in the distance, getting louder. She roared off, laughing hard now, on the motorbike faster than they would ever be. *Oh, how easy things were with the world on your side. How could they ever fail?*

*

'How about we wait it out in the bar? Joey said, eyes fixed on Daria's front door.
Franks didn't reply.
'What do you suggest then?' Joey asked, before continuing, 'you think she's still in there with a cup of tea waiting for the fireworks to begin?'
'Freeze, keep your hands where I can see them.' A man said, Joey slowly rotated his head then felt a forceful impact to his side below the shoulder, he fell face down in the grass and yelped.
A black gloved hand appeared before his eyes and he felt the soft material moving his arms forcefully behind his back, then his wrists clasped tightly in cold metal.
'Close your eyes' the man screamed. A hand grabbed his upper arm, forcing him up onto his knees, then he felt a rough textured material around his face and head.
'Now move,' the nuzzle of a weapon in the small of his back was joined by a forceful arm on the shoulder, he tripped and scrambled through the undergrowth, remembering a small gradient toward the road. A door slid open, then a palm pushed hard into his back. He fell inside, knocking his knee painfully; sweat and smoke filled the air as the vehicle screeched into motion.

Blinded, Joey found it hard to find his bearings. The vehicle drove erratically, he felt his shoulders touch someone else's a few times as they rounded corners too fast. He heard traffic and guessed they were on a main road, probably the A30 or A4, so still local. It wasn't long before they stopped and he heard the front doors open, then felt a breeze behind him as the vans side door opened. The same hand manhandled Joey out of the door and threw him down onto a hard floor.

'Stay quiet,' the man said and kicked Joey hard in the guts, winding him completely. Then a creek, a slam and some keys jangling before a light clunk from outside. The engine revved loudly and then there was quiet.

Joey tore off his head cover and blinked adjusting to the light. He was on his own. *How the fuck did this happen? They were right next to each other.* He tapped his thigh; no phone, but his keys were in the other pocket. Further searching revealed his lighter and the cross Cara had given him. He lit the flame and held the lighter up, panning slowly around the space.

The room was rectangular and approximately four meters long. The floor was cold grey concrete and there was a wooden shelf at shoulder height around the three internal walls.

At first glance there was nothing in it, Joey figured it was a garage, probably on one of the many estates around there. Nobody even had cars anymore so shouting was a waste of time.

He pointed the flame toward the door and revealed a light switch…it was not working. Underneath he frame he could see it was still light outside. He manhandled then kicked the door in frustration. Nothing. He shook it violently until his arm hurt. There was no give, he was trapped.

Joey fell back onto the rear wall in frustration, then sank down until he was on the floor with his head against the wall. He held the cross and closed his eyes.

Sometime later, Joey woke with a jolt to the sound of car wheels screeching then a loud crash. He moved backward as far as he could; it was dark now but he held up his lighter and saw the door had buckled in front of him. *Were the kidnappers back to kill him?*

Again, the wheels screeched and there was another impact, this time the door gave way allowing a dim yellow light into the garage, a scared mouse scurried away into the shadows.

'Quick, get out!' It was a familiar voice.

Joey squeezed past the twisted door and saw Abdul's damaged taxi with Franks sat in the front seat.

'Good timing.' Joey replied, before continuing, 'where were you, what happened, who were those guys?' He was out of breath and Franks signalled for him to calm down and passed him some water.

'We owe Abdul here our thanks, he saw you get taken and followed you here, then came and got me. Are you okay?' Franks said as the car moved off a little less silently than normal.

'I'm fine, we don't have time to waste. Did you see her? Joey asked.

'No.' Franks replied.

'Then what are we going to do have a cup of tea and watch a movie?' Joey said.

'Look I just saved you what's your problem? Franks asked.

'I want to know what's going on? Who kidnapped me? Why didn't they get you? How did they find us?' Joey said.

Franks looked up at Abdul then back at Joey and shook his head ever so slightly.

'You know everything is recorded here, whoever took you has permission from our government. I went for a piss in the river, when I got back you were getting thrown in the side of a van. Here, they chucked your phone away.' Franks said, then handed Joey's phone to him.

'I've just got here. I'm sorry they got you.' Franks continued.

'Were they U.K.S.F?' Joey asked.

'No, they wore casual clothes but they were built like soldiers,' Franks replied.

The cab stopped outside their block. Franks, delayed with Abdul, turned his head to see Joey jogging toward the Old Hat.

Joey walked in, grabbed Larry by the loose sports jacket he wore and man-handled him outside. A few regulars came to his aid but Larry waved them away.

'Who did you tell, you stupid cunt?' Joey said.

'I reported it; to the Report and Reward scheme' Larry replied proudly.

'You what?' Joey said.

'It's the government, at least they'll pay me, not like you!' Larry said.

'What did you tell them?' Joey asked.

'I gave them her address and said she was going to blow something up.' He replied quickly.

'And?' Joey said, grabbing Larry around the neck and applying pressure,

'And I gave a description of you.' Larry said, looking away.

He wasn't worth it, he was trying to help. Another member of the herd..

Back at the flat Joey sat down next to Franks, who had left his front door ajar.

'Larry told Report and Reward about Daria planning an attack.' Joey said.

'What a total wanker, they must have got her, that was a pretty heavy response.' Franks replied, pouring out a drink each.

'We don't know that. And who kidnapped me? They weren't U.K.S.F.' Joey replied. He got up with his drink and walked onto the balcony, just in time to see a plane disappearing behind a building in the distance.

Chapter 28
2050, America South

Daria woke abruptly confused about where she was, an old clock on the side table indicated the time was 2:13 a.m. She guessed it was still jetlag. The room was decorated with dark brown wall paper that matched the wooden furniture and garish orange carpet. She looked down at her blood-stained clothing and things started to become clearer. *Shit, now she remembered.*

There was a gown in the wardrobe, she threw it on and ran down the corridor, a sign indicated she was heading for the pool area, not long later the smell of chemicals that she had arrived. She headed through a wide double glass door into a well-equipped but deserted space; a health club with no patrons. A receptionist bot offered her a towel and a massage- she kept going in need of fresh air. She disrobed and dived into the pool, then swam freely and quickly; feeling her mind starting to work again slowly.

She swam toward an archway in the corner of the pool which led to a glass door built into the buildings outer wall. As she approached, it slid open and steam rushed outside. She swam through into an outside pool, gasping as the water temperature plummeted. She stood upright for a moment, water dripping from her, then quickly ducked back down. Snow fell gently around her the large flakes disappearing on contact with the water. For a moment she was mesmerized, in awe of the jagged edges of the mountain peaks that surrounded her outlined against the night sky. There was no moon.

She heard a low rumble, sounding like a diesel motor, then saw two headlights moving below her in the direction of the carpark. Her attention peaked at this late-night delivery. The truck turned and backed onto a large door at the edge of the main building. Two porter bots opened the door and began to unload a small titanium casket, followed by two massive titanium boxes. They wheeled them into the courtyard between her room and the reception area then covered them with tarpaulin. Do what thou wilt they said in training. And she had; they all had.

Later that morning Daria walked into a deserted restaurant area. There must have been fifty tables all perfectly set with nobody eating at them. There was an alpine feel to the room, with dark panelled wooden walls adorned with stuffed animal heads and large heavy looking wooden skis and hunting equipment. A large grandfather clock ticked loudly on the wall beside her. There were some black and white pictures of a family in various stages of its life too.

'He did say it was empty,' Daria remarked, to herself.

'Virtually empty,' a high-pitched male voice said, causing her to jump.

'Wait, you are…you look like..' Daria started.

'Yes, I am. How do you think I got here? We all had our missions. Mine were just, I don't know, more difficult. Now come and sit.' The man interrupted. He gestured awkwardly towards a seat opposite him in a cubicle with red coloured upholstery seats.

He wore a black rubber suit with shoulder pads and a ribbed design that made him look as if his body were not functioning in tune with his head; almost puppet like. His build was thick set without being overweight with a head that was squarer than usual that seemed too large for his body; a strong jawline just about kept him in the realms of looking human. Although his eyes, that looked as if they would escape from their sockets at any moment, surely betrayed some kind of unnatural modification. His aura made her uneasy, she couldn't get a read on him. Not even close.

'Stop trying, I'm the grandfather. Now explain how Joey defeated you twice, we trained you well, how did he fool you? We must know his power. He is making things very difficult.' Grandfather said.

'The first time he wasn't working for anyone, the second it was the bots, not him.' Daria replied defiantly. Almost immediately she doubled over, feeling a sharp pain in her stomach.

'I can read him but he thinks differently, not how we are taught they do.' She continued.

'I see, we knew these people existed within the programme; but they are few and far between. Our web should be too big for him to stop us alone.' Grandfather replied. The pain in her stomach disappeared as fast as it had arrived.

A waitress bot arrived with a menu card and handed it to Daria. The choice was wide-ranging but she wasn't hungry. Still trying to read Grandfather, she ordered coffee, and glanced at his plate, where she saw dried beef and a selection of fruit.

'How have you been since arriving here?' Grandfather asked, chewing with his mouth open.

'I'm getting stronger, why?' Daria replied. *Why hasn't he asked about the taxi?*

'Good, you must have noticed the members here are all, well, supercharged.'

'What?' she replied.

'It's the air- it's not polluted, we don't poison ourselves like we did the herd in the old world. The invisible rainbow that spread through the air since the Great War made them sick; many were diagnosed as mentally ill and became irrelevant. Others got incurable diseases. Towards the end-thanks to me; the coverage was so strong, they were no longer human and we controlled them like puppets on a string.' He explained.

'What about the pills?' Daria asked.

'All in good time. Oh and, that was just a test yesterday in the taxi. Until later,' Grandfather replied, then got up and motioned toward a flyer on the table.

Daria laughed, how ironic things turned out to be! The herd gave up their world for convenience and democracy. Now what was left of them made the bots that would rule over them for ever more. She laughed again when she thought of Freetime V.R., where dreams became reality, the ultimate Trojan Horse. They were actually happy to live in a virtual world, they thought it was cool. She popped a pill, backed her coffee and began to read the flyer on the table: "Fall Party, Main Hall, 6th June 6p.m."

Chapter 29
2030, London

Joey woke up sweating and with a headache. He was relieved to see no sign of Cara next to him, he couldn't remember getting home let alone work out how to explain his drunken state the previous evening. He put his head in the sink and let the cold faucet run, and run. Only after two minutes, as he was beginning to shiver, did Joey move from the sink and dry of a little.

Awake now, he pondered the situation as he made coffee - would this be the last day like Scales promised, would young Daria succeed or had he and Franks done enough? On the balcony Joey sipped the hot drink while looking out over an eerily calm landscape.

The airport was operating the irregular Easterly runway operations; taking off towards the city and landing from the West. In this configuration rather than watching the planes landing directly in front of him, Joey was able to watch them roar over head a little after they took off. He dropped the cup in the sink and made his way hastily to the bathroom and sat. Just after the initial release the doorbell rang. Joey ignored it. It rang again then someone started knocking. Joey cursed under his breath, tidied himself up and went to the door.

'Franks…' he began.

'Quick; the balcony,' Franks said, bursting in aggressively and past Joey toward the kitchen.

As Joey caught up and joined Franks, who was on the balcony, outside he saw three large black and grey plumes of smoke in the distance, it looked like a whirlwind or tornado, but rose upward slowly.

'There's something going on,' Franks said, pointing toward the smoke.

As they looked on in silence, a large silvery grey object emerged from the runway at a thirty-degree angle then banked left. It turned slowly but consistently then straightened out, heading directly toward them.

The wine of the jet engines grew louder as it approached, Joey counted two of them on the huge jet, it was closer now and still low in the sky, the added weight and drag causing a slower climb. Then suddenly the noise abated, for a split-second time stood still, until gravity kicked in. Like a jet of water from a hosepipe that had sprayed too far from the source, the plane's nose turned down and it began to descend.

'Go!' Franks screamed. Joey froze, open mouthed. Franks turned back and pulled Joey roughly by the shoulder. The shadow of the large machine loomed large overhead, Franks could read the carriers livery it was so close. The whistling and screaming of the speeding projectile became smashing, creaking and breaking then two large explosions boomed as the fuel ignited and the building and plane morphed together.

Chapter 30
2050, Capital City

From his control room in the future Scales watched the drama unfolding. It seemed unreal; like it had happened in slow motion, Scales looked down, covered his head with his hands and let out a deep sigh. They'd beaten him, again.

He gulped then realised his hand was shaking violently as he tried to zoom in desperately looking to find something to hold onto. *It's happened, save their souls.*

"U.K. GOV Emergency Alert. Terrorist attack in progress. Return home and stay at home."

The message appeared on one of the screens in Scales control room where he had cloned Joey's phone. The human robots glued to their phones would all receive this message simultaneously, and the fear would spread to every corner of the country within seconds. An idea began to form in his mind.

He also had access to the smart city camera network and it was this he tuned into frantically. From a camera in the control tower he could now see four large plumes of smoke, two to the east and two to the west of the airport. He switched cameras to a large supermarket opposite Joey's block for a closer view, the fire burned orange and wild; Scales watched emergency services making loud progress from their bases toward the disaster sight. *How could anyone survive that,* he wondered. On the high street, he noticed people moving around quickly; some were recording the event, others stood frozen by the horror they faced.

A security cordon had not yet gone up around the area; there were emergency vehicles stopped at locations between debris along the main road, their lights still flashing. Where the apartment blocks used to stand Scales could see a part of the tail section of an airliner with a blue logo in the rear section of the glass windowed gym that had been under the flats. It had been mostly destroyed by the airliners impact, but confused staff were wondering around still wearing identity badges.

Scales watched with interest as a group of U.K.S.F. vans arrived at the scene, their back doors flung open and swarms of armed troops emerged. It looked as if they were picking things up and bagging them, even amongst the flames. Scales couldn't quite make out what it was they were removing amongst the chaos; most of the rescue crews, dressed in fire protective clothing, were busy searching for survivors amongst the rubble. Where fires still burned large hoses sprayed vast torrents of water. There was a thick smog in the air.

The impact had destroyed the majority of the building and replaced it with a crater of varying depths. The angle of decent must have been such that the rear of the building survived and parts of the plane went down into the ground. U.K.S.F. troops continued to swarm the site. A large portable display screen flashed a message;

"Leave the area immediately; do not touch anything, medical assistance is available by the large orange light." While a troop with a megaphone repeated the message.

Scales noticed a bright orange light further along the main road with several men in U.K.S.F. uniforms gathered around it. They had shovels, large wheeled containers and industrial bags. They waited ominously. Scales watched on as survivors made their way toward the light. There was no sign of Joey.

Several large black trucks arrived with U.K.S.F. printed on the side in white writing, they looked like dumpsters with hoses on the top. Was this an investigation site or a cover up operation? Scales thought, although he already knew the answer and looked away, frustrated there was nothing he could do.

He looked back after thirty seconds or so to see the U.K.S.F. begin to herd survivors into a tent near the orange light. Behind the tent he saw trucks driving into position. Other troops continued to remove rubble and debris from the crash site into their various containers; destroying any chance of an accurate investigation in the process.

Scales flicked to another camera opposite the survivor's tent and zoomed in, he saw a slim guy with no hair, who quickly moved out of view.

The television broadcast screen Scales had also hacked into to his left distracted him by changing from white fuzz to a picture. The screen was divided into two with a large space playing a video of the four plumes of smoke after the crashes. There was a small information bar below which stated:

"6/6/2030 Live Broadcast imminent. Terrorist attack in progress; stay at home. Threat level Maximum."

'And now a live emergency broadcast by the U.K. Prime Minister,' the same female presenter said. The top part of the screen changed to a picture of a sombre looking woman in a suit; seated at a desk in a dark room with the Union Jack flag draped behind her.

'It is with great sadness that I deliver this message to you, fellow citizens of the United Kingdom. We, along with the rest of the world, are with immediate effect, at war with a malevolent Extra-Terrestrial race intent on destroying humankind.

Today, the 6th of June 2030, starting at 9:23a.m., we witnessed an horrific attack on our air travel system in London; four passenger planes crashed around London Heathrow Airport. Similar attacks have occurred around the world in several major cities including: Paris, Berlin, Toronto, Tokyo, New York and Rome. Intelligence suggests more attacks are likely to occur elsewhere and that these E.T.'s may have infiltrated the human form and are actively working to destroy us from within.

For this reason, under the 2026 Public Protection Act, all communications systems; mobile, satellite and broadcasting have been temporarily suspended and I am now declaring a level five State of Emergency and Martial Law. You must stay at home for your own safety. Travel is not permitted. The military and U.K.S.F. will enforce this rigorously. Anyone breaking curfew will be considered an enemy. Food will be delivered in due course. I implore you to follow these instructions for the good of this great nation and your fellow citizens, but I must warn you that this will be the most difficult time in our history. We must be strong. I reassure you that the government is intact and functioning. We are working with our allies around the world against this unprecedented threat. Goodnight. God save the King,' she announced.

The national anthem began to play and the screen switched to a hologram of the, now deceased, royal family on the balcony of a large palace. They wore military uniforms and there were Union Jack flags behind them. When the music stopped the screen returned to the previous emergency broadcast screen with a newsfeed ticker at the bottom.

They certainly weren't wasting any time sowing the seeds, a fearsome green bogeyman, living amongst them, put up to take the blame without delay.

Chapter 31
2050, America South

Daria was relieved to get that out of the way. *Fucking grandfather, what next Uncle?* Still that freak had almost singlehandedly enslaved the old world and even visited new ones, maybe he deserved it. An invitation was under her door when she returned to her room.

"*America South Founder Members Fall Party; 6/6@6p.m. Patagonia Lodge.*
Programme of events:
6p.m   Cocktails, pills and play.
7p.m.   Small-scale re-enactment of events in London 2030.
Those who attended will play their own roles.
8p.m.   Dinner
10p.m. Our Future; a demonstration.

*Note if there is an asterisk here * you have a costume which will be delivered by 4p.m."*

Daria smiled her crooked smile, for the first time she was beginning to enjoy this place, and now she'd get the recognition she deserved. She called reception and requested a ski suit, and snow mobile.

When she returned in the late afternoon it was almost dark and she could see her breath in the cold, dry air. Inside, the lodge was warm and busy, there were several groups milling around and Daria detected an air of anticipation around the place.

Back in her room, she laughed out loud when she saw the grey rubber costume that lay on her bed, the mask had wide eyes and no hole for the nose. With her features and this tight clothing…this was going to be fun evening.

As Daria entered the main restaurant, it appeared that there were only ten or so people in costumes and they were all sat at two tables at the front of the room, just in front of a stage.

At the table next to her one wore an expensive suit and glasses, another wore an overcoat and carried a microphone, then several wore black military style outfits and carried weapons that looked real. On her table there were a few others wearing the same style costume as her, but they were coloured green. Small plastic devices with metal aerials lay on their table, one for each of them.

Behind the top two tables was a meticulously constructed model of Heathrow airport and the crash sites around it. The buildings were as tall as a large man and were lit up and painted in detail. To the left and right of the model two rooms had been set up; one to look like a television studio, the other a grand office with a Union Jack behind a desk.

It wasn't long after six, when the room had filled, that the lights dimmed and a spotlight focussed on a dark area behind the model. Music played and a map of America South appeared on two large television screens. As the music got faster and faster, people started dancing and cheering until, eventually as they tired, a slow clap developed.

Then screams of joy as Grandfather appeared, dressed in a white suit with a sheep's head on, he danced in a demented fashion around the stage, milking the audience well until at the final crescendo of the music he tore off the mask to reveal another, this time that of a grey haired, blue eyed wolf.

'Thank-you, welcome, thank-you all!' he said over the exuberant cheers. Daria noticed two of her table friends in the green suits were fucking under the table.

'Please, yes its true. Those stupid fucking humans, eh! Give 'em a phone; they give you their mind!' He continued. The cheers became so loud Daria thought she might have burst an eardrum. Party poppers exploded and balloons released onto the stage.

Five fellow revellers aimed champagne bottles, then popped the corks simultaneously at Grandfather; who neatly caught two and dodged the rest with a crazed grin.

'Yes, you remember, don't you? I certainly do…they let me in. They welcomed me and let me become the master of their universe. Their money, transport and communications. All the while they believed I was doing it to help them. To make their world a better place!' Grandfather said. The crowd laughed.

'And all the while I was the wolf, waiting to eat them all up!'
He continued. The television screens behind him cut to a real video
of wolves devouring something that soon stopped struggling. Daria
couldn't make out exactly what it was for all the blood.

'With your help, we destroyed their minds, took everything
they owned and made them beg us for protection from an invisible
threat, beg us to turn them into the useless slave robot race they are
now!' Grandfather screamed. His eyes almost popped out. Bots
dressed as clowns set off fireworks all around the room then zoomed
in all directions, drinks flew into the air, fights broke out and corks
continued to pop. A clock started ticking down from 30 minutes on
the screens behind Grandfather.

'Join me for the glorious re-enactment of our greatest victory
in thirty minutes!' He shouted, his voice now harsh and throaty.
Pandemonium ensued.

Daria lit up a smoke and downed a bottle of something she
had had thrown at her, then clocked a guy next to her after removing
his hand from her crotch. *There was plenty of time for that later.*
She looked to the stage and saw three male clown bots engaged
sexually with each other, the final one engaged from behind with the
woman at the top table dressed in an expensive suit. The ironic thing
was the woman she was impersonating had likely done a lot worse,
and Mother had it all on film.

Next thing she knew a loud claxon went off and the music
stopped. The monitors switched to pictures of Big Ben and the
Houses of Parliament, then the U.K. National anthem started playing
before being drowned out by the sound of the whining motors of
model airplanes.

Daria and her table companions took up the baton and took
control of the small planes. The lights focussed on the four targets in
the model set up behind them. It took a while but eventually the
degenerate group celebrated four plane crashes into the model
buildings. As the fourth went down a larger than necessary
explosion destroyed the stage.

This caused Daria and her unearthly companions to flee away
from the scene. The crowd went ballistic. Some lay injured. A
small group of young men dressed in tatty clothes held up their
lighters, danced and took photos. One or two revellers were passed
out prone on the floor.

The top table was still intact where the woman in the expensive suit had decoupled herself and was busy adjusting her hair and ruffling some papers.

Chapter 32
2030, London

The news channel blared out from a screen in the make-shift field hospital; giving Joey a second headache as they sat on some fold out chairs waiting. Clouds of dust and smoke hung in the unusually still air with the slightly burnt smell of human flesh.

Franks, still in shock, kept his eyes on the goings on around them and was beginning to take it all in. The fire brigade officer, who moments earlier had guided them down via an extending ladder, stood adjacent to them.

'Definitely your lucky day chaps,' he said nodding up toward the small area of the block next to Joey's flat that had survived the impact, 'how did you manage that then?' he continued.

Joey and Franks looked at each other blankly. Neither knew, neither answered. There were several other occupied chairs next to them, in a sort of queuing system toward the front where there was a desk with two U.K.S.F. troops sat behind it taking details.

'Do you have some water?' Franks asked the fireman, in his most educated accent. The man looked around then walked off.

'Come on.' Franks said, nodding to Joey as he got up. As they exited the tent Franks broke into a jog. Joey felt his head, then followed, limping slightly. Out of the immediate vicinity, the men slowed to a quick walk. Joey turned to look back at the scene and shook his head in disbelief.

Franks turned left down a side road, after a minute he took out his keys and entered a black front door, beckoning to Joey to follow.

'A rental, we'll be safe here.' Franks said, as he climbed the stairs. His career had left him in a good financial position, and he had invested wisely. There was a sofa and chair in the sparsely furnished living room.

'What the hell is going on then?' Franks asked.

'Why are you asking me? I didn't ask for any of this. Could the Un-interruptible Autopilot have brought them down?' Joey replied with wild, glazed eyes; maybe from too much smoke, maybe because they were about to burst.

'Hmm, I never heard about it when I flew, then again most pilots wouldn't fly if they weren't in full control. So, they probably never told anyone.' Franks replied, shaking his head slowly, 'what do you think?'

'It doesn't matter now, I failed. She won. It's over.' Joey replied, sinking back into the chair.

Franks flicked on the television. A well-dressed woman began to speak.

'My fellow citizens, it has been four hours since my last address during this unprecedented International Crisis. Earlier, I announced a level five state of Emergency and curfew order to ensure your safety combined with a ban on communications and travel. Now I can confirm that food deliveries will begin tomorrow, supervised by the military and U.K.S.F. European and International colleagues will also assist. The state broadcaster, U.K. News, will begin to transmit a 24-hour news and public information service immediately after this broadcast. Regarding the Extra-ter ...'

The P.M. paused and Franks noticed a change in her facial expressions, she blinked several times and moved around in her seat looking uncomfortable. Before he had time to process anything two U.K.S.F. soldiers entered from each side of the screen and approached the PM's chair. They manhandled her to her feet and were in the process of removing her from the room when a loud single gunshot pierced the airwaves. The bullet struck the P.M. in the temple, her head reeled backward and blood began to emerge from the entry point. The screen cut out.

'Please bear with us while we try to regain the picture,' said an experienced sounding commentator. The picture switched to a male newscaster in a studio dressed in a suit and tie.

'Welcome to this live coverage of the Extra-terrestrial attack on earth from the studio and my colleagues reporting live from Heathrow, Chequers and across the country. We also have special reports from around the world during this unprecedented and uncertain crisis. First over to Chequers for the latest update.'

'Thank-you, following the horrific scenes earlier, I am now able to confirm that the Prime Minister, has been neutralised midway through only her second statement of this crisis. We await official word from the government, but my sources tell me that she had been behaving unusually over the past week and following some medical tests earlier today the decision had been made to neutralise the threat. When she went off script in her final statement the U.K.S.F. were ordered to move in. To repeat, the Prime Minister herself has been infiltrated by the enemy and as a result neutralised. Now back to you in the studio.'

Franks moved from his seat and had to steady himself. Despite his recent misgivings, his mind had been trained to take orders and listen to authority, that included the government, but this was too much.

All those years flying, and he had never seen a U.F.O., and neither had any of his buddies. This just couldn't be happening. He headed to the garden for some air, feeling slightly better until he looked up to the clouds. He recognised the heavy thudding sound of helicopters in the distance. Fighter jets and a large communications aircraft flew overhead, he watched in awe as the jets crisscrossed across the sky in a grid pattern. It did not take them long, he thought, and imagined being in the cockpit flying that slowly was a pain in the arse for the pilots.

'You want some company?' Joey asked.

'Sure thing, you were out cold,' Franks replied.

Joey slumped into a plastic garden chair. There were a few flowerpots with cactus style plants and an iron table between them.

'You know they are blaming this on Extra-terrestrials.' Franks continued.

Joey hardly flinched.

'I know, the war goes on until 2035.' Joey said.

'Look, something flew those planes into the ground, but I'm damned sure it wasn't the pilots.' Franks replied.

'And I'm damned sure it wasn't aliens,' Joey said. He sat up in his chair, before continuing, 'we know it was Daria, could they have flown them by remote control? The Uninterruptable autopilot?'

'I don't know enough about it but it wouldn't surprise me if something advertised to stop a terrorist attack actually facilitated one. Everything is inverted.' Franks replied.

'Now they will convince us that we could be infiltrated and offer a way to stop that threat that suits their plan.' Joey said.

'And they will repeat it over and over until we give in, they will never tire of it.' Franks replied.

'They must sit their laughing at how easy we are to control.' Joey continued.

'Tell me more,' Franks replied.

The men spent the next couple of hours talking. Joey explained everything he and Cara had been through in the past couple of weeks, to varying degrees of understanding and shock from Franks. For Franks, the linear thinker, things slowly started to add up; he had suspected global events had been manipulated since the turn of the century as they became ever more predictable. After all, didn't someone once say that the bigger the lie, the easier it is to fool them.

'So, you are telling me these bastards are going to put a chip in us that will control everything, and we will even beg for it?' Franks said, shaking his head.

'We gave up our minds for "entertainment," now we are controlled from the cloud like it or not. We don't deserve to be human. It's too late to stop it.' Joey said, head in hands.

'Scales chose you for a reason Joey.' Franks said.

'Maybe he chose you too?' Joey replied.

'How?' Franks asked.

'I don't know, he sent me here next door to you.' Joey replied.

Chapter 33
2050, America South

After several courses of the best food available on the continent and countless live pills, the debauched rabble donned jackets and blankets then moved outside into the rectangular courtyard around which the guest rooms were set.

The flames jumped and slivered around the edges of the overloaded bonfire set in the centre of the space, the inside lights dimmed; the sudden contrast seemed to hypnotise the group into an expectant silence.

An operating table with a sheet over it was wheeled out by a bot dressed in a white coat, the sheet was contoured as if it were hiding something. Daria thought she saw it move but couldn't be sure. Another bot wheeled out a dentist's chair with several tubes attached to it, then they began connecting the tubes between the two. Finally, Grandfather appeared with a white rabbit in one hand and a suitcase in the other. He had changed into a long Black gown with small silver and gold symbols and markings sewn into it and wore a miner's lamp on his head.

'And now for the evenings main event,' he said, as he tore the sheet aggressively off the operating table. He clicked his finger at one of the bots who whirred over and unlocked the magnetic restraints. The crowd gasped as the child sat up, then ran away. Some started to chase.

'No, stop, there's no need. Stop.' Grandfather said, smiling broadly before continuing, 'Our experiments have been successful. I need a volunteer, please who wants to make history?'

A hush descended upon the crowd. Grandfather clicked his fingers at the bots and they disappeared before reappearing momentarily wheeling out two large figures; at least twice human size. One was red with broad shoulders and toned muscles, the other silver with accentuated curves and real looking hair. They looked like a transformer/ superhero hybrid. A commotion erupted as the crowd jostled for position, they edged forward; some reached out to touch the shining objects. Shouts of 'me', 'yes', and 'I'll do it,' flowed into the cold air.

'Okay let's get the oldies out to the front now; one of you guys whose body is almost done.' Grandfather said, before continuing, 'yes that's it come on. Okay, you come up here and take a seat.' An old lady sat in the dentist's chair while the bots connected wires, cables and lobes between the volunteer, the vessel and two monitors.

'What's your name and what was your role?' he asked the volunteer.

'Geraldine, I worked interpreting their data.' She replied.

'There's nothing to be afraid of, my body has been a machine for years, I just had to look real to fool them. But now we have reached this milestone, over the coming months, you will all get your reward. Now silence!' Grandfather exclaimed.

He took the members hand, lifted it and allowed it to fall down limp. Her eyes were closed. He nodded to one of the bots, stood by a display unit, who pressed a button. Nothing happened. Then again. The large silver superhero body moved slightly, then its eyes lit up.

'What is your name and what was your role?' Grandfather asked the superhero.

'Geraldine, interpreting data.' It replied in exactly the same voice as the old lady moments earlier.

'And there we have it. Our mind lives on in an indestructible body. A toast to immortality.' Grandfather proclaimed. The crowd cheered wildly.

Daria looked on as other members surrounded Geraldine, and began conversing with her. One over excited male must have prodded her in the wrong place as he was literally sent flying into the far wall by a swipe of her arm. Grandfather made an indication to the bots who retrieved the body and hooked him up to the dentist's chair and began the process again.

Daria took a long look at Grandfather and wondered how old he really was and tried to imagine him when he was younger. The more she recalled seeing pictures or video of him at events she realised that he had always looked just like he did now. An entity stuck in a time warp leading humanity down the spiral toward a fiery end with his miracle inventions. A real wolf in sheep's clothing. She smiled at the irony and watched as the newly created machine awakened and set his eyes towards Geraldine.

Daria turned away and made for the front door, picking up a heavy coat as she passed reception. Outside the night was dark and the air still, her breath disappeared faster than the smoke from her cigarette.

'What body will you design?' A voice said from the darkness, startling Daria.

'I'm quite happy with what I've got.' She replied, turning to see Grandfather blending in with the dark evening.

'Well; *you* can't have one until you've had more injections anyway. This is a new beginning for us, now we have no limits, we can finally compete with them.' He said, looking up toward the stars.

'Tell me…why did you change your name? Everybody knows who you are from before. What you did.' Daria replied. Grandfather raised his eyebrows then laughed arrogantly.

'That's what you think you know. Why don't you just sort out this mess with Scales? Maybe then you will be ready.' Grandfather replied, he had already turned and opened the heavy front door as he spoke the last word. Daria checked herself in the reflection of a small window pane then threw her hand into it aggressively.

Chapter 34
2030, London

Joey woke with a curtain wrapped round him, laying on a single bed with no sheets nor pillowcase. There was no sign of Cara. How he longed for her embrace now after these awful days. Even the vision of her would be better than this hell; he knew what these people were walking right into but he could do nothing to stop it.

He turned over onto his stomach in a vain attempt to hide from the light flooding into the small bedroom. Something jabbed into his chest. It was Cara's cross. He took it out and held it for a moment, then turned over and lay staring at the wall. He imagined a young Cara, even more vibrant and headstrong, somewhere in the South of France, probably reading history while cursing the government.

Joey's malaise was interrupted by a beep from his phone. This was unusual. He reached down to his jeans and wrestled the device from the pocket without getting up.

"U.K. GOV Test. Reply Yes if you got this"

Joey threw the phone down and turned away in disgust. *Bloody communists.*

Next door, in the old-fashioned kitchen Franks found what he was looking for in the bottom drawer. He always kept emergency supplies for his new tenants. A couple of old mugs, sachets of coffee and tea bags. There was even some long-life milk.

A minute later Franks propped himself up on the wall in Joey's room and sipped his steaming hot coffee. Perhaps it was a moment of weakness, perhaps one of camaraderie or even of increased trust. Whatever it was it was a break from his more formal approach. He was tired, an old man now and having flown these machines all his life without even coming close to an accident and yesterday one flew into him. He'd laugh if his body didn't ache so badly. He burnt his mouth on the next sip of coffee but felt no pain; looking at Joey he wondered whether to wake him. The man from the future who wanted to avenge his dead girlfriend. This time he did laugh. Out loud.

Joey stirred, the feeling of someone watching him, he turned his head and was surprised to see Franks sitting next to the bed, on the floor, laughing.

'Nice one thanks,' Joey said, taking the coffee and sitting up leaning on the wall that filled in for the missing headboard, 'are you okay?' Joey continued.

'I don't know.' Franks replied, head down. Joey's phone beeped again.

'These fucking communists, can't they leave us alone for a minute?' Joey said. Franks picked up the phone and saw two messages exactly the same, fifteen minutes apart.

'They didn't message me, look' Franks pulled out his phone to double check, before continuing, 'weird-you can't normally reply to these. Go ahead.'

Joey did so, typing Yes and hitting send. The men sat, staring at the small screen, waiting. Oh, the irony. The phone beeped.

"Good. We may still have a chance! Keep the phone on and charged. Scales." Both men read as it arrived on the device.

'This guy can send text messages from the future now, that's impressive.' Franks said, before continuing, 'and bypass the government block on communication, come on let's see what's going on.' The men moved into the living room and tuned into the television.

"And now we cross live to Brussels for a press conference with the United Nations Secretary General," a voice said calmly. A man dressed in an expensive looking blue suit stood alone behind a lectern and addressed the camera.

'Citizens of the world, for the past two days we have been under attack by an extra-terrestrial force. We now face a common threat to our continued existence on this planet, one which can only be faced by working together. I have met virtually with your elected leaders who have agreed to place their trust in the United Nations to lead us through this crisis. As such we will join forces, one united world, working together to ensure our survival. All working age men will be conscripted, pro-creation banned and food rationed. We know the enemies are amongst us and we are working on a reliable test to identify them. Some early indicators to look for are blinking more than usual and contortions of the face and limbs. We must be prepared to make sacrifices to ensure the future of humanity. With your help we will succeed. Limited communications will be re-established for further instructions from your local government.'

The screen flicked backed to the 24-hour U.K. News channel, which was showing several reports on a loop being added to slowly. The first one started with a reporter located in an inner-city estate; where U.K.S.F. vehicles, troops and ambulances are in the background with several shocked residents scattered around. One of them is being interviewed by the reporter;

'Can you tell us what happened please?' The reporter asked. 'It was early this morning, I heard a commotion coming from Mrs Smith's house next door, then screams and bangs. Like things were being thrown around. We looked outside and saw her two sons fighting on the grass here; then one of them stabbed the other one with a kitchen knife. He just kept going. It was horrible,' the witness explained. Then the camera panned to a bloody stain on the grass.

'From what we can gather a family feud erupted over breakfast after one son accused the other of being an alien; after he blinked a lot while finishing off the last bowl of coco snaps. This led to a fight and the death of the infiltrated brother. Then, tragically, when the U.K.S.F. arrived; they saw several residents breaking the curfew, and they opened fire and shot them. The total death toll is twelve people. The U.K.S.F. refuse to comment or confirm whether infiltration has occurred but advise all citizens to adhere to the rules and stay indoors regardless.' The reporter explained.

Their phones chimed in unison. It was an emergency alert text from UKGOV, this time the real thing.

"Food rations. Your collection point is Dean Park at 11a.m. today. Bring attached QR code."

Joey's stomach rumbled, then he went back to his device, scrolling aimlessly, in only a few days he had become one of the zombies on the train.

There was a cruel meme of the Prime Minister wearing shades, then taking them off and looking in the mirror to reveal reptile eyes before being shot several times in front of a cheering crowd. Others depicted huge alien landing craft, like an episode of Star Wars, hovering over the planet with world leaders in the cockpit. Then things got real. People were posting stories and videos of an horrific nature. Pregnant women giving themselves home abortions. Families blockading suspected alien family members in bedrooms, garden sheds and worse. A hashtag "alien-proof" was spreading around saying if you drank cola then spat it out on some litmus paper and the pH was between 2.6 and 2.7 then you had been infiltrated.

To see Joey, a confirmed social media phobe, comatose in swipe city, you can bet your last carbon credit that the rest of the country was too. And for what good? None, they are just repeating and reinforcing the message they have been given and spreading the fear, panic and pandemonium faster than a Californian forest fire in August.

Next, he navigated to a headline story on the U.K. News website, the only website available, of a massacre in a remote part of Scotland, where the U.K.S.F. numbers were low. Apparently two men had acquired weapons and systematically slaughtered the whole village in their homes then appropriated their food. They were subsequently caught after one of the men released a video of the event on his social media titled, "E.T. went home."
Joey sighed, put down the phone, and began to drift away slowly.

*

'Okay let's go, we stick together no matter what. Don't engage with anyone you don't have to, our aim is to get back here within the hour,' Franks declared. Joey stirred, he stretched his arms then slowly got up, looking in the mirror he laughed at his large white bandage and wondered when the barrage of the last week or so would end.

They left and were on the high street minutes later, walking past the devastating crash site, Franks was surprised to see it deserted. The first aid tent had gone and the plane parts had been cleared; all that remained was the building's rubble, cordoned off by perimeter tape.

After a short walk to the pick-up point, they saw another large tent had been erected, with U.K.S.F. and Military troops mixed together. There was a que, but it was not too large, the ration collection times must have been staggered, Franks thought. Despite the circumstances the human robots experiencing them seemed to be behaving themselves.

'Four-day rations, scan your phone, take a bag and move away quickly. All rations are the same, take a bag and go home.' A U.K.S.F. troop announced repeatedly over a loudspeaker.

Franks was impressed with the organisation and began to think this could be a walk in the park when raised voices and a commotion broke out at the front of the que. He was tall enough to see a chubby, red-faced lady with a couple of children around her; one young enough to be held by the hand.

'What about the tests, I want a test, when are you giving us a test?' She shouted, disrupting the smooth-running operation. This was the reaction they wanted; now for the solution.

'She's blinking, look I can see it from here,' a voice from the que exclaimed, as the lady's children started to cry unharmoniously. A group of men in blue and white uniforms turned their attention to the woman. One of them looked agitated and moved his arm across to his automatic weapon, seemingly unable to deal with this unscripted question.

One of the U.K.S.F. troops moved across the military man and directed the lady away from the desk, taking he ration pack with him.

'Come away, Lady. You have your rations,' he said, confidently. The lady stopped mouthing off and looked up at the man in uniform in front of her with shock then walked away with her children following in silence. The look in his eyes required submission. The military men who had failed to deal with the situation shrugged and continued their roles allowing the man to lead the woman away towards the edge of the park.

'Don't ask questions, they will kill you. Go home.' He explained

By the time the commotion was over Joey and Franks had reached the front of the que and collected their box without fuss.

'Nice work there buddy,' Franks said to the U.K.S.F. troop who smiled and waved Frank's onward. He was stocky with long hair protruding from under his helmet, on his shoulder a nametag read "Jones." Humanity did still exist, he thought, even amongst the troops paid to control us.

'What do you think?' Franks asked as they walked out of the small park.

'He could be a one off, or we might be onto something.' Joey replied.

'He couldn't stand by and watch them get slaughtered,' Franks replied, 'maybe because of their civilian background, they aren't trained killers.'

'Or maybe he just has morals?' Joey said.

'But they are trained to take orders, and if some of them won't, then we might have a chance.' Franks continued.

Back at home, after a hastily thrown together meal of eggs, bread and cheese, the men took a seat with a steaming hot cup of tea. Franks turned up the television which had been on the news channel with a muted volume.

The scene was devastating, Manchester, the second most populated city in the U.K. had been obliterated. Pictures were being broadcast without sound. Co-incidentally, U.K. News had switched to their smaller London studio for broadcasting just after the Fall. A ticker at the bottom of the screen read:

"Manchester livecams; city under attack from unknown weapons. More to follow."

A shocked looking presenter appeared in the corner of the screen and the sound activated.

"Good morning from London, where we watch together to these hellish scenes coming to you live from Manchester, a city formerly housing 2.9 million residents that has been devastated over night during a suspected Extra-terrestrial attack. Reports are coming in from across the globe of similar attacks to large cities in a devastating first strike of this unprecedented war on humanity. We now cross live to a secret location and the Deputy Prime Minister for a statement."

A man in a suit appeared on the screen. He was sat in a dimly lit room with no desk and no Union Jack, it had been replaced with the United Nations flag; a white globe flattened out on a blue background.

'Citizens. It is with deep regret that I can confirm the total destruction of the city of Manchester. We are attempting to regain communications with our military and security forces in the area but have so far failed. Intelligence suggests the use of an unknown weapon, during the early hours of the morning, by the alien force is responsible for the devastation. Emergency crews are being mobilised to search for survivors but, sadly, we must prepare for the worst. As of 9 a.m. this morning I have activated the One World Act, as have my colleagues around the world. This transfers command and control of all the U.K.'s armed forces and government to the United Nations. This Act has never been revealed publicly, so as not to cause panic and because we hoped it would never be used. However, several years ago when the aliens made themselves known we developed a worst-case scenario to protect humanity. The U.N. has a highly secure location and can guarantee continuity of government regardless of what we face. I will continue to serve and broadcast directly to you, following on from orders from the U.N. However, I must be clear. We are at a crossroads, facing a challenge never before seen in history. The Lifepass and limited communications have been activated; rations are being delivered today. To all the brave men out there your service is required, conscription pick up points will be sent to you. We must stand together shoulder to shoulder, regardless of race or creed, and fight for our very survival together. Failure is not an option.'

The man bowed his head in silent reflection for a moment, then the screen switched back to the video feeds of the flattened city and a solitary bugle began to play. Buildings were destroyed, water pipes burst spraying their contents upwards vertically, fires raged beyond control but anyone could see survivors were unlikely.

'What next?' Franks asked, shaking his head. Before Joey could respond his phone beeped. It was a message from UKGOV.

"You have been conscripted. Pick up location R.A.F. Northolt. 11a.m. tomorrow."

'Good timing right.' Joey replied.

'Almost like it was planned.' Franks nodded.

Chapter 35
2050, Capital City

Scales closed the door to his control room and reversed awkwardly out of the massive wooden wardrobe that concealed it. Despite living alone, he always ensured that if anyone, human or robot did come to investigate the outskirts of the Capital, they would not find his life's work. He walked outside and took a seat on the traditionally carved wooden bench and admired the stunning view in front of him.

The old farmhouse was set atop a hill on the amongst green pastures and towering conifers. The old fences that demarked ownership had fallen into disrepair since the Fall thanks to the removal of their owners. Nature; its beauty, power and destruction, had taken over.

Scales kept a small herd of cows who assisted with the gardening, one of whom Mooed up a him as he watched the clouds closing in from behind the mountain peaks that towered over them.

Things hadn't gone to plan so far, and now he'd need to risk being found out to expose Mothers attack on humanity. He knew that communications were monitored, and that there were none except via the Lifechip in the Capital and Safezones. But such a large burst of radio energy would surely be noticed by someone, whether Freegov or Mother monitoring, more likely the latter. He calculated that by the time they found out after one round of communications, he'd probably be able to send one more before they got to him. Every word counted, so he began to scribble down ideas.

Reveal, Scales faithful Border Collie, enjoyed fetching the scrawled-up balls of paper as Scales threw them carelessly over his shoulder. The pile by his feet grew until finally he stood and held the paper up in front of him with a clenched fist. Rain began to fall forcing Scales inside, by the time he began to type he could hear the water pelting fiercely against the roof above him.

"UK GOV ALERT THE INVASION IS FAKE. ALL GOVERNMENTS ARE OCCUPIED BY FOREIGN AGENTS. THEY WILL OFFER YOU A CHIP THAT TURNS YOU INTO A ROBOT. DO NOT COMPY. DO NOT FOLLOW ORDERS."

*

165

Seconds later on the high-tech monitoring island just off the coast of America South a monitor flicked on with a world map, most of which was blacked out. A small red dot flashed just outside the Capital, which was coloured blue. Unusual Transmission detected. The operative read Scales message and hit the block button, then placed a call to the lodge in Patagonia.

Chapter 36
2030, London

Joey closed the door and walked away briskly in an attempt to block the pain he felt both physically and mentally having failed to stop the Fall. The past couple of weeks had been a rollercoaster, the only way he got through it was the constant action. And, more than likely, the fact that he hadn't really been able to feel any real emotion for years, indeed his whole mind had been numbed for years. It was only now, being alone, that he had the time to really think.

Before he'd even reached the main road that thinking left him in tears, floods of them to be exact. What had he done wrong in life to have so much given, then taken way so quickly. Was Scales just a cruel joke? All of his plans had failed so far and now Joey was on his own again. The whole thing seemed pointless, he wondered what was coming next as he absentmindedly kicked a piece of airplane debris down the high street. He doubled back and ran to where the piece had landed, Franks had been exasperated that the debris was removed so fast by the U.K.S.F. and Joey realised this could be important. He found the piece and grabbed it. It was around the size of a tea coaster and had the unmistakable logo from the Boeing Company stamped into it. Joey turned and sped back to the flat, knocking loudly a minute or so later.

'Take this I think it's from the plane that crashed,' he almost shouted as a surprised Franks opened the door, 'got to go I'll try and stay in touch.' Joey said as he turned and jogged back to the main road not wanting to be late for his next appointment with death.

The directions application on his phone showed a north-easterly journey to the R.A.F. base in Northolt, that would take two hours on foot. The weather was unusually cool and usually grey; Joey zipped up his jacket and headed east. The streets were busy with men walking, like zombies, towards their destination. He had seen that before somewhere. Some groups formed along the way but Joey chose to keep his own company as he approached a crossroads with a U.K.S.F. checkpoint.

He looked up ahead as a group of excited younger lads arrived. They had been laughing and joking on the road, like schoolboys going on their first trip abroad. After getting through the checkpoint silence fell; the human spirit crushed instantly by authority. Joey wondered what had happened as he waited his turn.

'Phone, I.D.?' A bored sounding U.K.S.F. troop said, not even making eye contact. Joey lifted his device.

'Keep walking, if you see a bus get on it they are all going to the base. Tests on arrival,' he continued, before handing back the phone along with a small piece of paper. Joey pushed through the makeshift barrier and instantly understood the reason for silence up ahead. Tests.

Reality kicked in, some of the conscripts could be aliens and they were about to find out who. The paper read: "R.A.T." A Rapid Alien Test would be carried out via a swab at the back of the throat. The results were instant and anyone who failed would be quarantined. Whether the infiltration thing was real or not, the fear would kill them either way. Joey threw the paper on the ground and looked ahead, no busses in sight. The remainder of the journey was uneventful, there were more men now walking, in silence, toward their judgement.

As he approached the base along a main road, minus any traffic, he could see a que had formed up ahead, it was twenty men across and hundreds deep, maybe even thousands as it spilled over from the base onto the empty roads. This was going to take a while, he thought, as he took a sip of water and checked his pockets. There wasn't much to write home about; a chewy bar and a penknife, he wondered how long that would last. In his trousers he still had some sustenance pills; and took a few to alleviate the hunger that the walk had created in his body and looked on.

Nothing of note happened for at least half an hour; the que moved slowly forward and he figured it would be another half hour or so before he rolled the dice to receive his personal judgement. He blinked and was glad the Lifechip had been removed, that, physical control of the human mind, was where all this was heading Joey knew and laughed at the irony of it all.

Suddenly, there were loud voices coming from the front of the que followed by a burst of automatic gunfire. Something had gone wrong, the blood drained from the faces of the men around him as he scrambled for a better view. Then a loudspeaker boomed into action.

'Conscripts, you will be tested and you will follow directions. Disobedience will not be tolerated,' shouted an authoritative voice in a foreign accent.

A murmur developed and spread around the group; there was a lot of swearing and cursing. Then, as if they had timed the move simultaneously, several men threw down their belongings and retreated backwards, away from the line. Some started running. Before Joey had time to think, a group of blue and white armored vehicles raced from the base toward the deserters. He crouched down instinctively and moved forward into the crowd wherever there was an opening.

Gunfire echoed in the air. Don't look back he told himself, keep moving forward. The inverse logic stood him in good stead as he approached the makeshift checkpoint quickly. There was a bank of approximately twenty desks with three men in uniform at each of them. Two wore all blue and white uniforms, the other all white. The group logic had been to turn and run, the que was no more, except a few brave souls around him.

Towards the left of the remaining que Joey saw a man wearing a baseball cap showing his phone, it being scanned then taken to the side where a man in white uniform swabbed the back of his throat with a long white cotton bud and put it in a small plastic vessel which he then shook. Then the man nodded, rescanned the phone and daubed the big man with green paint across his chest. The expressionless man's face reddened slightly and he moved on, not noticing the piece of paper the white coated man offered him. Whitecoat grabbed his shoulder and thrust the paper angrily in his face, the man took it and walked quickly away from the checkpoint, he had survived.

Joey trudged forward, trying his best to ignore the shouts, screams and now sustained gunfire behind him, took a deep breath and it was his turn. He headed for the same desk as the cap guy and leant back opening up his throat for the swab, giving away his dignity for a greater good. After a minute the guy nodded, daubed him with green paint and thrust a small piece of paper into his hand; it read; "Bus 13. Southampton."

A well-trodden pathway had opened up to the left ahead of him in the previously well looked after grass. A handwritten sign in the shape of an arrow read; "Busses this way." He turned and looked back at the checkpoint, the desks on the right led toward a similar pathway marked; "Quarantine camp." Looking ahead, in the distance, on a runway two large temporary structures had been erected. The men that walked that path looked at the ground and moved slowly, a red daub of paint across their torso.

Joey got on bus thirteen and found a seat towards the back, it was filling up with men wearing expressionless, blood drained faces. Robot- humans. Talk was minimal, except for a new arrival acknowledging a seat mate as they embarked. Joey was contemplating removing his jacket when the peace was shattered by a man at the front who spoke on the busses speaker system.

'Welcome to stage one of Operation Home Front, we will shortly be travelling to Southampton where you will embark ships in the defence of our world. You will be known as Conscript then your first name. Our estimated time of arrival is two hours from now, this is as good as its going to get so I suggest you get some shut eye.' Joey noted this man's accent was English.

Joey messaged Franks, "Destination Southampton," then started to properly assess his surroundings. He was seated on the right-hand side of the lower deck of the large double decker passenger bus, painted red. He imagined the happy tourists and not so happy commuters who could have sat here in the same space but in a different time with a different reality to consider. He strained his neck to the right, to see the runway and the back of one of the large quarantine tents. Every now and then a large flap opened and soldiers in blue and white carried out a stretcher with a body bag on it. It was as clear as day, they weren't trying to hide anything.

Joey felt sick…memories of the Freegov and their caskets of heroes on the conveyor belt to the furnace. He watched as the next stretcher came out, the soldiers walked twenty yards or so then went down a wide set of stone steps that were set into the ground at the end of the runway. The top of the structure was covered with grass and would be difficult to see unless somebody was actually using them. He couldn't see any further down, and could only assume there was an underground disposal facility there; out of sight, out of mind.

He turned back fully 180 degrees and could see through the back window of the bus that the que had reformed and the men who were tested towards the right-hand side of desks were all daubed red and sent to the tents. Right was wrong. Left was right. Everything inverse in this perverse world. Human beings just a number to their evil overlords, a lucky dip away from death at their command.

His thoughts were suddenly interrupted physically and mentally as a man almost broke the seat next to me as he sat down carelessly.

'Oh shit. I'll be damned!' The man said, shaking his head. It was Larry, disguised by his baseball cap, and squeezed in very tightly next to Joey, who was not glad to see him.

*

Franks put the phone down and mulled over the message he had just read. Southampton. He shook his head; he couldn't see Joey doing so well on a boat and he wished he was ten years younger and that he too had been conscripted. After the excitement and devastation of the past few days, he was now very bored and had nothing except the rations, his empty rental flat and the constant repetition from the old television set.

'Thanks Ian, yes video has come in from the Royal Navy of a battle in the channel, details are still sketchy but my sources tell me that the extra-terrestrial force was trying to land here earlier today, perhaps to gain a strategic base for further operations. A battle followed with one of our newest Destroyers; the H.M.S. Freedom, where this video was recorded.' A reporter explained.

171

A video played on the screen, the picture bumped up and down and the focus kept varying. It showed a massive cigar shaped craft, easily the length of a football pitch, firing streaks of white and blue light that lit the dawn sky toward the powerful ship. The aircraft moved quickly for its size, dodging return fire from the ship.

Then a huge explosion hit the centre of the unidentified aircraft and it deviated from its course, seemingly losing control before crashing into the sea where further explosions and a parting of the waves could eventually be seen. The video cut to seamen on the ship cheering, jumping up and down and hugging each other at this glorious victory. There were not many of them.

'As you can see there our Navy has downed a massive invading aircraft. We await official comment from the Ministry of Defence but it seems there is some hope today after the devastating attack on Manchester yesterday.'

Franks shook his head slightly, having flown for the United States Navy, he knew very well that video was propaganda, for more than one reason. He picked up his phone, which was receiving several notifications; Joey had signed him into the only working social media site as a parting gift. Franks wished he hadn't as he started to read and watch. The video was already trending with hashtags such as "#E.T. Down" and "#wegotem."

He knew any good news today meant it would get twice as bad tomorrow, like an abusive relationship; they reel you in with good news just to soften the blow of what's to come.

For a moment, he wondered how things could get any worse, until he remembered Joey's explanation of the future the other evening: A world without family, choice or love. Where humans became robots; slaves to time and the Freegov, in order to save them from the supposed alien threat. The monotony only tempered by a virtual world where total freedom existed to maintain compliance.

Franks considered what it would be like to have everything given to you; to not have to pay for anything. It didn't take long for him to realise that it would mean you no longer have any choice. If you don't do as you're told, you die. And all in the name of saving the world from this alien threat so you can one day get back your freedom.

He could see similarities with the current system and the Lifepass; it was an extension of the welfare system; destroy the economy making people reliant on the government, then gradually introduce conditions forcing people to comply or be penalised and eventually die.

It all added up now. Technology controls humans and the government controls technology with help from the media. As technology renders humans useless and therefore they offer less economic benefit to the government, so democracy becomes dictatorship and humanity faces extermination.

Glancing slowly between a tin of beans, another of tomato soup and finally a packet of rice Franks decided to skip dinner. He picked up his phone and placed a call to his elder brother, Chip, in the United States. Surprisingly the tone rang through as normal, but after a while Franks began to lose hope of it being answered.

'Howdy bro!' a distant voice said as Franks was about to disconnect.

'Is everyone okay there?' Franks asked, his voice breaking slightly as he realised how late his call was.

'We're just fine, San Francisco wasn't hit, only Washington and New York. I saw London took a direct hit, you okay there buddy?' Chip asked.

'I'm okay, my flat was damaged but I'm in the rental. Listen I got something I want you to take a look at, remember the secure email we had set up? Check it out in a couple of hours. Over and out.' Franks said and hung up. The whole call was completed in under a minute.

Franks headed out to the small garden where he had left the aircraft part to soak in and old container with some solvent. He was pleasantly surprised with the results. Back in the kitchen he placed the part on a piece of paper with a pencil next to it to reference the size then took pictures back and front, plan and elevation and a close up of a number that had been revealed by the solvent. His mind was still hazy after the Fall but he was certain the crashed plane was an Airbus A320, so why would it have left a part from Boeing onboard, unless it was part of the secretive Uninterruptable Autopilot system. A few clicks later the message was sent. All hail neutron mail. Franks pulled out his secret bottle and toasted his brother. Here's hoping him and his military buddies would be able to shed some light on the mystery part.

173

*

The bus engine rumbled into life shortly after Larry's arrival. The air conditioning welcome in the stuffy full vehicle. Larry looked uncomfortable.

'You were right,' he said.

'And you fucked it all up. For money. I hope it was worth it.' Joey replied.

'The plane smashed up my pub, why didn't they stop her? Why?' Larry continued.

· 'They are all in on it, your call gave them the lead on me, and they allowed it to happen,' Joey continued.

'Shit, I didn't know,' he replied and dropped his head, 'It's evil. No doubt,' he continued, 'bastards, the lot of 'em, at least we are in the clear right,' changing the topic masterfully as he glanced toward the que for the tests as we drove past.

'You noticed; everyone on the right failed and everyone on the left got through?' Joey murmured.

'I filmed it.' Larry said, holding up his phone, looking angry.

'I've seen no aliens, the only murders I've seen have been carried out by our own forces,' Joey replied, then signalled to Larry to lower his voice by putting a finger to his mouth.

'So, it's all fake, the lot of it. We've got to warn people.' He argued.

'Think about it, modern warfare is all about technology, especially if we are fighting aliens. What good is conscripting twenty million men? What are we going to fight them with, our fists? It's the perfect excuse to get rid of us all.' Joey continued. The conversation came to an end when some television screens at the front, middle and rear of the bus flickered into action.

'Conscripts. Pay attention,' a voice boomed over the loudspeaker.

The bus quietened. A poor-quality video showed a large cigar shaped aircraft, presumably alien, taking fire then exploding and crashing into the sea. The video repeated and the national anthem played.

'We've downed our first enemy ship, now sing after me,' the voice continued.

Some of the men around me started singing the national anthem in various awful tones while cans of beer were passed backward from the front of the bus in a well-coordinated manoeuvre. Joey took one and pretended to swig, spilling a lot of it on the floor accidently. He wasn't playing their game, Larry took out his phone and started recording Joey.

'What did you see at the airbase Joey?' he asked.

'The U.N. troops killed everyone who failed the tests and massacred anyone who ran away.' Joey replied. He stopped recording then started pressing buttons franticly. He was beginning to pay back his debt. Then Larry made his way around the bus undetected by the Officer at the front; beer delivery his cover. At each chair he squatted, pulled out his phone then pressed a few buttons, presumably with some convincing words and a nod and a glance back toward Joey. I had no idea what he was telling them, but I saw warmth in their eyes, not fear.

'I'll get this out to socials, you know any of our troops?' Larry said as he bundled into the seat next to me a half an hour later.

'No, well err, I met one the other day, but I don't have his number.' Joey replied.

'We need them onside, do whatever you can, we have support here. Some guys are passing it on to their mates on other busses.' Larry said.

Was this the start of a technological revolution Joey thought?

'Okay.' Joey said, looking out toward the vast sea. Perhaps there was hope.

The bus came to a halt in the large port. A sign indicated they had reached Southampton. Dusk was setting in, the sky glowed deep oranges and pink behind the wispy grey clouds set around the fading blues.

Directly in front of the bus a group of uniformed men stood around some bollards and fold out desks, beyond them two massive cruise ships with multiple floors and bright colours emblazoned on their sides. Funnily enough, the conscripts didn't have that holiday feeling as an Officer at the front looked nervously around the bus as the men began to rise.

Men swarmed off the bus over the sounds of the Officer on the loudspeaker, humans that survived 8 million years without constant nannying didn't need to be disembarked row by row. A que formed ahead of the improvised checkpoint, Joey felt eyes looking toward him but he knew this wasn't the time. He looked up at the huge ship nearest them, it must have been fifty metres high with endless decks; an awesome sight.

A movement at the far end of the ship caught his eye, it was a huge orange lifeboat being lowered carefully into a harness on the dock. He looked along the ship back toward the bus; all the other lifeboat housings were empty. On a scale of one to ten for bad omens; this got a ten. Nobody else seemed to notice and Joey had managed to get separated from Larry; turning back briefly he failed to spot him in the rabble of men shuffling toward the great ships.

The que moved quickly; when he reached the front, it became obvious why. First, there was a desk manned by U.K.S.F. troops.

'Follow the line,' a troop ordered over and over as the conscripts approached.

'You know they are murdering civilians in London; will you do that?' Joey asked the troop as he dropped to his knee to tie a shoelace.

'Follow the line.' The troop remained stoic, Joey moved on.

Joey found it strange that there was no search of his belongings, uniforms handed out nor instructions or orders given. Beyond the checkpoint there were two large steel turnstiles, one of which was in use the other had troops standing in front of it. They wore blue and white uniforms, with a logo he had seen somewhere before. They were armed with automatic weapons. As he got closer, he recognised the logo as a flattened world map, labels stuck on their shoulders said United Nations Peacekeepers. *Oh, the irony*.

Joey turned to see the lucky bus leaving and another taking its parking place, it said bus fourteen on the front; men started to emerge as he had done a few minutes ago. A conveyor belt of men progressing toward the abyss. Joey wondered how many more busses the ship could take, and how many were already on her.

The U.N. troops waved them through without a word. As they got closer to the ship, Joey noticed that the area where a name would normally be painted on the hull had been freshly painted over, disguising the identity of the great liner. It was not a good job, and he could make out a, "C," underneath the fresh paint which stood out from the old paint on the rest of the ship. Another que formed up ahead at the gangway, Joey slowed a little, still looking up, trying to take in every detail of his new home. Suddenly, he lost his balance and felt pain; then dizziness, then nothing.

Chapter 37
2050, Capital City

The small jet engine plane touched down with a bump just before sunset. The grass and shrubs that covered the disused runway, in the shadows of the mountains, remained flat enough for the jet to come to a halt eventually with its landing gear intact.

Daria checked her pockets and zipped up her suit as the pilot bot made his landing announcement. A new lease of life, she bounded out of the plane and made for the cover of some nearby trees. Safely under cover, she checked the device; a red dot flashed on the screen approximately three kilometres away. She laughed and broke into a light jog. *This idiot had led her right to him.*

To her right, the lights of the Capital reflected into the night sky. She thought briefly about Pablo. She didn't miss him or her dead-end life there; she trained to get what she wanted, now she had. She jogged on; thinking ahead now, this was a chance to end this chapter and they'd given it to her alone. Perhaps she'd get her own settlement or codename. She could be the face of Mother…a daughter to lead them into the next century and their next more ambitious, conquest.

Her mind ran away with visions of glory and time seemed to blur; before she knew it, she was approaching two dark buildings toward the top of a mountain, one of which looked like a dwelling and was set slightly into the side of the hill.

She slowed for a moment, not bothering to take out her binoculars, and checked her device, she was on top of the red blinking dot. Slowly she walked towards the thick set wooden door on the first building, as she pulled it open a noise from behind distracted her and she turned her head to look back. She saw nothing. She continued, feeling like Goldilocks, as she explored the small wooden chalet. She found nothing in the two bedrooms, bathroom or kitchen so she left and sat on a bench in the courtyard; lighting up and taking a deep toxic pull. Then another noise and she felt something by her leg, she looked own to see a medium sized dog, squealing slightly and waggling its tail. She pulled out her silenced gun and shot it.

Half a yelp emerged from the doomed mutt as Daria got up and explored the outhouse. There was nothing but hay and a space for the animals at night. She checked her device again, shook it and moved around. The tracker was working fine. *Where was the stupid old git?*

She looked closer at the dead dog and noticed its paws were muddy; back inside the house now and she was thinking again, following the mud trial into one of the bedrooms and to the front of a massive wooden wardrobe.

Pulling on the door it creaked loudly, she continued, inside another door at the rear was closed, she opened it and squeezed through; weapon drawn. There was no need.

The old man was out cold; head on the desk, while the three banks of screens in front of him blinked with light. Daria started to read with interest when a message appeared, it was to Joey.

"Message received, beginning to trend. Let me know where you go from Southampton. Franks."

Daria's frown was even more crooked than her smile, a bead of sweat appeared on her brow as she began to read more and punch buttons aggressively. There were other messages there too, it seemed like Scales was intercepting Joey's messages and somehow even communicating directly with him, in the past.

"Keep me informed, Scales." Several thoughts pulsed through her mind as she looked the helpless old man up and down. She slapped him so hard that he jumped up from his stool and screamed aloud.

'Welcome Daria, you finally arrived, but you're too late.' Scales said, breaking into a broad smile, before continuing, 'Joey is in 2030, to stop the Lifechip.'

A loud snap echoed in the small room. Scales screamed.

'Fake invasion, fake test; stupid sheep. Nothing can stop the Lifechip.' She declared, taking hold of his other arm.

He laughed. She pulled out her gun and shot him in the foot.

'Torturing an old man, what a hero you will be, you might even get a city named after yo…' Scales stopped short as Daria raised her weapon, he hit send just before the bullet exploded in his head. Then another and another.

Daria stamped her foot and dragged Scales out of the small room, bumping and breaking him unnecessarily as she reversed awkwardly out of the wardrobe then flung him onto the bed. Heart thumping, she retraced her steps and stared at the bank of screens with wild eyes.

*

In a small room in a different time and space, Franks added the hashtag "the real enemy" and hit send on the freshly made recording, launching the message far and wide for its interpretation.

Chapter 38
2030, Southampton

Joey regained consciousness on a hard slab of metal, looking down to his left he noticed that he was actually on a table with legs and wheels. Directly above a bright light, pointing at his head, blinded him. To the right, he was relieved to see the wax jacket Franks had given him slung over a chair.

He sat up and saw himself in the mirror, an even larger white bandage covered the top of his head, blood stained his white shirt. As he was about to get up a young man entered the room in a hurry.

'You're lucky sir; they thought you were dead, that's why they let me take you,' the thin framed man said excitedly.

'What happened?' Joey asked, as he felt his head begin to throb.

'You tripped over my foot and banged your head on a cleat, Ships porter, at your service sir. I did the best I could,' the man explained, pointing to the bandage.

'Thanks, I'd better get going,' Joey replied, looking down at his untied laces.

'I don't recommend that sir, they are floating death-traps, not sailed for years. The foreign bastards even took the lifeboats off; saving space they say; bastards. No man getting on that ship will ever come back,' he continued.

The small man was waving his arms as he spoke. Joey felt the truth in his words, the passion in his warning.

'I've got to get on that ship, how long was I out for?' Joey asked, doing up his boots slowly; it seemed a long way down, perhaps he was concussed.

'A good half hour sir. They are still loading, been at it hours now. It's dark, I can get you on if you insist,' he suggested.

'Who is in charge here?' I asked.

'New lot, in the blue uniform's sir. Arrived last week they did,' he explained.

Joey looked to the heavens as he made for the door; *everything was planned.*

'No, no sir, you get in there,' the porter exclaimed. He stopped me and pointed to a large wooden box on a trolley, marked "Supplies," in bold black lettering.

Reluctantly Joey squeezed inside; as the lid closed he coughed, realised there was very little air and hoped for a quick journey. The movement set him off balance and he hit the side of the box, he imagined the cobbled, uneven surface below as he tried in vain to protect his head from further damage. It was no use, then the trolley stopped and he heard the porter speak.

'Special rations, Captains orders sir,' he said, confidently.

'On you go,' a deep, heavily accented voice replied.

Joey felt an incline and the speed slowed, there were no more bumps. He imagined a smooth, wooden gangplank below him. Then a large bump knocked him upward into the top of the box, he cursed silently and wished for release. Seconds later, a door squeaked open and the movement stopped. He heard the sound of nails being removed then felt air, light...relief!

'Here you are sir, all the best,' he said then walked away exiting the room.

Gaining his bearings quickly, Joey reached for his phone and caught up with the porter on the deck.

'Wait, here pass this on to everyone you know.' Joey said, waving the device to indicate a transfer. He forwarded the video from Franks and his message from Scales and finally the video of Daria killing Scales.

The porter looked down at his screen and played the clips. He smiled then tapped a large white steel cradle on the wall to their left.

'Almost forgot sir, life rafts. Only enough for the officers,' he said.

With that the porter left; an angel exiting the entrance to hell.

Chapter 39
2030, London

'N.A.A.T. National Anti-Alien Testing to start today for all citizens.'

Franks shook his head as he listened to the news headline. *Not if I can help it.* It reminded him of the testing fiasco during the recent pandemics. He had read an informative commentary on the events somewhere. He pulled out his phone and after confirming there was no reply from his brother he retrieved the email he had sent himself and began to read:

"Millions of people were told they were sick after taking a test given to them by their governments even though they had no symptoms of illness. For the first time in history, symptomless people believed they could infect and kill each other, because their government told them. This allowed governments to shut down most of the world for months on end, over several periods lasting several years. The second virus was deadlier than the first; it spread globally overnight; as if it were transmitted over a recently installed, high technology network. The response was more draconian and uniform because governments had signed over Pandemic control to the World Health Organisation (W.H.O.); allowing them to dictate lockdown policy centrally.

Analysis of the W.H.O.'s funding showed that the same people control their main donor organisations as well as the think tanks that advise governments on the vaccines that were introduced to stop the viruses. It was like putting the wolf in charge of the sheep's pen.

The "Lockdowns" ruined economies and small businesses leaving millions of people financially dependent on their governments to survive. At the same time the economy became more automated and skewed towards massive multinational corporations, many of whom, via global investment funds, were in league with the very same politicians and governments who ordered the lockdowns in the first place. Government had been corporatized; and therefore compromised. With this scam they were able to profit financially from fear related to health.

With the benefit of hindsight, it seemed like the whole event was planned as a power grab by a privileged few to the detriment of the masses. Despite reams of information and evidence being reviewed during numerous public enquiries, around the world, the aftermath was never really resolved. Officially, nobody was to blame for the wholesale change in the worlds systems, economy and outlook. Nobody investigated the overbearing influence of the press and media on the mental state of the public; perhaps because it suited the governments and their corporate overlords to have total control.

A class of scared and sick humans had been created who relied on the state for their bread and butter. What they did not realise was that with advances in technology and Artificial Intelligence they had become surplus to the requirements of the state and therefore were far less important than they once had been for its survival. A cynic would say that the ongoing economic, environmental and security issues that plagued the world since the virus outbreaks were a clever way to distract people from what in essence was an outrageous power grab, both economically and politically as governments became more authoritarian in the name of public safety with the introduction of movement restrictions depending on people's health status. This was administered via government applications on people's mobile phones which eventually morphed into the Lifepass. A massive data grab that became a draconian social engineering tool implemented through a combination of fear and coercion. The type of activities that criminals are jailed for, yet the holier than though politicians and big pharma executives facilitated this with not one comeback, sentence or even dismissal.

The power grab even stretched to the physical body; humans gave up their genetic codes via the tests that most of them were coerced into taking where before you were only required to do this had you landed on the wrong side of the long arm of the law. Finally, experimental injections, labelled vaccines, were given emergency authorisation that they had never come close to achieving before due to their unacceptable side effects."

Hoping people wouldn't fall for it this time Franks tuned into his social media where a trending hashtag war was emerging between #scamtests and #testmenow. Many were starting to discuss Scales brutal death, speculating on who Daria worked for and why no Extra-terrestrials had actually been seen during the invasion.

*

Without knowing where Larry was on board, Joey decided he would have to continue the social media campaign himself. He pulled out his phone and recorded the spaces where the lifeboats should be with a voiceover explaining what the porter told him and that every conscript on this ship had passed the Anti-Alien Test. He sent it to Franks, the new tech man, and considered Scales' death.

It was all thanks to Scales sacrifice, but he had invented the bloody thing. What goes around comes around they say. If you start messing with things that shouldn't be messed with there will always be people who want to use it for their own, evil, purposes.

After checking out the ship for about an hour Joey found an empty cabin and made himself comfortable. It was on the same floor as the life rafts, having decided to ignore the handwritten signs directing conscripts to the; "luxury cabins on lower decks," that were placed seemingly everywhere he looked. Conscripts were wondering around freely, there weren't many crew or soldiers at all. There were no weapons either. Something didn't add up.

A loud clunking sound rose up the frame from the depths below followed by the continuous drone of the ship's engines, Joey shifted on the bed; it was still dark outside, his phone said 4 a.m. From the porthole he noticed activity down below. The landing ropes were being untied from their bollards by a couple of troops in blue uniforms. I couldn't see the porter who saved me.

He must have drifted off when a loud, long blast from the ships horn woke him up abruptly. He opened his eyes and looked up then out the porthole to the right, the motion of the sea confused him. *Where was he?* He saw choppy blue sea then remembered it all. A voice over the ships tannoy system invited all conscripts to attend the nearest restaurant for breakfast immediately.

He got up and splashed water over his face at the sink in the tiny, dilapidated bathroom. Maybe he had chosen a crew cabin. It smelled foul and he remembered the porters warning that the ship was old and hadn't sailed for years. The bandage was still in place, the bloodstain the same size. He turned on my phone, there was no signal, it was 11 a.m. He looked outside again and could see only blue. No land in sight. No spaceships either.

The hum of excitement in the corridors quickly turned to murmurs of discontent upon arrival in the restaurant areas. There was a buffet style canteen which the conscripts queued for and moved through. As they reached the serving area Joey understood why. The meal consisted of a bread roll, a banana, a cup of coffee and a tablet. There was some kind of conversation or barter going on at the end of the line.

'Iodine tablet first then rations. Full meal tonight at port,' a man in uniform behind the counter said repeatedly. Joey took the tablet, received a tray as recompense, then moved along. He spotted an empty area in the far corner of the room, turned towards the window and regurgitated the tablet into his hand, then his boot. Looking around it seemed he had gotten away with it.

'No, you don't. You, cheeky bugger,' a voice said from behind me. He turned expecting to see a uniform but instead saw a large unhealthy-looking man standing unnecessarily close to him.

'I saw you, you took two rolls, now give me that,' the man continued, while reaching for Joey's roll. Joey reacted fast pushing the roll onto the floor and stepping on it with his blood-stained boot.

'Go ahead, animal. Make my day,' Joey replied, standing up to reach the same height as him then staring coldly into his eyes.

The man wavered losing his balance, then collapsed into the seat opposite, looking distinctly unwell.

'I, I don't feel well,' he muttered, holding his stomach.

Before Joey could reply a loud alarm, tone started beeping over the tannoy system.

'Go back to your cabins, take cover, attack imminent,' a voice said.

Chaos ensued. Trays were sent flying, men shouted and swore, others ran, some stumbled and fell. Joey sat down again and watched his new friend get up, then sway towards the exit. There was a massive explosion sound from below. The voice on the tannoy kept repeating itself. The alarm grew louder and followed a pattern. The room was empty now so he got up and made his way toward the exit then up several floors to his cabin. He came across the odd straggler on the way but no soldiers, no crew.

Until he reached the cabin, where he found a hive of activity. He dived behind the door and into the bathroom, where he used an old toothbrush holder to smash the mirror and collect a piece no larger than a few centimetres wide. Opening the door slightly, he held the mirror up to see what was happening in the corridor behind. The life-rafts were being removed by soldiers and crew, their voices dulled by the incessant alarm signal, by now almost background noise.

The soldiers wore light coloured blue and white uniforms the crew a brown almost sand colour that matched Joey's trousers. Outside the sea looked as if it were bubbling around the hull and there was a lean to one side behind him. There wasn't much time. He opened the wardrobe, nothing. The drawers, nothing again. A small cupboard by the door was the last chance, there a yellow high visibility vest and an orange life jacket. There were some letters printed in black on the back of the high visibility jacket which he didn't have time to read. Scrambling into them, he ran down the corridor, all the life-rafts had gone so he followed it up to the deck, where a small group of crewmen stood around one of the empty lifeboat rigs. Others were being lowered down, two by two to a waiting life-raft. Joey blew the whistle attached to the life-jacket.

'What about the conscripts?' he shouted.

'Captains orders, sir abandon ship,' one replied, while another looked me up and down cautiously.

'What hit us?' Joey asked. The men moved away. A split-second choice.

It took minutes but felt like an age. The floor of the raft was wet and the sea a lot rougher than it looked. Joey was pleased to see no soldiers, only crew, in the raft as he made his way to a seat in the corner.

'Permission to leave, sir?' A voice said.

'Permission to leave sir?' The voice repeated this time with more urgency.

'Yes, navigate to nearest land,' Joey replied, not knowing what role he was playing in this tragic scene.

There was no talk as the life-raft accelerated away from the doomed vessel. Dark and wet. Joey lost track of time and space.

'Port of Amsterdam ahead sir,' the same voice said enthusiastically, sometime later.

Another man removed the overhead covers from the raft. In the distance Joey made out the stricken ships nose disappearing slowly into the choppy blue sea, he pulled out his phone and started recording.

'Now we go and do it all again Jim, where to next?' Another voice asked with a sigh.

'I've heard it's Harwich, Bob. They are infiltrated. It's for the best,' the robotic reply.

Chapter 40
2050, Capital City

The two rapid chimes coming from the middle bank of screens directly above Daria's head caused her to stir. Her long curly hair was all over the keyboard, looking down she saw blood on the floor then remembered quickly. *It was real.* The screen above her had intercepted a message and a video from Joey to Franks.

"In Amsterdam, suspect U.N. sabotaged the ship, check out the video." *That arsehole do-gooder was at it again. Fuck!* Daria let out a scream as she smashed her fist down onto the desk destroying a mouse. Before she had Joey, but Scales was still on the loose. Now Scales was out of the way but Joey was causing trouble. Someone was playing games with her and she didn't like it. She wanted all the glory; Joey, Scales and all his secrets. Instead of taking a deep breath and thinking things through rationally, Daria turned her attention to the bank of screens to her left. After turning them on, it didn't take her long to figure this was his time machine; there was even a green throne like chair behind a glass door in the corner.

The screens still had details of their last use; the top, origin screen; Amsterdam the middle; London; Joey's escape from the museum. Daria changed the information in the top screen to current location, and the middle, destination screen, to Amsterdam. On the bottom screen she filled in two dates; twenty years apart, selected one traveller and hit enter. The glass door in front of the throne like green chair slid open and a red button next to the chair illuminated. Daria made herself comfortable, the door shut automatically and she pressed the button.

Chapter 41
2030, Amsterdam

Joey's feet felt like lead as he got off the life-raft.

'Overnighting here, cruising back in the evening,' a troop on the dock said. He was dressed in white and blue uniform with identifiable U.N. tags. He pointed towards a white van with blue logo.

Amsterdam in the morning, deserted but for E.S.F.[18] and United Nations troops enforcing the curfew. On every corner and every crossing, they watched, weapons raised. A city under siege. For your protection. But from who? Nothing hit that ship, there was no attack. Only a cold callous plan to murder thousands of conscripts, in whose name?

Nobody talked, men contemplating their crimes; just following orders. The van pulled up to a six story, relatively narrow hotel in the centre of the city. Undressed; Joey finally understood the reverence the crew on the raft held him in. The life jacket and high visibility vest both had, "Third Officer," printed in large black capital letters on the back. He turned on the shower and looked over to the sink, where he had put Cara's cross, its jewels glimmered in the artificial light. Perhaps that was the answer.

Joey paused for a moment in front of the mirror and thought; he lost Cara then couldn't find Daria, now death was following him around like a bad smell. He didn't ask for this, he wasn't going to get back on another ship controlled by psychopaths; he was sure of that. He needed a way out, a way that they wouldn't come looking.

The small windowless room became misty with a hint of lavender; a brief respite from reality as he entered the cubicle. He thought back to the thousands of men on the boat, silently taken by the freezing water; thanks to the actions of men physically no different to themselves; only protected by the buffer of authority. Was it just lame obedience or something more sinister? He shouted loudly, punching the tiled wall hard. It remained in place. "It's for the best," the words of the officer echoed in his mind. No, it's not you selfish, stupid cunt. You might think it is now, but what happens when they turn on you? Will it be for the best then?

---

[18] European Security Force; merger of army and police. European equivalent of the U.K.S.F.

"It's for your health." "Just a few more years and you will be free;" corrupt, occupied governments. This one was just as bad as Freegov. He could see the future now; terrified people begging to be saved from infiltration, but a few dissenting voices. When enough people had been murdered the dissent would be no more and the United Nations would offer up a deal too good to refuse. A microchip fitted inside everyone to ensure that they could not be infiltrated; it was the only way to be certain, to have your body permanently monitored, fused with technology. A human robot. A new government would provide everything required; food, shelter and warmth in return for work. As a sweetener the microchip would allow free access to a virtual reality world of entertainment. It might take a few years but eventually the people would beg for it. There would also be a promise of returning to the old normal as a carrot at the end of a continually extending stick, never to be reached.

There was blood on his fist as he exited the shower. Through the mist in the steamy mirror he saw his outline but what was inside? Had he become like them, just following orders? He didn't need to be in this place anymore, knowing its secrets. Suddenly he thought of Cara, not a vision, just a memory; her full lips, soft skin. Her innocence. He could find her and explain their future. Maybe the 2030 version of her would accept him, after all he knew her secrets.

Chapter 42
2030, London

That morning Franks woke to messages from Joey, nearly choking on his coffee as he watched the ship sinking over and over. Those things could hold thousands. He felt sick as he followed the steps to post the video online, he was becoming quite an expert. But his account wouldn't open, no matter how many times he tried, frowning he turned on the news expectantly just in time for the early morning headlines.

"Mass testing success as quarantine camps fill."

"Missile Defence Shields activated in major cities."

"Trending Assassin video identified as fake news."

The newscaster went on to give more detail. Half the population had been tested and those who failed would be held in quarantine camps until a permanent solution was found.

The government saw this as a success and announced everyone would be tested by the end of the week.

The government announced a long-term plan to move advanced missile defence technology, linked to satellites, into the U.K.'s four largest cities in order to prevent another Manchester. They would provide free transport and accommodation for anyone who wanted to move into the cities.

Finally, they crossed to their Genuine Truth Correspondent, Mary-Ella Brook, for a special report.

'Welcome to the outskirts of Geneva, France where an investigation is underway today after a shocking video that was posted yesterday went viral. In it a scientist, supposedly from the future, casts doubt on the invasion and claims that it has been staged to scare humans into accepting a microchip. He is then brutally murdered by an unknown female assassin. Having spoken with the authorities here, who have identified the location the video was filmed, I can reveal that it is in fact a fake video. The security services are working on the theory that the video's poster is either an alien commander or an anti-denier whose aim is to sew discontent and discourage people from life-saving technology. The account that posted the video has been blocked and people are being advised to not to spread the content and report anyone who does. I have managed to get an interview with the unwitting star of the video, Dr Scales, a scientist who currently lives here in Geneva.'

The screen cut to a man in a white Scientist coat who looked a little like Scales.

'Dr. Scales, welcome. To confirm were you a part of this video and did you have any knowledge of it?' Mary-Ella asked.

'No Madame,' he replied.

'And what is your current role?' She asked.

'I am working on a neuro-link to help people gain control of troublesome aspects of their minds.' He replied.

'And have you ever seen this farmhouse before?' she continued.

'Yes, it belongs to a friend of mine, I come here to eat sometimes.' He replied.

'Thank-you Doctor. And there we have it: proof, that the viral video is a fake. We can but conclude that the aliens are so fearful that we will develop technology to resist their infiltration that they are already resorting to these tactics only days into their evil invasion.'

'*Now I've really heard it all!*' Franks thought, with a smile as he got up from the sofa.
'*Alien Commander! Left is right. Everything is inverted,*' He laughed again at the ridiculous messages coming from the screen in front of him, heading to the kitchen he made a start on breakfast and wondered what the anti-alien test today would be like.

As he did his phone chimed, and he opened the secure email site to a message from his brother.

"This is part of the Boeing Uninterruptable Auto Pilot system and the engineer I showed it to thinks this one has been activated. Considering that and the jet that went down in London was an A320, I'd say this is a smoking gun. I've sent the photos for further tests to confirm but that will take a while. Chip."

Franks dropped an egg as he read the message over. It quickly dawned on him that he might be in danger if they could trace his account. He called Joey; there was no answer. After donning his regular baseball hat, he set out for his test a little early. As he walked up toward the main road he heard noises that sounded like a crowd cheering and chanting, unperturbed he continued. At the main road he was surprised to see a U.K.S.F. 4x4 vehicle unmanned in the middle of the road, as if it had been abandoned in a hurry. Approaching the small, park, which had become the local headquarters for emergency operations, he saw a group of maybe fifty people, standing opposite the line for the tests, which was still orderly. Franks noticed there were no military troops, only U.K.S.F.

The group were chanting 'Scales was right' over and over. It seemed a counter-protest group had formed opposite them, with fewer people, holding banners saying, "we want the chip," and, "save us from E.T!" Franks interest peaked, he headed toward the larger group and struck up a conversation.

'Hey what's going on?' he asked a small vocal lady at the front. As she was about to respond he felt an arm on his shoulder and he was pulled back. Turning he recognised Jones, the conscientious U.K.S.F. troop, who led him away from the action.

'They think they've found the assassin from the video, only she's twenty years younger. I know that video was posted from your phone, there's an apprehend at all costs notice out for you.' Jones explained. Without thinking Franks got out his phone and showed the latest message and video from Joey of the ship sinking.

'Look, I don't know how involved you guys are but the U.N. are massacring civilians.
This is outrageous.' Franks replied.

Jones watched it a couple of times without speaking.

'Who is Joey?' he eventually asked seeing the message sender.

'My friend from the future, we were trying to stop her, the assassin, but we failed. Where is she?' Franks asked.

'She's dead. Found collapsed in a road, but she had a bag with some stuff in it that these guys opened. Passports, a weapon, two phones, a walkie talkie and landing charts for Heathrow Airport.' Jones replied.

'Sounds about right, she was responsible for the Fall, its nothing to do with aliens. Her organisation crashed those planes into the ground by remote control. Now everyone is running around scared while the world government commits genocide. And the solution, after the fake tests, will be to get fitted with the Lifechip, just like the video shows.' Franks said.

'Can you prove that?' Jones asked, his face several shades paler than when the conversation started.

'I'm working on it. Can you pass this on, my social media access is blocked. There's more of us than there are of them.' Franks said, then sent the message and video from Joey to Jones.

'Stay left for the tests, I'll be in touch.' Jones said. Franks joined the que, keeping to the left he secured a negative result then moved quickly down the back roads toward his flat. As he closed the door he remembered something Joey had said; when you travel back in time the younger version of you dies…the U.K.S.F. finding young Daria meant Joey was in danger.

Chapter 43
2030, Amsterdam

Daria laughed as she smashed her way carelessly through the Museums front door, with a figure of a bust she had removed from a display case. It was much nicer in 2030, she thought, rounding the corner where her colleague had shot Cara twenty years later. Joey was in her sights now, once and for all, she just needed to find that pathetic fools' hideout, which shouldn't be hard. She'd always had the tools to get what she wanted, especially from men. This would be easy.

Indeed, she was so focussed on Joey, she failed to notice the E.S.F. vehicle slowly following from a distance as she walked along the deserted streets toward Vondel Park. Alerted by the silent alarm from the museum, they had set up a tail and now followed on to see where the unusually dressed intruder was going.

A city on lockdown left few transport options, however Amsterdam had one thing in abundance; bicycles. Daria found one with a weak lock and was on her way, the E.S.F. were now more interested since receiving notification from the monitoring team who had reviewed the C.C.T.V. from the museum and reported the intruder had literally appeared out of thin air in the library on the third floor. A more organised surveillance group was now in place around their target, some on foot others in vehicles.

The tech team at headquarters in Brussels, who had been tasked with identifying Daria, were making scant headway; the facial recognition was a dead end, literally, as it pointed to a woman who died the day before in the U.K. That was until the media monitoring crew made a shocking discovery. Daria was trending on social media as the assassin who killed Scales, who himself was fast becoming a people's hero during these uncertain times.

For her part, Daria was still unaware she had company, whether it was sheer pig headedness or the number of live pills she had consumed in America South, she remained focussed on Joey alone. Her training had gone out the window. She had a picture of him which she stopped and showed to a group of people queuing for rations at a supermarket. Their blank faces indicated she was looking for a needle in a haystack. Suddenly a penny dropped and she decided to change tactics and head for the port.

When she arrived, there wasn't much going on, she stopped and observed a group of porters moving crates and items around on trolleys. A security guard was sat in a box by a barrier. She approached and noted he was older and his eyebrows raised as he lay eyes on her, she flicked her hair back and smiled. She could tell from his initial reaction that he hadn't seen Joey; but she needed to get in.

The E.S.F. troops watched on as Daria removed a small shiny item from her shoe and handed it to the guard. The barrier opened and she walked through. They set up watch above a stack of huge shipping containers that surrounded the port.

She approached two young porters in high visibility vests.

'I'm with the services, this man is highly dangerous, we believe he has been infiltrated. I need to find him, fast.' She said, showing Joey's picture. The porters stopped and stared as if they had never seen Joey or a woman before.

'Never seen him Miss.' One of them replied.

'Me too.' Said the other.

'Has anyone come ashore today, or yesterday?' she asked.

'Yes, the crew from the sunken ship.' The first porter replied.

'And where are they now?' she asked.

'Don't know, they are due back at this evening though,' the other replied. Daria looked around causing the E.S.F. team on the top of the container to drop down flat, they had become cocky and were trying to eavesdrop her conversation. She spotted a shelter with a bench, made her way over to it and lit up.

Chapter 44
2030, London

Franks; elated and fed up at the same time, he had tried and failed to get hold of Joey to warn him, and there was no contact from Jones or his brother. For now, he was impotent. The television it was.

The science correspondent, was on again, she must be earning overtime, Franks thought as he admired her dress until she began to speak in a harsh, accented tone.

'Scientists have made a breakthrough advance in anti-alien chip technology. Experiments have been conducted in a secret location to determine if implanted microchips can protect and monitor humans from alien infiltration. Early results are positive and the government is carrying out further tests on those who have been infiltrated in the quarantine camps. Volunteers are being sought who have tested negative in order to monitor exposure and transmission levels with the new devices.'

Then the screen switched back to the studio presenter who explained that they were now going live to their roving reporter, at a testing station in Birmingham for further opinion.

'Yes, welcome to the testing station where the first N.A.A.T.[19] tests for today will be getting underway shortly. I'm here with Jill and her daughter. Now what do you think of the news that a microchip could stop and maybe even remove alien infiltration?' The reporter asked.

'I think it's good news.' Jill, a large woman with ginger hair, said looking slightly nervous.

'And what about having a chip in your body, people are traditionally against that idea. Would you mind that?' The reporter asked, his boyish good looks and expensive suit giving him an air of trustworthiness.

'Well I...I'd rather a chip than an alien, especially if it can bring back everyone from quarantine.' Jill said slowly. She seemed distracted by something below her at first before moving her eyes up to the camera mid-way through her sentence.

---

[19] National Anti-Alien Test, introduced at Warp-speed by governments around the world following the Fall, 2030.

'And what about you, young lady, what do you think?' He asked, as the camera man panned to a small girl with curly black hair, no more than nine years old, wearing a bright pink tracksuit.

'I think that a chips is a good idea and we should all be given one by the governer. I like chips.' The girl replied. She looked nothing like her mother and spoke slowly as if she had been rehearsing all night.

'Well there you have it, thumbs up for chips, now back to the studio,' the reporter said, smiling unnervingly at the camera.

Franks sighed and turned down the volume. As he walked out toward his garden he caught sight of Joey's cigarette box by the door.

Franks had never smoked, but he wanted one now, there was something wrong with that report; it was aimed at the masses and featured basic language and everyday people that were easy to identify with. The "working class" were the largest group numerically therefore the one with the most power, but also the one historically subject to endless propaganda and social engineering to ensure the seed of revolution never saw daylight.

A hundred miles or so to the north none of the other television viewers saw the boyish man in the expensive suit nod to his camera crew, who then began to unload bag after bag of food into the ginger haired ladies flat. Nor did they see the child holding her hand discard a piece of paper with a line typed on it onto the grass nonchalantly.

Chapter 45
2030, Amsterdam

Joey woke on his front with a damp pillow wedged awkwardly under his face. He struggled under the tight sheet then pushed the cover away onto the floor. He could see their anguished expressions now; hear their feint screams as the water furiously replaced the air around them. Taking their last breath before their bodies were strewn around like a cruel child's rag doll. He sat up and took a gulp of water, a deep breath. What it would be like to suffocate? Torture. At least those poor souls could find peace now, away from the polluted air and the devil it relentlessly transported into their minds.

His phone kept buzzing, he wondered what bad news it could bring next, so let it be. Nothing mattered anymore. They could stick their conscription and their ghostly voyages where the sun didn't shine. He wasn't going to follow orders anymore. He'd make a record of all this, so their deaths might mean something. Finding a pen and paper in the drawer he began to write.

"It was a good a point to start as any; reality. We each have our own and we are all different, but how far can our realities be affected by the messages we receive and the environment we inhabit? Irving's death on the monorail, witnessed by myself and Cara, became something far more gruesome; fitting well with Freegovs narrative a few hours later. The power of the message amplified by the singular dominant transmission format, i.e. the respect and remember broadcast. The altered facts, based on the truth; became reality for the survivors. Perhaps this is how it worked; reality an altered truth determined by the dominant messenger. Is our reality a lie? Could a similar illusion be underway here in 2030? Could it have been underway since time began, whenever they say that was.

By 2050, survivors are no longer different after they have given away their bodies and become human robots. The political system works perfectly because there is no need to trick anyone anymore with promises of Democracy or free speech. There is no voting or elections because there is only one government; the Freegov, which is nothing of the sort. However, it still relies on the human desires and wants in the form of Freetime V.R. in order to maintain compliance, a tacit acknowledgement that numbers still trump technology.

In 2030 freedom has become fascism disguised by multicoloured flags held up by smiling pixelated avatars; with no idea those flags are tightly wrapped around the eyes of their human counterparts. Who are these evil messengers? Dancing through the air… An invisible army hidden in the clouds; allowed in beyond our defences to destroy us from within.

In 2030, the herd follow a dark path. If only they could see that they are being led a deadly dance toward their own downfall. The modern-day pied piper, staring down at his digitized palm, a legion of likes following him around. His altered reality becoming their everything. The herd, still human but so easy to control through a combination of technology and psychology that has been utilised by corporations, governments and media in a trident like attack on its livestock; utilising their own data unwittingly given away. The years of transition saw coordinated Global events that combined to remove the last bastions of freedom and pillars of hope. Terror, Pandemics, War, Energy, Climate and financial crises morphed into one another from day to day. Reality controlled by the dark messenger.

It's a wonder any government official had the cheek to stand up and say anything considering the state they had left the world in by 2030. Any sane person would say: 'sack the lot of them- they failed miserably.' But by then the sane were insane, labelled as anti-deniers and brutally silenced by the three-pronged attack. And the insane; sane. Given high messenger status, platform and loudspeaker, to further the plot as they grazed the pastures.

Maybe that was one of the reasons politicians were wiped out in the flood and the G7 attack; they had served their chaotic purpose and their masters had reached the next stage. And that goes for the multinational corporates; their economies of scale made obscene profits thanks to globalisation. Their smarmy overpaid C.E.O.'s, experts in word-soup who spout vocabulary that nobody understands about sustainable development goals. Resource management is really resource theft. Everything inverted."

The phone buzzed and Joey picked it up without thinking.

'Joey at last, you alright?' Franks asked.

'There's nothing left.' he replied despondently.

'People are saying Scales was right! It's spreading, you have to keep going!' Franks said.

'Really?' Joey asked, standing up he drew the heavy curtains, light flooded in illuminating the tiny dust particles in the air around him.

'Yes. I sent your video from the ship to the U.K.S.F. guy, Jones. If they stop taking orders, there is hope.' Franks said, before continuing, 'Watch out; Daria came back too, its likely she knows where you are.'

'What? Okay, speak soon.' Joey slammed the phone down, no time to lose. It was early afternoon now; his stomach rumbled in anticipation of the energy it required.

Looking for his boots something under the door caught Joey's eye. It was an envelope; inside a hand-written note asking if he would be willing to give a paid interview for U.K. News about the sinking of the, *"Carnival Illusion." How appropriate.* Another note from the hotel informed him the pick-up for today's journey was 6 p.m. That should give him enough time before they started searching. His hand didn't feel too bad as he pulled up his trousers and splashed some water over his head. He'd kill her with his bare hands.

Chapter 46
2030, Amsterdam

Daria jumped as the huge cruise ship basted its horn. She looked over and saw it being guided in slowly by two strategically placed tugs. It was approaching 3 p.m. Not much longer and that idiot would present himself for duty. His final duty.

She lit up another smoke and watched the vessel carefully come to a halt in front of her; only for a hive of activity to break out as porters secured the moorings and began carefully loading crates, some were marked fragile. Others boarded and began to work on the lifeboats; a massive flatbed truck pulled up behind some containers and the first lifeboat was lowered, via its own winch system into a cradle on the port, then driven by a small motorized pick up to the flatbed, which then drove away. The process repeated.

Over to her right she observed a small white van approaching. The word, "Press," was painted on its sides in black letters and there were two dishes on its roof. It stopped briefly at the security gate then drove through and parked in a bay opposite her, not far away. A man and a woman exited. Then man started setting up a camera, the woman looked in one of the wing-mirrors and began to beautify herself. A few minutes later some men in high visibility vests, the type ship's crew wore, approached the van.

Out of sight on the container just behind Daria, two members of the E.S.F. observation team received orders.

'Abort mission. Target not of interest. I repeat abort mission. Return to base immediately.' Troops in various observation posts around the port packed up and left, more than ready for some refreshments and a break.

'My shifts done, tell the boss I went home yeah.' One of the troops on the container said.

'Okay, don't fuck up, Boris.' The other replied and shimmied down the container toward his vehicle. The remaining E.S.F. troop lay flat and pulled out his phone; free at last from his colleague's glare, he set it to video mode and hit record He focussed in as the camera man made a signal and turned on a bright lamp pointing at the woman. He estimated she was in her mid-twenties, with long brown hair and wearing a lot of makeup. She looked a little like *the Joker* and spoke in a condescending tone.

'Welcome to this special report for U.K News, I am Mary-Ella Brook reporting live from the Port of Amsterdam where I have an exclusive interview with two crew members from the *Carnival Illusion*, which sunk here yesterday.'

'James, you were the ships First Officer. What can you tell us about the tragedy?' she asked.

'Good Afternoon, I can categorically deny that the ship was scuttled. We took fire from enemy craft and evacuated the ship. Unfortunately, not everyone escaped.' The larger of the two men said.

'And what did this craft look like?' Mary-Ella asked.

'It was massive, like a cigar shape.' He replied.

'And Michael, a deck hand, what can you tell us about the man who filmed the ship sinking?' She asked.

'Well Miss, he was on my life-raft and he kept blinking, he had wild eyes and well that's it.'

'Thank-you gentlemen. Well there we have it, proof that the rumours circulating on social media are fake news, propagated by our enemy. The suspect is Joey Styles from London; a known anti-denier.' Mary-Ella said.

A picture of Joey filled the screen before she continued, 'stay with us for a special analysis of the enemy's disinformation campaign.'

Joey heard the phone buzzing in his pocket but there was no way he could answer at the speed he was cycling. By the time he stopped, it had too. The display read, Franks. Joey called back.

'Where are you?' Franks asked.

'On my way to the museum.' Joey replied.

'No, get to the port, she's there.' He said.

'How do you know?' I asked.

'I'm watching her on television.' He replied.

'Are you sure?' Joey asked.

'Yes. She is dressed all in black, sitting under a shelter by a massive cruise ship at the passenger terminal of the port. I'll tell you if she moves.' Franks said, before continuing, 'oh and be careful they are after you for the ship video,' then hung up.

Joey was no tour guide, but he knew the port was north. He turned the bicycle around and pedalled for all he was worth.

A haze of summer rain was falling in the port as the camera cut back to Mary-Ella Brook for her special report.

'Following my interview with Dr. Scales in Geneva yesterday, I have just received this report from the Department for Media and Genuine Truth,' she waved some papers in front of the camera with widened eyes and raised eyebrows, before continuing, 'experts have been analysing yesterday's viral social media clip that seemed to show a female assassin, named Daria, killing the scientist, Scales, who claimed that the invasion was fake and that the chip he invented had been altered as part of an evil plan to enslave humanity.

The experts here have now concluded that this video was produced on a computer and is a C.G.I. fake. As we know Scales has given recent interview to confirm this and I can reveal that the assassin is entirely made up- **she does not exist**.' Said Mary-Ella with a vindictive smile.

The camera man panned out slightly and two figures, one male, one female could be seen in the background.

'It is thought that the technology to make this so realistic must be otherworldly; our enemy is again trying to influence us using social media,' she continued as the camera now focussed in on the figures in the background. The woman wore an all-black jumpsuit, the man and yellow high visibility vest and light-coloured trousers.

'Hey what are you doing? The camera…why are you pointing it over there?' Mary-Ella asked as she turned around slowly.

'Move cunt!' The cameraman replied, barging her out of the way as he moved closer to the action. She fell onto the wet ground and burst into tears.

'Well if it isn't the superhero himself, Joey Styles, how is saving the world going? Daria asked, holding the gun steady aimed directly at Joey's head.

'I don't fear you.' Joey replied, with a cold smile.

'You liked the planes, right?' She chuckled, before continuing, 'we are untouchable and now it's over. All those years of social engineering, playing both sides and false promises. *None* of you realised! The herds begged for the chip that enslaved them; put the mobile phone into their mind and made them into machines. And all because they are scared… of nothing!' She exclaimed, with wild eyes, waving the gun upward as she spoke.

Joey saw an opportunity and reached into his pocket.

'The game is up Daria; you lost,' Joey shouted above the sound of another lifeboat being winched down.

'Say hi to Cara from me you fool.' Daria said, levelling the weapon again.

The air ripped apart; two rapid thuds then a splatter of blood covered Joey's face and he lurched backward.

The E.S.F. troop suddenly came into view on top of the container and jumped down into the action, landing just behind the bloody mess that was now all over the shelter too. He stood behind Joey and began to haul him up.

'Sorry it took so long, I just needed the confession, you know.' The E.S.F. troop said.

'That's okay, someone's looking after me,' Joey replied, looking down at the cross Cara had given him with a glint in his eye.

A few hundred miles away, Franks television screen went blank with a no signal alarm before he could turn it off. 'Just turn it around, everything is inverted,' he whispered to himself with a rueful smile.

Chapter 47
2030, Unknown location

This was becoming a bit of a habit, Joey thought to himself as he opened his eyes in an unfamiliar location where he was forced to squint to avoid the bright light from almost blinding him. He sat up easily, pleased there were no new injuries to report but concerned at the plastic tube attached to his wrist from a beeping machine next to him. Instinctively he pulled out the tube and the device that housed it then felt immediate pain and a saw drip of blood flowing down toward his palm. He was vaguely aware of some further machine-like noises around him then a bustle of activity as the door burst open and the room became a madhouse. After a brief kerfuffle a syringe made its way into Joey's arm and released its payload.

'It's to calm you down, there's nothing to worry about you have my word.' A female voice said softly. Joey was flat out and couldn't see the origin but he liked what he heard, she had a soft accent that reminded him of someone. He felt dizzy and couldn't get up despite his best efforts, so relaxed and allowed the fuzzy warm feeling to send him away to a happy place.

'You need to stay with him at all times, keep him dosed, you understand?' An unforgiving male voice said.

'Yes sir, I understand.' The lady dressed in a white outfit replied.

Joey woke abruptly, cold sweat covered his overheating body as he sat bolt upright and wondered where the hell he was. The main lights were off now, the only dim light source came through the glass window in the top half of the door and the quietly beeping machine adjacent to him. The door swung open and Joey made out a figure approaching him, bracing for an impact that didn't come, he felt a firm but gentle push back onto the bed. A sidelight came on and the figure pressed some buttons on the bed, raising Joey to an upright position.

'I thought you'd wake up soon, how are you feeling Joey? I'm your nurse.' The lady with the soft accent said.

'Where am I?' Joey asked.

'You are in hospital, in France; goodness what were you dreaming about?' She said as she approached Joey with a hand towel and began to dab his head gently. As she leant toward him her dress opened slightly and Joey noticed a cross dangling above her ample bust.

'Where's my clothes, my things?' Joey asked more alert now.

'They are safe don't worry,' The nurse replied, placing her hand onto his and looking slightly uncomfortable,

'Where? I need my things,' Joey exclaimed.

'You had quite a bang on the head there, do you remember anything that happened?' she asked. Joey paused as he scanned her uniform for some sort of identification, but there was none. She raised a finger and left the room briefly, moments later she returned and placed a pencil and notepad on the table next to Joey where an empty fruit bowl and vase stood.

'That's the best I can do for now, you had some things on you but they took them. Here you can write things down as you remember them.' She said.

Chapter 48
2030, France

In the less populated rural areas to the south lockdown and rations were a little harder to manage than in the big cities. Even in 2030, despite the best efforts of the globalists, many still lived with a barter and subsidence economy where farming was king. For this reason, there was more of a sense of normality as the news flickered onto the old television screen in the top room of the dilapidated four-story house.

The viewer's, who normally paid little attention, interest was piqued by an appeal for information regarding three items. This was highly unusual especially given that earth was under attack by alien forces. The first two items, a penknife and a wax jacket, did nothing for her, however the third caused her to go over to the window, lean out and take a sharp intake of breath then steady herself on the cracked wooden sill.

It was a gold cross with three jewels indented into it, the picture had been taken on a blue background with the United Nations Logo and a contact number and email address.

After a minute the fresh air did the trick and she moved quickly down the creaking, uncarpeted stairs to the third floor. She retrieved the key from above the frame and pushed the stiff door open, it resisted on the brown ragged carpet and a cloud of dust enveloped her like a gas. She coughed, then reached for the light. The bulb blew instantly with a puff. Navigating herself toward the outline of light by the window she lifted the clasp and pushed outward, it was no good, these windows hadn't been opened for years. The room had been left, like a shrine, since that terrible day.

She let out a curse in her native tongue which swiftly turned into a coughing fit and she was forced to retreat. Moments later kitchen drawers flung open and a box of matches became her first target. Check that and back up to the room. Striking the tip allowed sight of a candle on the chest of drawers, the old methods were always the best, she thought as her goal became closer.

The bottom drawer of the dark wooden chest of drawers creaked and angled down, almost resting on the floor as she pulled it open. There was an array of papers, photos and smaller boxes, that she recognised from happier times, way back in her childhood, when her grandmother and her would play make believe with her jewellery sets.

Everything was just as she remembered it from the day of the funerals, packed carefully and orderly, in its correct place. There was a great deal of value there but she hadn't ever considered selling, they were after all unique and the only memento of her family.

The purple box had faded but she was sure that was the one. On the front two initials, "B.L," were inscribed in gold and the green felt could be seen escaping from the insides. Heart racing now almost uncontrollably she turned the tiny brass handle and fingers shaking, tore open the box. There inside was the outline of a small cross, indented in the felt, but the cross was gone.

She gasped, then fell backward onto the side of the single metal bed frame which creaked under her weight.

'Merdè!'

How could it be, she thought to herself, as she hurdled stairs back down to the kitchen and poured out a large glass of red wine. Her Grandmother, Bertice, had been given the cross as a communion gift by her father, who was a jeweller, and it was the only one ever made. Specifically, the three Jewels embedded in the cross were highly unusual as they represented Bertice's birthstones and that of her father and mother. A Sapphire, Diamond and Ruby.

210

Common sense directed her to the thought it could have been stolen, but she rarely had guests and the room was always locked. Outside now, smoking, her mind drifted to some of the social media posts she had read; "a man from the future, destined to save humanity", she finished her cigarette and settled in the living room with another glass of wine and opened her laptop. The internet was severely restricted, but the amount of vitriol aimed at Joey and Scales for being the enemy rang alarm bells in her questioning mind. She remembered something her old History teacher had said: "whatever you aren't allowed to think about, you should think about very carefully." Could they really be alien commanders? After a while she found the video's she was looking for and viewed them over an over until her eyes grew heavy and she lay back on the comfortable old chair.

It was an unusually quiet location in the middle of a legion of high-rise buildings that all looked the same. As her view zoomed into the bench next to a canal she immediately recognised herself sat next to a man. She was older, and had no hair, but her beauty spot and lips gave her away without any doubt. Her viewing angle did not show the man's face but she saw him handing her something which she refused to take. Then she heard him speaking to her calmly as she appeared to become upset and pound his chest with her fists. After sometime she calmed down and they left the bench abruptly as a drone approached. The man turned around and she got a brief glance of his face- it was Joey-the man from the future.

She startled upright in the chair and returned to the conscious world with eyes wide open. She rushed to the bathroom and doused herself with water. In the reflection around the beauty spot and full lips, she saw determination etched into her face, she must find him.

Chapter 49
2030, London

A feint knocking sound caused Franks to stir in his chair, that bloody doorbell battery had always driven his tenants mad. As he descended the stairs he made out a burly figure through the pane in the glass panelled front door. It was late evening and Franks didn't immediately recognise Jones, dressed in civilian clothing, with a cap pulled down low over his face.

Moments later, in the sparsely furnished living room, Franks beckoned Jones to sit.

'You are a prime target for the U.N. now, it's only a matter of time before they find this place, I can take you somewhere safe.' Jones said.

'I'm not so sure it's in my ex-wife's maiden name…and she's dead.' Franks chuckled as he replied. Jones was unsure how to respond and paused before responding.

'Look your face is on the news, you are enemy number one now they've got Joey, I'm only going to ask you one more time, this is dangerous for me too you know.' Jones said. The mention of Joey seemed to alter Franks attitude and he shifted in his chair.

'What? Isn't this over? Everyone saw the news report, she confessed.' Franks said looking shocked.

'No, The U.N. pulled rank on the E.S.F. and took Joey in. The media machine is in overdrive telling everyone Joey is an alien commander.' Jones replied.

'Do you know where he is? We have to help him?' Franks replied.

'I'm working on it, there are several possible locations. For now, I need to get you out of here.' Jones said, getting up from the sofa and looking out of the window nervously. Franks took the hint, nodded his acceptance and the men left.

Now under cover of darkness, Jones put on his uniform jacket and drove his U.K.S.F. jeep through the deserted streets, only stopping briefly at a checkpoint to show his I.D. Franks had squeezed his considerable frame into the rear and covered himself with a tarpaulin sheet.

They hadn't been driving more than ten minutes when the Jeep came to an abrupt halt amidst a chaotic scene. There were hundreds of protestors blocking the road outside a large building which looked like the townhall. The crowd held up placards and banners and pushed towards a line of U.K.S.F. troops in front of the building. Jones cursed under his breath, wondering what to do momentarily until the decision was taken out of his hands. A loud thud then the windscreen shattered in front of him, he looked away instinctively then opened the door and scrambled to the rear. He opened the boot and shouted to Franks to get out, by the time he had the men were immediately surrounded by angry protestors. Franks made out a "Scales was right" banner up ahead before a voice from the melee said:

'It's him, Joey's buddy from the Fall'. A man in a balaclava was pointing directly at Franks.

'They've arrested him, the bastards!' Another said waving his arm at Jones.

'Save him!' Screamed a desperate voice. By now the other U.K.S.F. troops had noticed the situation and Jones saw his opportunity to act. He removed his helmet and raised his arms.

'On behalf of the U.K.S.F. I declare that we are with you.' Jones shouted with all his might. The other troops, seeing his rank and precarious position, began to copy their Captain. Whether this was a last-ditch defensive move or coordinated plan was hard to say. But within seconds the atmosphere changed and became celebratory.

Protestors lifted Franks up onto their shoulders and took position on the top step in front of the Townhall. The U.K.S.F. troops lay down their weapons, removed their helmets and made a ring around the protestors. Someone brought a wastebin into the centre and placed a small placard on top of it. It read, "Anti-deniers tell the truth." A man hustled through the crowd and took his place at the make shift lectern. A U.K.S.F. troop handed him a megaphone and he began to speak.

'Friends, thank-you. Please…' the crowd began to quieten down slowly.

'Friends, we have succeeded here today thanks to you and these brave men from the U.K.S.F.' Cheering erupted as the man held Jones arm aloft.

'But this is only the beginning. And now let me ask you some questions. Has anyone seen an alien?'

'No!' The crowd responded enthusiastically.

'Do any of you believe a word the government or media say?'

'No!'

'Has anyone here taken a test?'

'No!' The shouts grew louder and more enthusiastic. The speaker paused until the noise abated.

'Now tell me…are there more of us than there are of them?'

'Yes!'

'And was Scales right?'

'Yes!'

'Scales was right, Scales was right, Scales was right' The speaker chanted. The crowd grew delirious and continued the chant. While they did so a screen flickered on behind the speaker, it was one of those installed by Local Councils in the early 2020's to ensure fear and propaganda passed into its citizens during the continual, "emergencies and crises". One of the protestors had got into the building and taken control. The screen played the videos of Scales being murdered by Daria, then Joey's video of the sinking ship and finally the news report where Daria admitted everything before being shot. The videos continued to play on a loop as the speaker signalled for calm with his hands and the crowd drew silent.

'Thank you, thank you…Now I have some disturbing news for you all. Joey, the man from the future who enlightened us all, has been taken into custody by the U.N. We do not know where he is being held so I ask you all to help find and free Joey…free Joey…'. The speaker began.

'Free Joey, free Joey, free Joey…' The crowd chanted louder and louder, almost eclipsing the thudding sound of the approaching attack helicopters. Jones', always alert, training kicked into action and he grabbed the microphone.

'Take cover, take cover,' he screamed before grabbing Franks and leading him towards to the vehicle where they watched the two white helicopters approach and then open fire on the crowd. Jones fired up the engine while Franks looked on in disbelief.

Chapter 50
2030, San Francisco

The man who would become known as grandfather sat watching the massacre event on a screen making rapidly exaggerated hand movements as if he was being electrocuted. None of his army of employees dared to speak. He stood up and paced the underground command centre that he had installed in the California headquarters of his largest business. Luckily, they had escaped the worst of the "alien assault" and had free pass to do as they pleased over and above any curfews or emergency laws put in place by the US government or United Nations.

The discovery that young Daria had died, followed by the news broadcast of future Daria's murder by the E.S.F had sent him, and his main companies headquarters into a meltdown worthy of this type of megalomaniac capitalist. The amusing thing was that all that was a charade; the rockets, cars and data mining. None of it really mattered to him but America South did. That was the reward for all these years of work, all the planning, and now, somehow, this upstart civilian and a crazy scientist were throwing obstacles in their way.

'Good, put them down. Instantly. Any protest, any opposition. Anywhere. You hear? Close the airwaves. Find Franks. And what...what are they doing with Joey? Do we have anything yet? Well!' he screamed.

'Sir, the general is due to check in today.' An underling dressed in an expensive suit said.

'Get him now. We need progress otherwise he dies.'

'Yes sir.'

Chapter 51
2030, Paris

Joey was propped up in his bed now and looked on with curiosity at the appeal for information about his jacket, penknife and cross on French television news. As he pondered the nurse breezed in and flicked of the screen.

'Hey, I was watch...,' he started.

'No time for that, you need your medication,' she said, appearing uncomfortably close to him with two pills and a glass of water. She watched him swallow the pills and picked up the paper and pen on the bedside table.

'Now why don't you be a good boy and write down everything you remember for me?' she said, handing them to Joey. Joey looked at the paper for a moment and wondered what was in the pills, he hadn't had the speed of thought to fake swallow them, partly because he liked the nurse, or at least he thought he had liked her the first time they met. On reflection her manner had become slightly abrupt and frosty on this occasion so perhaps his initial assessment might change. It was sad how people disguised their feelings and intensions he mused. Somehow before he had the time or inclination to decide who he might be writing for and whether they were friend or foe he picked up the pen, opened the notebook and began to write.

'Nurse, nurse!' Joey shouted. The buxom nurse returned with a slightly flushed face as if she had been doing or thinking something that she ort not to have been.

'What is it?' She replied sternly.

'This pen is kaput.' Joey said smiling broadly, holding up the poor-quality plastic biro, feeling the effect of the pills. The nurse grabbed the pen, tutted and about turned leaving the room in a huff. Momentarily she returned and placed an identical poor-quality biro on the table next to Joey, ignoring his open hand.

'Hope you aren't so careless with the medication,' Joey landed as she left the room for a third time in a huff. Whatever was in the pills he liked it, honesty and clear thinking abounded as he picked up the replacement poor-quality biro and began to write.

"Dear Cara,

Joey's creative snap was brought to a stop abruptly as the lights turned out and the room, with no external window, was pitched into darkness. After a moment to adjust his eyes, the dim lights from the medical equipment that monitored him allowed him to see.

Well fuck this, Joey thought as he swung his legs out of the bed with the intension to go and investigate. He stepped on the cheap biro, which had landed on the floor, and almost tumbled backward as he moved forward towards the door. Outside, the hallway too, was in darkness, perhaps this was part of the energy crisis Joey wondered as he edged his way cautiously down the corridor. As he moved he corrected his thoughts, no this simply must be a part of the alien attack, as he remembered the propaganda dutifully he laughed aloud to himself. Man, he was enjoying these pills. Now if he could just get out of here then he'd be okay.

He opened the door to a conveniently located locker room and found himself amongst a sea of personal belongings. It wasn't long before he found his own: the cross, penknife and jacket. There were some magazines on a desk by the far wall written in French. Joey put two and two together and realised he was no longer in Amsterdam, maybe that was why the nurse had been coy about telling him where he was?

France meant Cara, to the south…where did she live again…somewhere near …Toulouse. He picked up a Surgeon's hat and mask in an attempt to disguise himself. Donning the mask, he felt inhuman and struggled to breathe, still at least he was doing it for himself, not because he had been told too for others.

Outside the building, Boris the E.S.F. troop who had shot Daria, was leading a small team sent to rescue Joey from the clutches of the United Nations. The team were unaware that Boris had set the mission himself, after rejecting his own dismissal by his superiors in a hastily called meeting following the broadcast to the world of him killing Daria. He had also received a message from Jones, his brother in law, that protests were growing in London and that they were expecting proof that, "the Fall," was faked.

Boris, now rogue, didn't expect to have long until he and his merry band of men would be discovered. He had disposed of his Commander in Chief in the old-fashioned way a quick and violent neck break which, after years of pointless ear bashing, had felt good. Still the curfew and alien war had its advantages: there were few civilians on the streets, only E.S.F. and U.N. and there weren't nearly enough U.N. troops to be everywhere at once. Indeed, it appeared to him that they were concentrated at certain locations where they had advance warning they would be needed. Now that disorder was spreading through the continent, the U.N. were under severe pressure and the E.S.F. were slowly breaking apart, the sheer horror of firing on their own citizens was having a devastating effect on morale. That, combined with the unusual events left many in the security forces questioning their place in the ongoing unprecedented emergency. Just like with the first virus in the early 2020's people who were asking themselves the very basic questions found the answers didn't make sense. In that case it was something like; "where has the flu gone?" In this case it was: "Has anyone seen an alien?"

Being part of the E.S.F. gave them carte blanche for now so getting to the converted chateaux on the outskirts of Paris was a doddle. As was getting in. Now he just needed to find and extract Joey. The only problem was where to take him. This guy was target number one for whoever was behind this plot. He'd find him first then improvise, but it would need to be good.

Another benefit of the fear inducing circumstances for Boris was that anyone would believe anything he said. A few moments earlier he had put the whole facility into lockdown effortlessly with a few words indicating there was an alien-based security threat; faces whitened, staff acquiesced, doors opened and they were in. He wasn't stupid enough to ask for the patient list so split his team up to search the annex floor by floor; they'd take one each. As he bounded up the stairs to the fourth floor he stopped as he entered the building through the emergency exit. There was a guy wondering around.

'Hey you!' Boris shouted, his English poor and accent heavy.

'Zut- Alors,' Joey replied still at a distance from his rescuer.

'What are you doing, everyone is locked down due to the threat.' Boris said as he walked slowly toward Joey who comically turned his face away but continued to talk:

'Ahh, yes I am seeing a patient now,' Joey replied speaking in a dubious French accent and started to walk away. Boris caught up within a couple of strides, restrained him and turned him around.

'It's you, my saviour!' Joey said as he removed his face nappy, his eyebrows almost touching the ceiling.

'C'mon, there's no time to waste,' Boris replied leading Joey back the way he had come.

Joey couldn't believe his luck and followed Boris eagerly down the emergency exit and into the waiting E.S.F. vehicle.

'Are we in France?' he asked as the engine fired up.

'Yes, why?' Boris replied.

'I know someone near Toulouse, can you get me there?' Joey asked. The vehicle roared into action without further ado and they were on their way. It was soon dark and the men, except Boris, slept on the long journey south.

Joey contemplated the past 24 hours and wondered what Cara's reaction to him would be, that was if they even managed to find her. He did have a couple of trump cards though so he was feeling confident. If the cross didn't do it then surely his intimate insider knowledge would.

Chapter 52
2030, London

Franks and Jones sat in the damaged military vehicle in silence, taking in the chaos and death around them, both unable to make the links required for speech. Jones had aborted his original plan to take Franks to his family home, deciding now that that idea was far too dangerous. In fact, he sat wondering if he would ever see his family again momentarily, picturing his beautiful wife and child, hoping for their safety.

Franks mind had slipped back in time to the wars where he flew F15's for his country, acting as world police, but instead normalising death and destruction on a devastating scale. He thought about a book he had read a long time ago where one of the governments sayings was, "war equals peace," and he wondered how the author could have known so accurately what was to come. As he replayed the carnage in his head, he wondered how men kept killing each other in more elaborate ways after all this time. How dare man claim to be intelligent when these massacres still occur? Just because they are part of a group that disagrees with the dominant force, or doesn't do as they are told. What happened to freedom of speech, and thought? Oh, it's a threat to national security- that makes it alright then, yes you can declare a state of emergency, suspend the constitution and do what you please. A little like Germany in 1933, that was a democracy and look what happened! Really, that humanity had not managed to work out, perhaps with the aid of free thinking or philosophy, that war is evil, was the biggest disappointment. He shook his head, and allowed his eyes to close momentarily until a vibration in his pocket woke him.

It was an email notification from his brother, Chip. There was no writing only a series of attachments. Franks nudged Jones and the men read the small screen together.

Part Description	Boeing Honeywell Uninterruptible Autopilot
Patent no.	US7,142,971B2. Nov 28/2006.
Part Serial no.	5180-01-154-8945
Carrier	British Airways
Tail no	G-TTNA
Aircraft type	Airbus A320-neo
Fitted date	11/11/2026
Mechanic	Mr. F. McConnell
NTSB assessment	Part activated and used
NTSB assessor	Mr. N. Davies

Franks scrolled to the second attachment, which contained two pictures of the part in question. The first a new undamaged part to compare with the second actual picture of the part Franks had found. The second picture had a red circle annotation over a small lever with the word, "Proof of Activation," written next to it.

'Damn, there's our proof,' Jones said, letting out a long slow whistle. Franks shifted uncomfortably in his seat. All those years flying and he hadn't known about this. He brought his fist down angrily into the vehicle's tough dashboard, opened the door and kicked it outward with his left foot. In the fresh night air, he took several deep breaths, his eyes darted around like an injured bull for something, anything to take a hold of and destroy. The "smart-bin" on the pavement became his target and before he could engage and ask it how much carbon it had saved he had kicked and smashed it violently from its pathetic foundation.

'Now that's a service to society if ever I saw one, come on get in,' Jones said, walking toward Franks, confident the strength of youth would prevail over that of rage. Franks turned and Jones, seeing the rage in his eyes, instinctively took a step back. This old guy was not done yet.

'Bastards, how could they?' Franks cried, arms waving unsteady on his feet. He tripped and fell, landing neatly on the curb. Jones risked it and sat down next to him, putting his arm around Franks shoulder. Franks didn't explain it but his problem was that pilots are responsible for the souls on board, fully responsible, and to be fully responsible they need to be in control. This secretive technology meant that their airplanes could be remotely flown so they were no longer in control. No wonder he, and thousands of other pilots, didn't know. If they did they wouldn't fly it was a simple as that. And now this, "safety device," had become responsible for the biggest air crash disaster in history. *Everything was inverted.*

Mind still racing but now rapidly joining the dots, he opened the email again. Patented in 2006, that was only five years after the second biggest air crash disaster in history. Could it have been fitted then…a secret prototype? It was all making sense; now it was Aliens…then it was terrorists from a cave who got a do not fly recommendation in ten hours of flight school then were able to create events that changed the world forever. The speed and trajectory of their recorded flightpaths would have made any Top Gun pilot proud. *Bollocks they did.* More likely years of planning to shift the geopolitical balance and edge the world closer to the end.

'It's all a lie. Everything.' Franks finally said, face as white as a sheet. Jones had been busy on his mobile device and now looked up.

'I think you might be right. My brother in law has Joey, they are in France.'

'France eh, that rings a bell, come on we need to get this information out there. Do you have that protestors number? Jones scrolled through his phone and sent the information on with a short explanation, then silently said a prayer the guy was still alive. *Those helicopters meant business.*

The men got back into the vehicle, Franks walking with a slight limp after his altercation with the bin.

'Where to now?' he asked as Jones fired up the noisy engine.

'France.' Jones replied confidently eyes fixed on the small part of the windscreen that wasn't cracked as he pulled out into the dark, empty road.

Chapter 53
2030, San Francisco

'Gone, what do you mean gone? Gone where for fuck sake. He's dosed up in a secure unit for psych tests. Get me the General…now!' Young Grandfather screamed, his large eyes barely remaining in their sockets as his veins pulsed blue.

'He's gone too, re-assigned to another mission.' The underling squeaked quietly edging closer to the control rooms exit door. As he did a red dot on one of the screen's enlarged and a fuzzy picture of two men in a military vehicle enlarged on the screen next to it.

'Sir, we've got something sir. We've intercepted unusual communications from a civilian and a soldier and we are tracking them now, they are on the move in a military vehicle.'

'Well who the fuck are they? What communications?

'We aren't sure yet sir but they refer to the situation, we think they are involved.'

A lady in a long white coat entered, as if she had been summoned, carrying a tray. She led Young Grandfather to a large expensive looking leather chair in the middle of the room and sat him down. He didn't resist. She adjusted the collar of his robe like garment then injected him with a syringe in the back of his neck then passed over a large steaming hot drink. He laid back in the chair and seemed to relax…after a couple of sips the woman took the drink back and his eyes closed.

Chapter 54
2030, South of France

After five hours or so driving on empty highways Boris decided to pull in at a deserted service station for a rest and to swap driver. The other men stirred as he halted the vehicles motion. The vehicles built-in navigation system was not functioning due to blocks on civilian satellite's so Boris had been using the old-fashioned methods so far, but now they were approaching a little more detail was required. He pulled out the military issue PDA from his pocket and nudged Joey.

'Where are we going then?' he asked.

'I don't know exactly; her name is Cara Leclerc.' Joey said almost instantly as if he had been awake for a while. In fact, he had been, thanks to a severely dry mouth and hunger pains in his stomach.

'Can we get some food?' he continued. Boris nodded to the three troops and they left the vehicle then typed in the name Joey had given him into the search screen of the E.S.F. intelligence database. A picture and crib sheet style details screen loaded rather slowly a few seconds later.

'Is that her?' He asked, lifting the screen above his shoulder so Joey could see it from the back.

'Yes, she-' Joey started before he was interrupted by the sound of automatic gunfire coming from the service stations shop. Boris hit the gas immediately and accelerated away, checking back in his rear-view mirror for anyone following. He didn't see one of his troops pulling himself onto the open rear of the vehicle as he sped off. Those men were well trained and could look after themselves; his precious cargo took priority. The device had fallen to the floor in the excitement and Boris couldn't reach it. Joey moved into the front with difficulty and retrieved the device as well as a gun from the footwell.

'Okay hit location, then directions,' Boris said. Joey did so and a route planner overlaid a map on the screen. They were close, in fact, only minutes away but they needed to get off the highway. Joey began to wonder how Cara would react to him, she looked more beautiful than ever with hair and carrying a normal weight, when a sudden flash of orange-red light blinded him. He felt an accelerated motion then cold fresh air before a rapid deceleration and finally wet, dark and pain.

He struggled to sit up, looking around it appeared he was in a ditch surrounding a field full of perfectly straight vines. He could do with a glass now, he thought. To his left, about fifty meters away, his eyes were immediately drawn to a raging fire which he identified as his former carriage. A helicopter and two four-wheel drive vehicles were stationed around it. The helicopters blades were still rotating. Soldiers in blue and white uniforms surrounded the vehicle with machine guns raised. Two of them began to extinguish the flames from opposite sides of the burning vehicle, moving slowly their chemicals did the trick and the flames subsided. Three of the soldiers moved forward, two with weapons still raised, the other held a torch to illuminate the dark smouldering vehicle. One of the four-wheel drive vehicles drove around and illuminated them with its lights.

'All clear Sir, two bodies, one in the front, one in the back.' The soldier with the torch shouted.

The helicopter's engines whined and it lifted unevenly from the road. An older man dressed in a smart uniform finished typing his communication;

"Mission accomplished- target eliminated."
and slammed closed the laptop with a satisfied grin.

Joey sighed deeply, then looked up and silently thanked Boris and the unknown body in the back, his ghost, and latest savior. He stayed perfectly still and watched while the remaining soldiers dragged the E.S.F. vehicle out of the highway, swept the area down then piled into their vehicles and sped off. As he contemplated a red light in the night sky drew his attention. It was Boris' P.D.A. with Cara's home address blinking on it. Joey smiled, someone up there was definitely looking after him, as he brushed himself down and started across the field.

The sunflowers created almost human like shadows in the moonlight as Joey pushed them out of the way with his hands and dodged other larger ones. Some of their faces seemed to turn as he passed and he wondered what messages they told and judgements they had reached. As he reached a clearing at the side of the field he looked out towards a group of houses clustered around a few larger buildings one of which looked like a farm, another a church. *That must be it!* No food or drink for hours and his throat raw he sped up, using his last ounces of energy, to propel himself forward toward his future, her past. Time sped up, he heard himself lifting the knocker on the old unvarnished wooden door at number seventeen. He heard footsteps and the door opened inward and he entered, tripping on the step up and collapsing into her arms.

The young Cara fell back as Joey's bodyweight leaned into her but she was able to react and cushion their fall onto the bare floorboards in the narrow hallway. Before she had a chance to curse she heard a feint pinging noise and noticed a movement out of the corner of her eye.

She followed the trajectory and it led to the wall where the now stationary item glimmered in the light shining down from the bare bulb. It couldn't be, could it? She struggled with the man who was out cold and managed to lever his weight off her with her legs, as she did he fell backwards and she drew in a sharp intake of breath. It was Joey! The man from the television and her dream- the man from the future.

She edged herself across to the wall and picked up the item and examined it. There was no doubt- it was her ornate cross. She read her Grandmother's tiny initials engraved into the rear of the post then almost immediately dropped it in shock.

'Zut alors!' She finally said aloud, how could this be? She heard a groan and turned her attention to the injured Joey, moving to him and gently rubbing his cheek. Nothing happened so she began to strike him with a little more vigour.

What a beautiful symmetry life had.

'Stop Cara, stop, I'm alive,' Joey groaned, whilst wondering if he had landed with some kind of sadist. But this time he knew the answer and smiled a weak smile then squeezed her hand. It felt good to be close to her again.

'How did you get this?' Young Cara asked, lifting up the cross into Joey field of vision.

Joey's eyes fluttered open and the couple made eye contact briefly. Cara realised his predicament and went to get some water; which she then fed him slowly after perching him on the wall in a sitting position.

'Well?' She probed.

'You gave it to me, in the future, as a gift for saving your life.' Joey relayed in a matter of fact tone, before continuing, 'we were friends, nearly lovers.'

Joey had always had a loose tongue but the look on Cara's face did make him wonder if he had gone too far, too soon. He smiled on the inside as he watched her emotions mirror those he knew so well from the future; the slow progress from anger to disbelief to confusion. He chose that moment to continue.

'You have a birthmark on your stomach.' Cara instinctively touched her naval with her hand, then realised she was fully clothed. She shot Joey a glance, his kind but knowing smile disarmed her and she sighed.

'How can this be?' she asked again shaking her head. Cara hauled herself from the floor and put out a hand to Joey. Together they moved into a sparsely furnished living room and sat down on an old sofa. Cara pulled on a knitted blanket that had been resting over the back of the sofa and tucked it around Joey carefully. She looked into his piercing blue eyes as he began to speak.

'It's a long story, I'll start at the beginning...'.

Chapter 55
2030, San Francisco

The outside world, indeed any onlooker, would deduce fairly quickly and to a high degree of certainty that young Grandfather was asleep in a comfortable chair in his San Francisco H.Q.

However, that was as far from this reality as anyone could guess. They did not see the wrinkled lady in the white gown shooing away his closest aides nor the room transform form a high-tech command and control centre into something resembling more of a shrine of sorts. The main lights dimmed leaving low level L.E.D.'s that pulsed between neon blue and green. Once the room was clear the lady in the coat pulled a cable from the luxury chair and connected it to a receptacle hidden under the collar on young grandfathers' neck.

Young grandfather awoke in the virtual reality space and watched as his perfectly-made avatar sat in the chair waiting. His breathing became uneven as he waited impatiently for something to happen. He had only been summoned once before.

He looked on as the display screens in front of him turned on and slowly tuned into a barren landscape. It was a grey white colour with a dark black background. The land was hard to identify clearly; there were patches of light and dark rocks with deep scars and high peaks. There were no visible beings, but young Grandfather knew they were there.

'We have eliminated the threat, the Fall was a success and we will deliver humanity to you, under the Freegov, by 2035.' He said confidently, eyes bulging.

'You risk our plans with your incompetence then dare to report everything is fine. You think we don't see everything from here? We do. We withdraw our offer of Mars and put you on notice that the America South deal is at risk.' A high pitched, slightly unhinged sounding male voice said. Young Grandfather's jaw clenched and twitched, he used all his force to stop his arms flailing around.

'I will deliver you humanity. I am on track.' He replied through gritted teeth.

'How? We see the protests, the anarchy. They know the invasion is false. You have wasted our trump card... fear. They don't believe, they are no longer scared.' The voice said pitching higher now sounding almost lunatic.

'I'll get you more of them, now, give me a chance!' Young Grandfather pleaded.

'You know our deal, all of them chipped and handed over by 2035. Make it work or all your privileges are history, no more pioneering technology gifts, no more idolising fans, no more world's richest man, no more!'

The screen faded back to black and Grandfather woke up in his Headquarters. He had a splitting headache and began throwing things around the room uncontrollably. All he was really looking forward to was America South and the new colony and now that was in jeopardy. He knew he was a front man, that none of these inventions or ideas were really his...but the colony thing was going to be great- when earth was about to implode he'd get his people out and start afresh on the solar systems blueprint for Earth...Mars. And there he would be the supreme leader, with nothing above him to steal the glory. There was only one thing for it, he turned to his old manual and began planning a dark ceremony.

He knew these foolish sheep still couldn't see that everything they gave up to the cloud was used against them; and everything sent back was harmful, a means of control; the ultimate deception...that the devil was in the air.

THE END.

Printed in Great Britain
by Amazon